SWAPPING
PAINT

FORTHCOMING BY JOYCE & JIM LAVENE

Hooked Up

OTHER SERIES BY JOYCE & JIM LAVENE

Sharyn Howard Mysteries

Peggy Lee Garden Mysteries

A STOCK CAR RACING MYSTERY

SWAPPING PAINT

JOYCE & JIM LAVENE

MIDNIGHT INK
WOODBURY, MINNESOTA

First Edition
First Printing, 2007

Book design by Donna Burch
Cover design by Kevin R. Brown
Cover driver image © Colin Anderson / Brand X Pictures
Cover flag background © PhotoDisc

Midnight Ink, an imprint of Llewellyn Publications

Library of Congress Cataloging-in-Publication Data
Lavene, Joyce.
Swapping paint : a stock car racing mystery / Joyce & Jim Lavene. — 1st ed.
p. cm.
ISBN-13: 978-0-7387-1020-4 (alk. paper)
ISBN-10: 0-7387-1020-2 (alk. paper)
1. Stock car racing—Fiction. 2. NASCAR (Association)—Fiction. 3. Stock car drivers—Crimes against—Fiction. 4. North Carolina—Fiction. I. Lavene, James. II. Title.

PS3562.A8479S93 2007
813'.54—dc22 2006053073

Midnight Ink
Llewellyn Publications
2143 Wooddale Drive, Dept. 0-7387-1020-2
Woodbury, MN 55125-2989, U.S.A.
www.midnightinkbooks.com

Printed in the United States of America

For my brother-in-law, Don Harmon,
who taught me everything I know about cars and racing.
Thanks for spending time with a scrawny kid
who had too many questions.

—Jimmy

ONE

"SHH! DO YOU HEAR that?"

She shoves her hand against my mouth, pushes me against the wall, and waits.

"I'm not talking," I mumble through her fingers.

"I was making sure."

"We can't break into someone's RV!"

"The Branfords took our Rusty Wallace plate last year, and I mean to get it back."

"This is stealing."

"This is taking back what's rightfully *ours*, Glad."

You don't argue with a woman like Ruby. At least *I* try not to. She's got a race car engine inside a Rolls Royce body. She's not a little thing, but she's someone you can hold on to. Unless she's up and running in another direction, like now.

We finally move away from the side of the hot dog stand. It's closed for the night—or what's left of the night at three in the morning—but the smell of beer and bratwurst lingers. The lights on the towering superstructure of Lowe's Motor Speedway still illuminate the sky.

We're camping on the infield this year for race week leading up to the Coca-Cola 600. Every year, a group of us put in some money and pick a name. I won the draw this year after five years of putting in money. The only other speedway I've stayed inside is Talladega. Too expensive.

A hundred thousand fans will eventually line up to see if their driver of choice wins the races on the narrow circle of blacktop. Around us is a sea of RVs and buses, some of them special-order, which can cost a million dollars. Not mine, but they do exist. The infield is just one of a dozen campgrounds around the speedway. I'm sure the hotels are full too. And if you're rich, there are always the VIP suites and condominiums. But even if I had ten million dollars, I would still want to camp to see the race.

My wife, Ruby, and I are searching for a license plate that someone else took after a race years ago. Ruby's parents, Zeke and Louise Furr, were leaving a race at Darlington, North Carolina, when popular driver Rusty Wallace lost his personalized plate during an off-track wreck. The Furrs "pulled" for Rusty before he retired. One of the first questions out of any racing fan's mouth in conversation is who you pull for—like I pull for Joe Nemechek. Good driver who gets a lot of bad breaks. I still like him.

The Furrs passed the plate down to their youngest daughter, Ruby, on our wedding day. For anyone *not* into racing, it's a little like catching a home run ball at Wrigley Field during a Cubs game. Or reeling in a record-breaking swordfish. Or finding a diamond in a can of soup.

Rusty is next to Sunday clothes and fried chicken in the Furr household. Giving Ruby the plate that was solemnly enshrined between the kitchen door and the china cupboard for fifteen years was a tearful event. It was hard for me to tell which the Furrs hated losing more. But one thing is certain: Ruby has waited for this moment since we left Lowe's last year. Nothing I can say is going to stop her from getting Rusty's old plate.

How did the Branfords get Ruby's plate? I'm not sure. I wasn't there. I was playing poker with some friends. It has something to do with Ivey stopping by to talk to Ruby. Rusty's plate was on the wall when Ruby went to get a beer for each of them. When she came back, the plate and Ivey were gone. Ruby had a security guard search Ivey's motor home, but the plate wasn't there and Ivey swore she didn't take it. And that's why we're here tonight.

We sneak around the campground in a left-to-right fashion, hiding behind trash barrels and motor homes. In the distance, someone else is awake, torturing an old guitar and baying at the dark sky. It seems like fifteen years as a cop in Chicago would've prepared me for this undercover operation. But, like meeting Ruby in the first place, nothing from my former life can help me here. I'm on my own.

"I see it!" She points one perfectly manicured pink nail toward an orange-and-black-striped Bluebird Custom LXI motor home with the words TIGER IN THE TANK emblazoned across the side. The green awning is still up over some deserted plastic lounge chairs and a lighted fountain where the water cascades from a tiny version of Jeff Gordon's number 24 car. A few empty Pepsi cans lie on the flattened grass, but no one seems to be outside anymore.

"What now?" I'm looking at the closed door to the motor home and seeing myself doing eighteen months in a county jail for breaking and entering. Will they be harder on me because I understand the law and did it anyway?

Ruby shrugs, her large blond curls bouncing on her shoulders. "We go in and get the plate. I saw Sam go in a couple of hours ago. He's dead to the world by now. And Ivey sleeps with a mask and earplugs. I know where the plate is. We can be in and out in a minute."

"I'm *not* going in there. Come on. Let's go back. If you want, I'll smash Sam in the jaw tomorrow. But I'm not sneaking into their RV."

Ruby has a face for everything. It's something I love about her—except when I'm annoyed. Like now. I don't appreciate her petulant frown or her big blue eyes looking up at me like I just drowned her cat. She calls this her boo-boo face. I call it a pain in the ass coming my way. It must be the age difference. Ruby is twenty-five, seventeen years younger than me.

"Fine." She huffs and sighs. "We'll go back. But when my daddy asks how Rusty's plate is doing and wants to visit it, I'm gonna feel pretty stupid. You'll feel worse, because we were right here and didn't get the job done."

"I'll take that chance." I glance around the sleeping campground. It's only been five years since I was working the street. It's true that old habits die hard, I guess. I never say things like that out loud. It sounds too much like something my old man would say.

I take Ruby's arm and bend close to kiss her ear. "Come on, baby. Let's go back home and find something else to do."

She smiles at me. It was definitely that smile that changed my heart and mind. I met her after a bad divorce. I swore I'd never marry again. I was free at last. Then Ruby smiled at me one afternoon at Talladega Superspeedway in Alabama. We were married on the track of the Infineon Raceway in Sonoma, California.

But that pretty smile can mean trouble. In this case, Ruby bends down, looking like she's checking her sandal. Distracted, I admire her ample hips in tight jeans. When she pops back up, she looks past me and her eyes get big. "What's *that*?"

I know. I can't believe I fall for it. But in my own defense, there are some *really* weird things happening at these races. At Bristol Motor Speedway in Tennessee, a man put on a pair of wings and tried to fly off a grandstand. Ruby called my attention to that one. Most of the time, her surprises are legitimate.

But this time, before I can turn back to look at her, she's gone. I hear her giggling as she runs toward the Branfords' RV. "Dammit, Ruby!" I yell after her, hoping to wake the Branfords before she can creep in the door. No one moves. Not a light comes on. Maybe they locked their door for a change. Then I hear it squeak open. No such luck. She's already inside.

I figure I have one of two choices. I wait out here and hope nothing happens, or I go inside and try to *keep* something from happening. Knowing Ruby is a frequent flyer in the land of trouble, I opt for the second choice. The RV sags under my weight as I step inside. I can see Ruby's penlight flashing across the living area in the back. I know Sam and Ivey are asleep behind the folding doors that separate the space.

I can't call Ruby now. She's too far back. It would give us both away. I follow her shadow and the bouncing light, promising myself some fantastic form of retribution when we get back home. Not that it will ever come to pass, but it gets me through the experience.

I manage not to groan too loudly as I squeeze between the tight-fitting furniture. If we can make it out of here without getting caught, I'm going to chain Ruby to our RV.

There's a small noise, somewhere between a sigh and a giggle. She's found the plate. I can't see her or the penlight anymore. I realize she's in back with Sam and Ivey. Better and better. I hesitate before I draw back the folding doors, but it doesn't seem to matter so much now. I remember a car thief once told me that after you steal a watch, a car is just something bigger to hide. That's how I feel. I'm already breaking and entering and trespassing. It doesn't matter if I see Sam and Ivey in bed together.

But Sam isn't in bed with his wife. Instead, he's in bed with Ivey's sister, Holly. I don't see Ivey. God knows, I don't want to see *any* of them. I want to be home in bed with Ruby. My wife is taking out her camera, the Rusty license plate pressed close to where I would be if we weren't in this damn mess. I can't believe she plans to take a picture.

My heart is racing until I hear the shutter click and realize she was sneaky enough to turn off the flash. Now if we can only get out before Sam wakes up. Holly groans in her sleep as Ruby steps across her. Apparently, the plate was on the wall behind the bed. How Ruby got up there in the first place without waking them is a miracle. The couple on the bed must be too worn out not to notice her walking between them. I don't want to think about it. I whisper, "Can we go now?"

"I got what I came for!" Ruby waves the plate and hops off the bed. She wiggles her feet into her sandals. I take her hand and we slip out toward the door.

Life takes another strange turn. The door opens again and Ivey steps up into the motor home. I'm about to confess to everything and beg for mercy when Ruby pushes me down on the leather sofa. She pulls a blanket over both of us and straddles my waist as she puts her lips on mine. Ivey doesn't turn on the light and creeps by us in the dark. It's a miracle. I can't believe it! Then I realize what's wrong. She *knows* Sam is in here with Holly.

It only takes a minute. Ivey's screech is first, followed immediately by her sister's howl. Sam's low-pitched pleading turns to begging just before the sounds of a scuffle rock the RV.

"Let's get out of here," Ruby urges me.

I follow her lead, and somehow we manage to make it out of the motor home before anyone realizes we're there. Ruby's laughing and hugging Rusty's plate.

"Don't *ever* do that again." I'm so damn grateful to be out in the cool night air, my voice isn't as authoritative as I'd like. I sound more like a boy who lost his trunks in the pool. *Please, God, just let me get out without anyone seeing.*

She smiles up at me and slips her arm through mine. "You know it was fun. And we got what we came for. Plus some. Who ever thought about Sam and Holly? *That* was interesting!"

"I don't want to think about Sam and Holly." The picture of the two of them is still fresh in my mind. It's hard to believe Sam is so stupid that he'd take his sister-in-law back to his own place. Why didn't he go to *her* RV? People don't think much about what they do. But I already know that from my previous life.

"We have my treasure back again, anyway." Ruby sighs and rests her head against my shoulder as we walk. "Sam and Ivey will be surprised when they see it's gone. Ivey might even suspect Holly of taking it."

"You're lucky we're not both in jail with your treasure." Even to my ears, it sounds like sour grapes. We *did* get in and out without getting caught. And the Branfords *did* take Ruby's plate and claim it was their own. There must be justice there somewhere.

"You *know* you had a good time." She laughs. "How about when we were under the blanket on the couch and Ivey walked right by us? That was exciting, wasn't it?"

Sighing, I admit it was *great* fun. Sort of like having a tooth pulled. I guess I should be happy none of the guys from the 22nd Precinct saw me hopping back and forth like a damn ballerina trying not to be seen. I'd never live that down. All I want to do is go home and get in bed.

Life, however, has other ideas. It always does. We're almost home when Ruby's brother, Bobby, pops up at us out of the shadows. "Ruby!" He grabs her and swings her around.

"Bobby!" She starts to laugh and hugs him back.

I look longingly at the closed door to our 2000 Holiday Rambler Navigator that I got such a good deal on after my ex-wife and I sold our house. Still, if it wasn't for my Uncle Lech and his shrewd investments, my medical pension wouldn't let me live this lifestyle.

So close. If we were inside with the lights off, maybe Bobby would've gone away. I sit down in a green plastic chair and light a cigar while they laugh and yell at each other. Ruby's relatives are the only people I know who can make the wind chimes she hangs around the awning tinkle without touching them. There's a certain decibel they reach that could probably allow them to communicate with dolphins.

"Glad!" Bobby finally notices me sitting there. It's my turn. He hugs me and probably would swing me around if he could. I outweigh him like a Great Dane outweighs a poodle. He starts to kiss my cheek and finds himself staring at the end of my cigar.

"Good to see you too, Bobby. You looked good out there on the track during practice. You and Sanders developing a rivalry?" Bobby is driving in the Coca-Cola 600 for the first time if he qualifies. It's the one subject I know I can talk about with any member of Ruby's family.

"Yeah, Ricky and I swapped some paint. But there were four other boys who kept scraping each other too. It's part of being a driver." He sits down in the chair beside me and settles in to wait for the glass of iced tea Ruby went inside to get for him. "Crew chief says I better watch my step or they'll fine me."

So I can probably figure he's going to take up what's left of the night. "Ricky ran good too. And you're gonna do Team Hamilton proud," I say.

"Ricky Sanders is a loser, Glad. You know he dated Ruby, right? They went out for a few months before she met you. Daddy always liked the idea of the two of them being together since their farm sits next to ours."

I didn't know that. I lean forward and listen a little more intently. Who is this Sanders guy anyway? "What made them break up?"

"Ricky got some girl pregnant, and Ruby wouldn't give him the time of day. Mama and Daddy both cried about it. That fence between our properties has always been a sore spot. Now their only hope is Betsy and Davy, Ricky's little brother. Maybe it'll work out between them."

"Don't wish the Sanders family on Betsy!" Ruby hears us talking when she comes out with the iced tea. "She's too good for them. The Sanderses are trash."

"So why'd you date Ricky?" I take a can of Budweiser from her.

"I was mixed up in that whole land thing." She sits down beside me and crosses her legs as she drinks her tea. The tiny lights around the awning—she calls them fairy lights—glint in her hair. Ruby was a beautician before we got married. She's very careful about the color and style of her hair. Changes it almost every month.

"Don't fret, Glad." Bobby slaps my knee. "She's all yours now. What passed between her and Ricky doesn't matter anymore. Isn't that the way it's supposed to be? That's the way it always was with the King."

I nod wisely. "Elvis Presley."

"No." His face contorts at the name. "Richard Petty. All I ever knew about women I learned from watching him. Nobody had moves like the King."

Of course. I should've known. For a racing enthusiast, there isn't another king. Richard Petty might not race anymore, but his legend continues.

Ruby laughs, putting a hand to her nose as she almost sprays tea. "That sounds like a book, Bobby. But since I know you don't read, I'm sure it must be a song."

"Since you mention it, I could do a few bars for you." He starts humming and finally launches into song. Did I mention that Bobby thinks of himself as being a country-western singer once his career as a driver is over? It's part of his twenty-year plan.

I finish the Bud, knowing it's going to be a long time until morning. Surprisingly, when Bobby finishes the song, he decides to leave.

"You're not going already, are you? It's not even dawn yet." I hope he catches the sarcastic tone in my voice, but it's unlikely. Ruby's family understands sarcasm about as well as they understand vegetarians not eating pork rinds.

"Sorry, son." He stretches his slender frame and yawns. "I got a pole to win tomorrow. I gotta get some shuteye. But I appreciate you wanting me to stay. Whenever Mama and Daddy start complaining about Ruby marrying a Yankee, I tell them you're okay."

Ruby hugs him and wishes him luck. We wave to him as he disappears into the RV forest around us. It's four a.m. before we close the door to our motor home. You can be sure I lock it up tight. By the time we crawl into bed, I'm too tired to do anything but fall asleep. The last thing I see is Ruby polishing her Rusty plate with a cloth.

A piercing shriek punctuated by a loud scream wakes me from a dream about me and Ruby in the back seat of a race car. I glance at the clock. It's nearly seven. The light streaming in from the windows is sunlight.

"What *was* that?" Ruby yawns but doesn't move, stretching her curvy limbs around me. "And how do you turn it off?"

Another scream rends the air. "Something's wrong." Probably the understatement of the year. I pull on my jeans, slip my feet into moccasins.

Ruby is already at the door, taunting me in her shorts and tank top. "And they say *women* take a long time!"

She's out the door before I can reach her. I follow as quickly as I can. Will she still be the same when she's ninety? Having met her great-grandmother, who lives in the mountains, smokes a pipe, and plows her fields with a mule at the age of eighty, I'd say I'll never be able to keep up. I'm just a forty-two-year-old Polish ex-cop who shaves his head to keep people from noticing his bald spot and can't run on the bare ground without shoes.

The group outside is gathered around a race car. For a minute, I think Dale Earnhardt Junior must be here to sign autographs. Even the big-name drivers make the rounds to talk to the fans. That's one of the things I love about racing. Nobody gets too big for his britches. The drivers are as likely to sit down and drink a beer with you as they are to get mad when someone bumps them into the wall.

But the color of the car is wrong and the number is 110, Ricky Sanders's car. Ruby is already pushing the crowd aside and sticking her head through the driver's side window of the Ford. She's not a petite woman, and she has the strength of a bulldozer when it comes to getting where she wants to be. I push and shove to get close to her, wishing I could still flash my detective's badge and get people out of my way.

"I think he's dead." Ruby finds my eyes with hers as she stands up straight. "There's a lot of blood and I think Ricky Sanders is dead."

TWO

"Not Ricky Sanders," the woman beside me says, with shock in her voice. "He was such a good-looking boy too. Bless his heart."

I hear the gasps from the crowd around me as I stand beside the car. Nothing looks unusual. The driver is wearing his helmet and jumpsuit. He's strapped into his harness. It's not until I look closer that I can see blood on his neck and arm. It's pooled on the floor, dripping down his fingertips.

Ruby's face is pale, her lips trembling. "Who would want to hurt Ricky?"

I take her hand as I call 911 on my cell phone. I can see Ricky's face behind the protective shield. His eyes are open and staring. He looks about twelve years old. One of his hands is on the steering wheel. No doubt someone posed it there. Nobody dies that pretty. He was probably already dead when he was put in there.

"Do you think he got all dressed up and then killed himself?" Ruby asks.

"Not many people cut their own throats, but I can't tell for sure. The crime scene people should be able to find out what happened when they get here. I can't imagine why he'd put on his gear, strap in, and drive over here to kill himself, but I've seen weirder suicides." It seems to me like this isn't a suicide, but I'm not saying any more right now. Let the cops take care of it. I'm retired.

I step back from the car and notice a line of blood that looks like it dripped down from the window. There's a large smear where someone might have leaned in too close, but there's nothing on the ground.

Even though security is tight this year, from the track to the campgrounds that surround it, the police are taking their time getting here. There have always been security teams at the races, looking for problem drinkers or the occasional rowdy fistfight, but since 9/11, it's been worse. Now they're looking for possible terrorist activity. With an American flag on every bumper and a rifle in every truck, it would be a bad place to be a terrorist. But I suppose you never know.

The campgrounds are crowded this year too. It seems like there are more people every year. Most people stay out here in motor homes, but there are always a few tents too. Along with the crowd, the motor homes get bigger every year. I saw a bus yesterday that was as big as a house. If they get any bigger, they'll have to develop more land to camp on during the races. It's the only way to really experience everything. A few people might not want to brave the mosquitoes and the noise of the cars on the track, but most do.

People continue to gather around the car, wondering what happened. The late-night party people are getting up and starting to wander this way, popping open their first beers of the day. The smell of coffee and fresh Krispy Kreme doughnuts seems to be everywhere.

The PA system reminds everyone that they can drive a race car around the track or be driven around by a professional driver. Lowe's Motor Speedway is great about setting up exciting pre-race activities for everyone. I took a drive last year on the track. Going 180 miles per hour is about as exciting as I can stand. I couldn't pull my teeth apart for an hour after it was over. When Ruby did it, people could hear her screaming outside the track. It's as close as we'll ever get to being professional drivers: in other words, heaven.

"What are you doing?" Ruby asks as I look at the inside of the car again.

"Once a cop . . ." I squeeze her hand and smile at her. "There are short, black fuzzy hairs on his shoulder."

"Maybe he was with a girl before he killed himself."

I glance at his gloves. Everything he's wearing is so clean, except for the blood. Along with the hand posed on the steering wheel, the whole thing looks staged to me. "I don't know. This hair doesn't look human."

Ruby lowers her head and looks at the dark fuzz. "It looks like something from a boa."

"A boa? You mean a snake?"

"No. It's like a scarf you wrap around your neck."

She starts to touch Ricky and I pull her back. "You can't touch anything. It's a crime scene. We can only look."

"What's there to see? He's dead."

"Yeah. But look at his hand that's on the steering wheel. No one dies like that. Everything is so perfect. I don't think he killed himself, Ruby. I think he was murdered."

"Murdered?" Her voice is loud enough to be picked up by the crowd. "Who'd want to murder Ricky?"

As the people closest to us start murmuring, "Ricky was murdered," an unpleasant thought pops into my brain. "You knew him."

She takes her hand away from me. "I did. So did a lot of other people. That doesn't mean I killed him."

"Rule of thumb, sweetie." I quote her from the Police Bible: "The first person at the scene of a crime is usually involved in some way."

"But I didn't find him, remember? I ran out like you did when we heard everyone else screaming."

"Let's hope one of those screamers was another ex-girlfriend."

Blue eyes already wet with tears raise to mine. "Are you saying you think *I* did this?"

"No. I'm saying the detective who has this case might think that." The sound of several sirens punctuate my words. I put my arm around my wife as we move back from the car. "I'm not volunteering that information, Ruby. Just don't be surprised if it comes out anyway."

A large detective in a wrinkled brown suit and tie takes out his badge and starts toward the car. Several uniformed officers accompany him, pushing back the crowd and making room for the ambulance. "I want a name and phone number for everyone in this group around the car," the detective says to the officer standing beside him.

From my vantage point, I notice several people slowly easing back from the crowd. Force of habit causes me to notice their faces and where they go. They're probably bail jumpers or have some other reason to stay outside the police radar. Most people want to be there and talk about what they've seen and heard. Enough information means you get to talk to the TV cameras later. No one wants to miss that.

“Shouldn’t we leave now?” Ruby pulls at my hand as I watch the detective stoop down to look in the driver’s window.

“We’ve got nothing to hide. Don’t worry. I’m probably paranoid. If I’m right and Ricky was killed, it was most likely one of his sponsors who did it.” I laugh. “Except for bumping your brother out of the race yesterday, he was pretty unremarkable.”

We see Ivey and Sam Branford at the fringe of the crowd. Both of them are sporting black eyes. For once, Ivey isn’t hanging on her man. There’s no sign of Holly. She might be in worse shape and not willing to come out.

When Ivey sees Ruby, she makes a quick stab through the crowd to confront her. “I don’t know how you did it, but that plate you claimed was yours last year is gone. If I knew for sure you took it, I’d tell that officer and he’d arrest you.”

“I don’t know what you’re talking about, honey,” Ruby drawls. “But that’s one heck of a shiner you’ve got. Want to borrow some makeup?”

Ivey grits her teeth and makes a low growling sound in the back of her throat, but she doesn’t say anything else. She turns away and struts past Sam, who shrugs and follows her.

I can’t help feeling sorry for Ivey. I went through the same thing with my ex. Came home from work early one day and found her with her aerobics instructor in our bed. It took me a few minutes staring at them to understand what happened. I wonder if Ivey will stay with Sam anyway. Some people seem to want to blame the outside person. All I could see was my ex-wife’s face.

"Hey!" Andy Andersen's chubby pink face pops up from the crowd. "I knew you'd be down here. What happened? I didn't get here until after the cops."

"Hey, Andy." Ruby hugs him. She hugs everyone. "Glad thinks I killed someone."

"I didn't say that." I glance around uncomfortably. Leave it to Ruby to do a 360-degree turnaround in record time. "It's Ricky Sanders, Andy. He's dead."

"Wow! Did you get a look at him?"

"I think his throat was cut. Probably not a suicide."

"And what makes you think that?" another voice demands. The detective in the brown suit takes off his latex gloves and invites himself into our conversation. "You must've gotten a pretty good view."

I look him in the eye and put out my hand. "Glad Wyczsnewski. I used to be a homicide detective in Chicago. I'm retired now."

He shakes my hand and smiles at Ruby. "I'm Detective Frishburn from Concord PD. I thought I heard the sound of a Yankee cop. Down here for the race?"

"That's about all I do now," I say. He keeps smiling at Ruby, his eyes resting in the hollow of her cleavage. Lucky for him I'm not an insanely jealous man. "Looks like you've got yourself a homicide."

"Looks that way to me, but the medical examiner is on his way out. He'll have the final say." Frishburn looks out across the crowded campground, then stares at Ruby again. "This is a mess. Not like we can close down the race to search for a killer, if there is one. Did you notice anything when you were looking in the car?"

"Not really." I shrug and put my hands in my pockets. I'm not *insanely* jealous, but if Frishburn's eyes don't go back into their sockets in a few seconds, I'm going to have to have a private conversation with him behind my RV. "I saw the kid race yesterday. Maybe somebody didn't like the way he did it. Or maybe he had some other problems. This isn't an easy life."

"Hard to say." His gaze flashes up to mine. "Some people will do anything to get into a race. Maybe he crossed the wrong person."

Andy takes the opportunity to introduce himself just like anyone else who has nothing to hide. "I'm Andy Andersen. I'm a retired stock broker. I didn't see anything, but I'd be glad to help in any way I can."

Frishburn shakes his hand. "Thanks." He swivels to look at Ruby again. "And you are?"

"Ruby Wycznewski." She takes his hand. "My family lives in Midland. Maybe you know them. Zeke and Louise Furr."

"Furr's Auto Supply?" He shakes her hand vigorously. "Who doesn't know your daddy? He's been working the racing circuit almost as long as Humpy Wheeler. Isn't one of your brothers racing this year?"

"Bobby." She giggles with pride. "He's the baby, but we have high hopes for him."

"I'm sure he'll do fine. I met your daddy once when I was working in Harrisburg before I moved to Concord. He's a good man. Always hear good things about him."

"Thanks."

"So how'd you end up married to this boy?" He jerks his head toward me. "Shouldn't you have married somebody from down your way?"

Ruby puts her arm through mine and presses against my side. "After I met Glad, there wasn't anyone else. He doesn't eat grits, but he loves racing. Nothing wrong with that."

A shadow crosses Frishburn's face. "Your brother and the deceased swapped some paint yesterday during practice. Almost cost Bobby his car. Sanders lost an engine. I remember hearing about the two rookies going at it. There was a fight after the race too, wasn't there?"

Ruby glances up at me with a worried frown between her eyes. "It happens, Detective," she says. "Everybody knows that. Bobby was lucky he could control his car and didn't hit the wall. Ricky wasn't that lucky."

Frishburn jots down a note in a greasy little book, which he then puts back in his pocket. The morning sun is making his face red. He mops his brow with a large white handkerchief and smiles. "Gotta check everything. I'm sure your daddy would want me to do the same if one of you were dead. Excuse me. I have to check in with my captain, let him know what's going on out here."

"What was that all about?" Andy asks as we start back toward our motor home.

"Nothing much," I answer. "Ricky Sanders and Ruby's brother, Bobby, got into it off the track yesterday after practice. It doesn't mean anything."

Andy's shuffling gait keeps up with us. "Yeah? But Detective Frishburn seemed to think it meant something."

"He's looking for anything to make his life easier right now. Like he said, this race is too big and there's too much money involved to shut it down. He's going to have to sift through a bunch of crap to get any answers."

"I'm sorry I said anything," Ruby says. She sits down in a chair under the awning when we reach our RV. "If I wouldn't have told him about Bobby—"

"He would've found out anyway if he didn't already know," I finish for her. "Don't blame yourself, sweetie. He'll have to do his job."

"But who's gonna protect Bobby?" Her eyes meet mine as I sit beside her and pop open a cold beer.

"Don't look at me. I'm here for the race. I don't do that anymore."

"But Ruby's brother could go to jail," Andy says, arguing with me too.

"Not if he didn't do anything. Relax, you two. Let's enjoy the week. Ruby and I are going down to pit-crew school this morning, Andy. Want to go?"

Andy decides not to go. Probably a good idea, since he isn't signed up and he'd just have to watch us. Ruby and I suit up with three other members of our pseudo pit crew: Jack and Ruth Mullen and their daughter, Stacy, from Dubuque, Iowa. This is the Mullens' third race, all at this speedway. They explain that they love the sport but haven't been able to venture further. Jack tells us he'd like to go to Sonoma, and I tell him about the race where Ruby and I were married. The Mullens are clearly envious of us being able to follow the racing circuit around the country. It doesn't surprise me. It's the best life I can imagine.

We suit up in fire-retardant blue jumpsuits just like a real pit crew that works on the cars during the races. Pit-crew school is another activity Lowe's has added for die-hard race fans who want to know exactly what it's like being on the track. After we're ready, we're introduced to our pit chief, John Staple, and five real-life pit-crew members who will show us how to change tires, add gas, and take care of everything else a race car requires between laps.

"What does it take to have a successful NASCAR Nextel Cup pit stop?" Staple, a big man with a hard face and thinning brown hair, sounds like a drill sergeant. A particularly obnoxious drill sergeant.

The Mullens look at us, and Ruby raises her hand. "Really fast hands and no regard for your personal safety." The real pit crew laughs and agrees with her.

Staple, on the other hand, is more to the point. "Interesting answer, but not correct. It requires four tires, twenty-two gallons of fuel, seven team members, and fifteen seconds. It's the pit crew that gives the driver the winning edge." The Mullens' mouths all make Os.

I find myself wishing I'd worn my hat. The sun is hot on my head for May, and my days of having hair that protects it are over. They're back there with my misspent youth and jumping fences to chase young car thieves. I focus back on what the chief is telling us.

"Working together, the pit crew decides whether the car needs gas, tires, or a chassis adjustment. In the old days, crews held rubber hoses lined with lug nuts in their teeth. Buckets of gasoline and a funnel covered the fuel stops. There was no speed limit, and the pit crew had to be careful they didn't get pinned between the wall and the car."

"That had to be tough," Mr. Mullen gushes. "Separates the men from the boys."

"Rules save lives, sir," Staple tells him. "Like everything else, there's a right way and a wrong way."

One of the pit team continues the information. "There's one jack man in a seven-member team. That's my job. I jack up the car so the tires can be removed. I signal the driver by dropping the car after service is complete."

Staple picks up the pace after we admire the jack man in our presence. "There are two tire changers. Tire changer one changes front right and front left tires. Tire changer two changes rear right and left tires. There are two tire carriers. Tire carrier one carries two new seventy-five-pound tires and rims to the front tire changer. Tire carrier two carries two new seventy-five-pound tires to the rear tire changer."

Another young man from the pit team smiles. "I'm normally the gas man. I empty two eleven-gallon cans of fuel into the car. The full fuel can weighs ninety pounds. The catch-can man controls the overflow of fuel. Both the catch-can man and the first gas man wear fire-retardant clothing. Sometimes we have a windshield cleaner. It all depends on the race."

"That's amazing," Stacy says. "How do you get all that done in such a short period of time?"

Staple looks at her like she's got a bug on her forehead. He continues with his canned speech. "People wonder how we manage to do so much in such a short period of time. Today, I'm going to show you all the tricks we know. These boys are going to help me out. After they show you what *they* can do, you'll have a chance to show them what *you* can do. For safety purposes, we won't have a gas man. You all will just be changing tires and checking the car out. I'll start the clock as soon as the team starts working."

True to his word, Staple starts the clock just as a race car slows in front of us. He narrates the pit stop. "The car pulls into the pit. The front tire changers and the jack man are already standing on pit road. They run around to the front of the car while the car's still moving. The jack rolls under the car as it comes to a stop. Both right-side tires are changed in a few seconds. The tire crews head to the left side of the car. The gas tank is filling while this happens."

The five pit-crew members are amazingly fast as they work. They manage to do exactly what Staple says as he's saying it. It's incredible to watch and daunting to think of trying. I look at Ruby, wishing I had a cold beer. But she's totally engrossed in watching the pit crew. From behind us, the distinct roar of engines starting up scratches at the clear morning.

"It's the job of the front tire carrier to find some time to clean debris from the grill of the car. He waits at the pit wall with a new tire until the jack man comes around to the other side. The rear tire carrier and the gas man also wait at the wall for the rear tire changer to come around to the rear left tire. This is all done in total synchronization to avoid anyone getting in anyone else's way and slowing down the pit stop." Staples stops speaking as the crew stops working. He smacks his hand down hard on the top of the clock. It registers everything having been done in nineteen seconds.

"How do they get the tires on and off so fast?" Mrs. Mullen asks in disbelief. "We won't be able to come close to that!"

"Definitely not," Staple agrees without a hint of encouragement.

The man is obviously not tourist-friendly. It makes me wonder how he got the job. I seem to recall him being a crew chief at one time. I'm not sure what happened to him. The same thing is probably as true for old crew chiefs as everyone else. Those who can, do. Those who can't show wide-eyed race fanatics like us how to do it.

We're put in position as the car spins around to come back and pit again. I'm set to be a tire carrier with Mr. Mullen. Ruby and Mrs.

Mullen get ready to change the tires. Stacy is the jack man. The car pulls close to us and we're off.

"This takes better hand-eye coordination than your average video-game-playing six-year-old," Staple shouts, harassing us further. "Most of you are probably lucky you can change a tire in an hour." He pushes down on the clock to set it.

Our real pit-crew member is more help. He squats down beside me and Ruby and says, "There are a few tricks the teams use to make things faster. When a new tire is put on the car, the five lug nuts are already attached to the wheel by an adhesive. The studs are different. They're long and have no threads for the first three-quarters of an inch. This way the lug nuts don't get cross-threaded. That makes it easier for a tire to be positioned properly."

Stacy finally manages to get the car off the ground. Ruby tries and fails to remove the tire. One of the pit crew finally steps in and helps her use the air wrench. The tire comes off and I put the new tire on. Ruby secures it and we repeat the process on the other side. Stacy drops the car and we look at the time. Ten minutes. Not a great start.

"Not bad," our pit-crew member tells us. "You'll do better next time."

"Are we doing it again?" Mr. Mullen wheezes.

"Can only give you a certificate for less than five minutes," Staple tells us. "We'll keep doing it until you get it right."

Staple is sounding more and more like my sergeant in the Marines. All of us are sweating and breathing hard when the car comes to the pit again.

"Wasn't this supposed to be fun?" Stacy asks as she trips over her jack.

"*Fun?*" Staple demands. "This is supposed to show you the reality of what it takes to win a race. NASCAR has a pit-road inspector for every two stalls. It's his job to apply penalties like a stop-and-go freeze for running over a jack. A crew that jumps the wall too soon can be penalized. A car with missing lug nuts has to return to the pit, which can cost your driver the race. Do you think those pit crews out there are having *fun*?"

"She's just a kid who admires what gets done out there," I jump back at him. I don't know if it's just his attitude or that I'm ready to move on to something else, but this guy is starting to bug the crap out of me. "Lighten up!"

Staple glares at me and pushes the clock to start timing us. Stacy starts jacking up the car, so I go back and do my part. But no matter what the time is, I'm through with this. They need to get someone a little less abrasive for this job.

We move faster and better at getting the job done. It's like the synchronicity of it finally hits us. Stacy drops the car as we finish. Ruby manages to get her hand out just in time.

"Four minutes!" Staple stops the clock and smiles at us. At least I hope it's a smile. "Good work! You made your certificates. Now you have a working souvenir to show your friends."

I'm not sure who's more relieved at his words. The real pit crew looks uncomfortable, and the rest of us are just glad it's over.

From the corner of my eye as I receive my certificate, I notice Detective Frishburn coming to stand at the edge of the group. Staple gives me my piece of paper as Frishburn starts talking to Ruby. From the look on her pretty face, I can see I've underestimated the man.

"So why didn't you mention that your family is feuding with Ricky Sanders's family off the track, Mrs. Wyczewski?"

THREE

"Call me Ruby, Detective. It's too hot out here to use that whole mouthful of a name." I watch as she smiles and lays her hand on his arm. God, she's good. The bright blue jumpsuit fits her tight in all the right places. She's one spectacular hunk of a woman. Not that I'm willing to share her with Detective Frishburn, but I have to admire her style.

"Okay, Ruby," Frishburn says, starting again in a different tone of voice. "Your family has some history with the Sanderses. Didn't you think that might've been important to mention?"

"No. That was a while back. I'm surprised anybody remembers. We *do* have history, and not all of it is bad."

"Ricky's family remembers. I talked with them this morning." He looks at her in that way all cops have, sizing her up, wondering what she's guilty of. "They said there was more than just the land dispute too. You two had a big argument because Ricky was cheating on you. Then you married on the rebound. Is that true?"

She nods her head. "All except the 'marrying on the rebound' part." She smiles at me around Frishburn's head. "I wasn't in love with Ricky. It was a family thing. Our families' lands are side by side. My parents have always hated the fence between them and the Sanderses. They thought if I married Ricky, the Sanderses would take it down. It's like a standing joke in my family. If they had a daughter, my daddy would've expected Bobby to date her too."

Frishburn writes everything down and then looks back at me. "Sorry. You know it's just my job. You may be from Chicago, but we don't do things that different here in Concord. We have to check all the possibilities."

"I'm not worried about it." I put my arm around Ruby's waist, and she moves closer to me. She's cool and sweet as watermelon on the outside, but her heart is beating fast. "And just for the record, Ruby was with me all night."

"I know you know I expected you to say that." He shrugs. The heat has seeped sweat into his shirt collar, leaving it wilted. His tie is loose around his neck and has a stain on it. Looks like mustard. "How many men did you ever ask about their wives' whereabouts who *didn't* say they were with them?"

"Only the husbands who wanted to pin something on their wives," I point out. "And you know that I know you'd expect me to say it. So I had to know I was better off *not* saying it if I was trying to hide something."

He opens his mouth to speak, then shakes his head, looking confused. "I'm not sure I follow that logic. But we're at an impasse. Your brother-in-law could be a suspect in all this. You two both knew there were other factors that could point toward Bobby. If you wanted to be up-front with me, why didn't you say so?"

"Maybe because Bobby didn't have anything to do with what happened," Ruby explains. "Ricky's always been popular, but since he became a driver, he's had his choice of women. Maybe there was someone who thought she had a good reason to kill him."

"Maybe." Frishburn smiles at her. "Or he broke *your* heart a little more than you want to admit. Especially with your new husband standing next to you. Maybe Ricky bumping Bobby was just one insult too many."

"That's ridiculous!" she declares passionately. "Ricky got the worst of that, anyway."

"Yeah. And maybe that was how it started."

"No way!"

"Are you saying Bobby *couldn't* have done it? Do you have an alibi for him, Ruby? Was he right there with you and your husband all night?"

"No." She backs down, but she doesn't give up. "Bobby wouldn't hurt Ricky over any of those things. We grew up with the Sanderses. Families fight sometimes, but they don't kill each other."

I hold Ruby a little tighter. She's shaking like a rough-idling car. I ask Frishburn, "Have you talked to Bobby about all this?"

"No, I haven't been able to find him. Do you have any idea where he is?"

"I haven't seen him since early this morning," I admit. "But since he's racing today, I'm sure he's somewhere getting ready. Maybe you should talk to him and see if he has an alibi. You might be barking up the wrong tree."

Frishburn scratches his head and looks away. "It's just a theory. I'm checking out all the angles."

"In that case, let me give you a few other angles," I insist. "Sanders obviously wasn't killed in the car. I know you noticed the blood on the door. There was none on the ground."

"Why did you say you retired from the job?" He puts away his notebook. "You sound pretty sharp to me. We don't know yet if Ricky was killed in the car or not. The ME hasn't made that call. You know how that goes. I can hypothesize all I want, but he has final say."

I smile at him. "It hasn't been *that* long, Frishburn. I know the problems dealing with forensic evidence. But we both know a good cop has instincts. You see things too many times. You notice things other people miss. I know you already have a gut feeling about this case. Is that what's telling you Bobby did this?"

"It's possible." He shrugs. "He had motive. We don't know yet if he had opportunity. I think he makes a good suspect. That's what my gut tells me. What does yours tell you, Wycznewski?"

I know he's baiting me, but I can't resist the opportunity to talk shop. "The blood smeared on the outside of the car door might be on the killer's clothes. That would be one angle to check out. I bet whoever did it cut Ricky's throat, then lifted him up and stuffed him in the car. He pushed the car into the campground to display what he did. He wanted everyone to notice."

"None of those things might be important," he retorts. "A little blood on the car. No blood on the ground. Maybe there was a tarp protecting the ground and the killer moved it."

It's obvious he didn't see what I saw. Rookies. "Did you see how much blood was in the car? You should be looking for some blood somewhere else. Maybe you should check someplace where the car was easily accessible."

Frishburn moves close enough to me that I can see the beads of sweat on his upper lip. Not a pretty picture. "You mean one of those places I should be looking for Bobby? No matter what the incidentals are of this case, the fact is that your brother-in-law very likely played a part in it. Unless he has a better alibi than your wife, I might pull him out of the race and take him downtown for questioning."

"That's almost as ridiculous as charging *me* with the murder."

"Is that a confession?"

I can't help it. I laugh. Ruby pokes me in the ribs, but I still can't help it. "You and I both know if I decided to kill someone, you'd never find the body. I wouldn't put it out for show at the camp ground or pose him pretty for pictures."

We stand almost nose to nose for a few seconds. I know what's going on in my mind, but there's no way to know what he's thinking. I can only hope I've convinced him to look for something that makes more sense. Could I have killed Ricky Sanders? Sure. Would I have gotten out of bed with Ruby to kill him? No way. And I don't think Bobby wasted that much thought on what happened during practice either.

Finally, Frishburn backs down. "Yeah. I suppose so." He looks up at the cloudless blue sky and squints into the sunlight. "It's gonna be a hot one. Dry too. We could use some rain. Hope you two plan to stay for the whole race."

It's his way of telling us not to leave town. We're not exactly suspects, but we might have information he needs about Bobby. I know this is as close to an apology as I'm ever going to get. I hand Ruby her certificate from pit-crew school. "If there's anything else we can do, Frishburn . . ."

“Thanks. I’m sure we can handle it. Don’t know how they do things in Chicago, but down here, we just keep on pushing at the dirt until we find what we’re looking for.” He glances at Ruby and nods his head. “Mrs. Wycznewski.”

Ruby and I stand with our arms around each other while we watch the detective amble away. A new group of students are being treated to Staple’s brand of charm. The smell of gas is strong in the still, hot air.

“That was close!” Ruby takes a deep breath and sags against me, then punches me in the side. “And *you*! Were you trying to get us arrested?”

“What was close?” I kiss the top of her head, inhaling her personal scent mixed with White Diamonds. “Oh! You mean he almost found out we killed Ricky and shoved him into the car?”

She punches me in the side again and glances around to see if anyone is listening. “Don’t *say* that! That man was *serious*. He thinks Bobby killed Ricky.”

“And did he?”

“No!”

“Then how was it close? What did he almost find out? Some deep, dark secret only the Furr family knows?”

I’m sorry immediately when I see the drawn, dark look on her face. There *is* something. Something she’s held back from Frishburn *and* me. Something that could make Bobby more than a passing suspect in the murder investigation. I draw her away from the noise and the possibility of interested ears.

“Bobby shot him,” she says.

Nothing could make me more likely to hit the steamy concrete right now. I feel like a man in a cartoon. My jaw drops. My eyes become the size of saucers (well, large gray marbles anyway). "What are you talking about? Are you telling me he killed Ricky? When did he do it?"

"Don't be ridiculous, Glad! I said he *shot* him. I didn't say he *killed* him."

I have to sit down on the bench beside her. I need something to drink. There's a Coke machine nearby. Why don't they make beer machines for emergencies like this? I'd take the Coke if I had correct change to appease the flashing red light, but I don't. "Tell me the whole story. From the beginning. Maybe we can go to the DA with Bobby. Make a deal for him before they prosecute. We could make it easier on him."

She shoots to her feet. "Would you *please* stop being a police detective for one minute?" I know she's gathering her thoughts as she paces the short, broken sidewalk. "Bobby shot him when we first found out Ricky got that other girl pregnant. He only wounded him in the shoulder. It was a .22. He barely felt it. It was more like a bee sting."

My heart stops beating for an instant, then surges back to life. I crush her against me. "Don't *ever* scare me again like that. Next time, start with the important part, like *when* he shot him."

"You don't see this as being important?" She glares at me. "If Detective Frishburn thinks Bobby makes a decent suspect now, what's he gonna think when he finds out Bobby shot Ricky before?"

"He's not going to think anything. The three of you had a fight, and Bobby got mad. Obviously, he's over it. That doesn't make him part of what happened now."

"There's plenty of bad blood between the Furrs and the Sanderses. He's bound to come after one of us. He's already asking questions about Bobby. I could be next. It looks to me like we might stay on his suspect list."

"Would you like to clarify 'bad blood' for me so I have some idea what to expect?"

Bobby drives up at that moment. He hops out of his beefed-up 1966 Mustang convertible that I'd give up my RV for even if it *would* be hard to live in. We'd get used to it. "I heard that police detective was looking for me, Ruby. I've been trying to stay clear of him until after the race. I have to concentrate and court a few sponsors. Does he think I killed Ricky?"

She hugs him and tells him what happened while I admire the new red paint job on the Mustang. "He thinks you did it. If he finds you, he'll take you in for questioning. He'll be even surer once he hears about you shooting Ricky. Maybe we should leave."

I only pay attention to the last part. "We can't leave. None of us can leave. Frishburn would know one or both of you are guilty. You're making too big a deal over it, sweetie. He doesn't have anything concrete because there *isn't* anything. Let's enjoy the race and let Frishburn find Ricky's killer."

Bobby brushes his hand over the ten coats of paint and Klear Kote it took to get his car looking that way. "You know I'm not a runner anyway, Ruby. I might not put myself in his path until after qualifying, but I don't have anything to hide. Once it's over, he can take me and question me until next Sunday. I didn't kill Ricky."

"Then you don't have anything to worry about. Just a family feud won't hold up in court as a motive," I assure him. "Out of curiosity and because Frishburn will ask you too, where were you this morning after you paid us a visit?"

"I was looking at my car. Imagining myself on victory lane. That's how you have to do it, you know. Thought power."

I nod, not sure if that will really work if everything else isn't already in your favor. "Anybody stop by to talk? Was a mechanic there?"

"Nope." He adjusts the bill on his ball cap to shade his freckled face from the sun. "Just me and the power thoughts."

"That's not good." I don't want to bring him down before the race, but Frishburn is looking for a better alibi than Bobby sitting around thinking about his car. He's going to dig deeper when he hears Bobby was probably alone when Ricky was killed.

"I didn't do anything. Just because there's some bad blood between us doesn't mean I killed him." Bobby's tone is arrogant, belligerent. It won't win him any favors with the police. "I'd like to stay and talk, but I better keep moving. Talk to you after the race."

Ruby hugs him and wishes him luck. When Bobby speeds away, she turns to me. "So what do we do now? What's the first thing we should look for?"

"Look for?" I puzzle over her words. Not too bright, I guess. I should know by now. She can't stay out of anything for long. "Oh no! You're not talking about . . ."

She sits down on the bench again as a group of people stroll by on their way to pit road. She crosses her long legs and smiles at me. "Well, Frishburn isn't gonna get the job done if he's trying to convict Bobby. He has to be looking for the right person. I was so mad back there! I could have wrung his neck like Aunt Ada used to wring her roosters' necks when they started crowing in the middle of the night."

I hope she's not thinking what I think she's thinking. "I don't do that anymore, remember? I retired. Pension. RV. New life." I should've known she wasn't trembling because she was *scared* when we were talking to Frishburn. Thinking back on it, I haven't known her to be scared of anything.

"You don't have to do it," she tells me. "Just tell *me* what to do, and I'll do it."

I take a deep breath and count to ten. Then I look at her, take another deep breath, and count to a hundred. "Let the police handle it, Ruby. They know what they're doing. Bobby won't be the only suspect. Frishburn will figure it out."

"Maybe. But probably not until he causes my family some grief. *We* have to figure it out, honey. You did this all the time back in Chicago. We can solve one murder. How hard can it be? We poke around. Ask everyone if they saw or heard anything. We find that blood you were talking about. Frishburn arrests the killer. Just like on TV."

If you could compress all the hours it takes to do the list of things she's outlined, it *would* be easy. But the fact is, it can't be done just like that. "It's not the same as on TV, sweetie. They start and finish a whole murder investigation in an hour. Sometimes it can take weeks, even years, to solve a homicide. And that's with forensics. I don't know about you, but I'm not willing to give this that kind of time."

"Well, *darlin'*, we better get started then, don't you think?"

"It's impossible, *angel.* The best thing we can do is lay low and enjoy the race. Bobby can lay low too. Frishburn is bound to figure it out."

"I can't do that, *sugar.*" She surges to her feet and glares at me. "Are you gonna help me with this or not?"

I fold my arms across my chest, angle my head, and gird my loins. (I'm not sure what that means, but it sounds like something I should be doing right now.) "I'm not going to help you investigate a murder, Ruby. And I don't think you should do it either. It's not a game or some reality TV show. People's lives are at stake. It could be dangerous. We could make it even harder for Frishburn to look at someone else. That wouldn't help Bobby."

We stand there staring at each other, oblivious to everything else going on around us in the carnival atmosphere of race week. Trucks are revving their engines as vendors are hawking everything from T-shirts to souvenir NASCAR sandwiches. People are yelling and babies are crying. The Goodyear blimp is flying overhead. There's something unreal but exciting about being here. It's the buildup to what we all want to see: forty-three cars racing around the track, trying to find out who has the nerve and ambition to be the next winner.

I know Ruby will back down. I know she'll see that I'm right and that the best thing is to leave it alone. I know we'll end this with a hug and a kiss and go on to the next event.

Yeah, right.

Ruby's face gets animated. She holds up her arm and waves to someone behind me. "Kim! David!" She hails her best friend from high school and the friend's husband. "We're gonna solve a murder. Want to help?"

And all I can do is stand here with twenty cents in my pocket and the sure knowledge that I'm going to help find Ricky Sanders's killer, despite my better judgment.

FOUR

I'll admit I'm happy when Kim and David laugh and wander away, disappearing into the crowd that smells like sunblock and beer. I don't want to take care of this problem in the first place, and if I am, I sure as hell don't want Ruby's friends thinking they're going to help me. That is a sure recipe for disaster.

Ruby looks innocently at her perfect nail polish like she thinks she can find a chip somewhere. I know that game.

"All right. We'll ask a few questions. I don't know if that will help, but—mmmsshh." Ruby squeals a little and plants a kiss on me. With her pretty mouth pressed up against mine and her arms wrapped around me, I don't mind so much that this is happening to ruin my fun-filled race week.

"You're the best, sugar! I know we can do this!" She winks and uses her thumb to take lipstick off my mouth.

"I'm glad you're so confident. I'm not even sure I know where to start."

"Of course you do! We'll get a notebook and start writing things down that people say." She wraps her arm through mine as we start walking toward the track. "That's what they do on TV. Didn't you do that when you were a detective?"

"Sure." How can I tell her that most of the time I forgot my notebook and wrote on the back of Twinkie wrappers or on my hand? Besides, getting a notebook and writing things down is probably the safest thing she can do. Bogging her down in paperwork might make her reconsider.

"Who should we interrogate first?" she asks, tapping her cheek. "Let's see . . . there's the team owner, Paul Massey. Everybody said yesterday he couldn't have been very happy with Ricky's performance on the track. Maybe we should question Ricky's parents after that. Mama said we should come out for supper before the race is over."

"Ricky's family might not want to talk about this yet," I suggest, not wanting to burst her detective bubble as we approach the garage area. "They just lost their son."

"Maybe." She considers it. "I suppose they're still in shock. Of course, that might be the best time to talk to them. Who knows what they'll say!"

"Or they might think Bobby did it. Just because *you* think he's innocent doesn't mean they will."

"I doubt it." She slips on her sunglasses. "What would be the point of Bobby killing Ricky?"

"I don't know. Sometimes people get worked up and things happen. No one means for those kinds of things to happen, but they do."

"I know what you mean. But you know that detective is all wrong. Nobody was mad about Bobby shooting Ricky that time. Everyone understood what happened. It was like that time Dale Sanders, Ricky's daddy, accidentally cut off my daddy's toe with the hedge clippers. We didn't go over there looking for revenge—although Bobby *did* cut down Mr. Sanders's apple tree. But that wasn't directly for him cutting off Daddy's toe. Bobby and Ricky were good friends. As good as our two families can be and still be kin."

"Kin? Am I wrong about this? Doesn't 'kin' mean family?"

"Not close kin," she admits. "But somewhere back in our great-great-great-grandfather's time, the land was all one piece, and it all belonged to our combined family. Then it was divided when someone got married, and the feuding started. I can't recall exactly how that went. Mama would know all the details."

I know I'm going to sit down to supper with Ruby's family. That's coming no matter what, since we're at Lowe's and they only live about twenty minutes away. It might even work to my benefit. Ruby's parents might talk her out of trying to investigate Ricky's death. Surely they won't want their daughter put in harm's way.

Ruby has her cell phone out already. She's talking to her mother about supper. I'm looking at the program for today and watching two rookies on pit road working on their cars. Not all drivers start out here with everything handed to them. Some really have to work at it. A pretty smile only goes so far.

It strikes me that killing Ricky and framing Bobby for it pushes the other four rookies up in standing. That could be a motive worth exploring. There's nothing easy about being at the bottom of the ladder. The drivers on top don't want to give way, but maybe the drivers on the bottom could be pushed out.

It's thready, I know. This is only one race out of two thousand race events in forty-one states. Even winning this one would only go so far, and none of the rookies have a chance to do that. Still, people do strange things for reasons that make sense at the time. Later they might want to take them back, but they're stuck.

"All set." Ruby closes her cell phone and smiles at me. Her eyes lose focus and go past me. "There's Paul Massey! We should talk to him, Glad!"

Massey Auto Sports owns the number 110 car Ricky was driving. It could make sense that he might want to see Ricky out of the way, although it would be easier just to fire him. It's always possible Massey tried to fire Ricky and things got ugly. "We have to be careful what we say to him, Ruby. Nothing openly hostile. This needs some finesse."

She rolls her eyes. "You don't have to talk down to me! I think I get the idea! I know how to sweet-talk when I have to."

We wade through all the picture taking and hand shaking going on between the garage and the pit area. Massey is talking to his lead driver, Derek Spencer. Ruby is sashaying in front of me.

One of the rookies takes his truck out on the track to check it out, and I follow it with my eyes, eager for the big race. The sunshine glints off the windshield, almost blinding as it comes around. Something is wrong with the engine, and it sputters and dies. Five pit-crew members rush out to see what happened. Bad luck when your vehicle won't run. Even though a crew usually has more than one engine for the lead driver, some rookies only get one shot.

I realize I've lost track of Ruby. I glance around and finally see her blond curls. She's standing with Massey and Spencer. I come up in time to hear her "sweet-talking" him.

"What do you know about Ricky Sanders's death?" I hear her asking Massey with her usual bull-in-a-china-shop brand of charm.

"Pardon me?" Massey stops talking to Spencer and stares at her.

I step in with, "What my wife means is, what a shame it was to lose Ricky. He showed a lot of promise."

Spencer laughs. "Except he was afraid to put his foot on the gas. Otherwise, he was great."

"Shut up, Derek," Massey says. "There is no reason to speak ill of the poor boy." His eyes narrow suspiciously at Ruby and me. "Ricky was a promising young driver. It was a loss to our team. Are you with the press?"

"No, not at all," I assure him. "Just fans."

"Oh!" Massey's eyes widen as he smiles. "Let me introduce you to Derek."

Spencer flashes his bleached-teeth smile, flips his longish blond hair out of his eyes, and shakes my hand. "Good to meet you."

"Where were you when Ricky was killed?" Ruby asks him.

Spencer grins at me. "Is your wife from another country? She has a funny way of saying things."

"I said exactly what I meant to say," Ruby says in defense. "Ricky was killed and stuffed into his car. Where were you when that happened?"

"I think you should be careful what you're asking, lady."

"Derek!" Massey silences him before he turns to Ruby. "What are you getting at? Do you think Derek killed Ricky? What would be the point?"

"Probably none." She shrugs. "Unless *you* told him to do it."

"Ricky wasn't the best driver in the world, but he was learning," Massey tells her. "I would've kicked him out if I felt differently, not killed him."

"I hear Bobby Furr is the official police suspect," Spencer tells her. "Maybe you should ask *him* those questions."

Ruby balls up her fists and takes a step toward him. Before she can tip our hand, I put my arm around her and pull her back. "Thanks for talking to us."

"Sure."

I have to pull Ruby away from Spencer and Massey. When we get away from the pit area, I stop and growl at her, "You can't do it like that! You put them on the defensive before we had a chance to ask any questions! If you want me to help you do this, you're going to have to do it *my* way!"

"Glad—"

"I mean it, Ruby. We won't get anywhere if you sound like you're out for blood. We have to have a conversation and listen to what they say when they're not suspecting. Can you do that?"

She jerks her arm away from me. "I suppose."

I don't know why I'm bothering to ask her. I know she can't hold back when she gets going. I love that passion in her. I'll just have to make sure I start the conversations from now on.

We stand near the garage, where mechanics are working on various cars. Dale Junior's car is down here for last-minute tweaking. So is Jeremy Mayfield's number 19 car. Rookie driver David Stremme took his car out around the track earlier. It didn't look so good either. I wonder if anyone bothered to bring a decent automobile. Don't they know what they're competing against?

I see another one of Ricky's teammates from Massey's organization as I light a cigar. He's Massey's pit chief, Joe Blalock. He's coming toward us, probably looking for Massey or Spencer.

"Okay. We have another chance, sweetie." I nudge Ruby. "Let me set the pace, and maybe we can find something out about Ricky and Massey."

"Okay." Ruby sighs and I give her arm a squeeze before the chief gets to us.

"Chief!" I hail him. His eyes glaze over when he doesn't recognize us, but he smiles wide and reaches to shake my hand. "Hey, how's it going?"

"We're going good with the new engine," he replies. "I think we'll be hot on the track come the weekend."

"Great! I sure was sorry to hear about Sanders. He was on his way. Tough break."

"Yeah. He was a good kid. Big loss to the team."

They all have that speech down. "I heard someone say he was murdered."

The chief shrugs broad shoulders inside a black-and-white team jacket. "Don't believe everything you hear. I heard suicide."

"No!" Ruby finally speaks out. "Not little Ricky! Why would he do such a thing?"

The chief sidles up next to her and smiles in a greasy way that has nothing to do with his dirty hands. "He owed some people money, you know? He liked to bet big, but he wasn't good at winning."

"And you think he killed himself for that?" I ask, hoping I look amazed and troubled by that knowledge.

"Chief!" Massey calls through the crowd. "Could I have a word with you?"

The chief leaves us with a rueful smile. Ruby giggles and comes close to me as he shuffles away, talking to fans as he goes. "I see! I can do that, Glad. I was doing that with boys since I was twelve."

"That doesn't surprise me." I kiss her briefly, then put my arm around her waist. "So what did we learn from that conversation?"

"That Ricky had money problems?"

"Exactly. Not that it necessarily has anything to do with his death."

"Then what was the point of sweet-talking the chief? If what we learned doesn't make any difference, I could have accused him of killing Ricky and learned the same thing."

"Maybe. But chances are the chief told us something he wasn't supposed to tell us. Maybe Ricky having a gambling problem doesn't matter. Maybe it does. We have to find other things that go along with it. Either you find supporting evidence that holds up your theory, or you move on to the next."

"What do you do with the theory that doesn't work?" she asks.

"You throw it away," I explain. "There's no point in holding on to a bad theory. You learn from them, then put them aside. At least you know what didn't kill him. Sometimes it's only a process of elimination."

"So do we still think Massey was involved?"

"I don't know. He could've tried to fire Ricky and it took a bad turn, I suppose. I don't think he would've wanted to advertise it for everyone by driving the car to the campground. But you never know."

"So whoever did it wanted everyone to know, to show it off?"

"Exactly, my dear, sweet Watson."

Ruby wrinkles her cute little nose. "That's terrible, Glad."

"That someone wanted to show off Ricky's death?"

"That too. But I was thinking of Sherlock Holmes and Watson. I don't think they went that way."

I laugh and take her hand, happy we're on the same page now with our investigation. "There's Bobby." I point to her brother's Dodge Intrepid coming out of pit road.

He makes it around the track, more than I can say for some of his competition. We both see Detective Frishburn standing outside the pits, watching Bobby's car go around the banked track.

"Think he's looking to arrest him?" Ruby asks me.

"Not yet. He wouldn't be standing around like that if he had anything. He'd take Bobby in. Let's see if we can find something else for him to look at before that happens."

"What do *we* look at from here that doesn't involve Bobby?"

"We check out the gambling theory," I explain as we go back toward the infield campground. "If Ricky was gambling and lost money, someone could have made an example of him."

"So we could ask some of the other drivers, since Team Massey won't say anything else bad about him, right?"

"Exactly! We can't talk to Bobby about it because of his position with the investigation. But we can ask those other two rookies. I'll take the one with the busted car. He'll be standing still for a while in the garage."

Ruby stops walking and puts her hands on her hips. "How am I supposed to slow down the other driver?"

I smile and let my eyes take an enjoyable tour of her Cadillac body. "You'll think of something."

Her eyes widen. "Are you saying . . . ?"

I suddenly realize what it sounds like I'm suggesting. "No! I'm not saying that! Just get him to stop long enough to ask him a few questions! You don't have to—"

Grinning, she kisses me and then starts to walk away. "Just checking to see how far I should go to get him to stop."

I don't like the sound of that as I watch the sway of her hips walking away from me. I knew this was a bad idea. Why did I let myself get suckered into it?

"So you don't know anyone in particular who might have bankrolled Ricky's gambling?" I ask the rookie driver again. I'm beginning to think I'm wasting my time.

"I never saw him gamble," he says, wiping grease from his hands on a dirty rag. "But I don't have much time for that sort of thing."

"Thanks."

"But Ricky always had a thing for the ladies." He grins and rocks back on his heels. "Everybody knows that."

"Any particular lady?"

"Not that I ever saw. It was always a different woman. Ricky was a sweet talker, from what I've heard."

"Any of them ever get mad about the others?"

"Maybe. I don't know." He stops screwing down a spark plug and nods. "There was that one lady at Pocono last year. She scratched his face pretty good. He wasn't so popular for a few weeks, until it healed."

"Got a name?'

"Nah. I remember what she looked like. Tall, blond, nice legs. She hung out with some of the owners and drivers for a while. I've seen her around lots of times before. Some of the drivers like that kind of thing. I've got a wife and kid back home."

I smile. "Where's home?"

"Sweetwater, Mississippi." He shakes his head at his car. "And the way this is going, I'll be home pretty soon."

"Thanks for the info, anyway. Good luck with the car."

I walk back out into the sunshine. Hundreds of people are already scrambling around the pit area. Some of them are in uniforms that identify them as part of a team. Most of them are fans dressed in shorts and T-shirts, kids riding on their fathers' shoulders.

The atmosphere is loud and boisterous everywhere from the pit to the Bojangles. Tons of food vendors dispense everything from coffee to slushies as fans look for their favorite drivers and pose for pictures with team owners.

I look for Ruby, thinking about the tall blond with the long legs who scratched Ricky's face. It couldn't have been Ruby, since we were already married last year. But it didn't surprise me to find out her reaction to Ricky getting another woman pregnant. Having been on the other end of that predicament, I know what I felt like doing.

Ricky had a history of lady problems. Maybe one of those problems was strong enough to take him out and stuff him into the car. Or, like Frishburn suggested, maybe there was an accomplice who was there to help her. Or we're looking at it from the wrong direction. It would be nice to have access to that information. I'm sorry Frishburn and I are adversaries. We could have helped each other.

I finally see Ruby near the media center, talking to Dale Junior. I know his father was friends with Ruby's dad, so I'm not surprised.

Ruby hugs him and waves when she sees me. Junior nods and whispers something in her ear before he leaves her. She laughs and playfully slaps at him. Thankfully, I'm not jealous enough to ask what those soft-spoken words are.

"Glad! I might have found something!"

"Great!" I take her arm as we walk away from the media center. "What did Junior say to you?" Okay. I'm wrong. I *am* jealous enough to ask. Come on! The guy is good looking, knows her family, and has plenty of money and a hot car, besides being closer to her age. What's not to be jealous of?

"What do you mean?"

"At the end there," I clarify, leaning close. "When he whispered something to you."

She smiles and puts her hand on my cheek. "You can't be jealous of *Junior*! We practically grew up together."

"And that makes me feel better?"

"Glad, never mind that. I found out something about Ricky."

"All right. What did you find out?"

A loud engine starts up close to us as the Food Lion car comes in to pit with a smoke-filled hood. We duck inside the media center, the sound muffled by the building.

"John said—"

"John?" I ask her.

"The rookie," she explains, keeping her voice down, although the crowd inhabiting the media center doesn't seem to notice. "The one I talked to."

"Doesn't he have a last name?"

"I didn't ask. Why?"

"Did you tell him *your* name?"

"Glad! Focus!"

"Sorry."

"Anyway. John said Ricky told him he'd gotten notes from some woman he met at Pocono. He said she was threatening to kill him."

"My rookie said the same thing." I grin at her. "His name is Murdock. *I* don't know what his *first* name is."

She rolls her pretty blue eyes and I laugh, giving up my sulk about men reacting to her the way they always do. Ruby can't help it. She's just that kind of woman.

"Think we could be on to something?" she asks.

"Maybe. Did John know the woman's name?"

"Yes." She looks around in case anyone is listening to us. "He said her name is Jeanette Almond. And Glad, she's here at the track."

"With ninety-five thousand other people."

"She's camping in the infield. She could have killed Ricky and then shoved him in the car and pushed him into the campground."

I put my arm around her shoulder. "You should've been a cop, Ruby."

She looks smug. "I still could be a cop. Or an FBI agent."

"Whoa, Agent Starling."

"You mean Agent Scully!"

"Hey, you two!" Bobby calls us from the door. He looks around the center and then hurries over to us. "I've been looking for you everywhere! That cop is looking at *me* for killing Ricky!"

"You already knew that," I remind him.

"No, I mean *seriously*! He got a search warrant to look through all my clothes at the track and at home. What's he looking for?"

FIVE

"The police are looking for evidence that you killed Ricky, and how you did it," I say as we walk back outside the media center. "That's how this works. When Frishburn finds enough evidence, he'll haul you in for questioning."

"There can't be enough evidence. I told him everything I know already, Glad!" Bobby complains. "You can't get blood from a turnip."

"That may be." I push back the number 01 cap on my head. "But he has to do his job. Somebody killed Ricky and left him out for the whole infield to know about it. Frishburn has to find out who did it. If you look like the most likely suspect, he'll take you in."

"How can I look not guilty? You're an ex-cop, Glad. Tell me some tricks."

Ruby cuts off our conversation. "Do you know anything about Ricky gambling too much? We heard he might owe some people money, and that might be what happened to him."

"Not me!" he denies a little too quickly. "I wouldn't be involved with that stuff. You know me better than that!"

"That answer isn't gonna help you," she says. "If you know *anything* about Ricky gambling or a woman named Jeanette Almond he had a run-in with, you better tell us now."

"Aw, Ruby, you'll tell Mama!"

"If you get arrested, I won't have to tell her anything! She'll know more about you than you ever wanted. Do I have to do all the thinking for both of us?"

"You really think it's that bad?"

She takes his hand. "I do, honey. You should tell me whatever you think might help. We have to get you out of this mess."

"Okay." He glances around the crowded area. The only way to be heard above the sound of the cars revving their engines is to shout. "But not here. Let's meet back at your place in about an hour, okay?"

Ruby glances at me and nods. "All right. Just be careful, huh?"

"What do you think *that* was about?" I ask as he walks away, disappearing into the crowd.

"I don't know, but I didn't like the way it sounded." Her worried eyes follow him. "Bobby never minds saying anything, anywhere. You know that. Do you think he could be involved in this in some way?"

"I hope not." I don't know what else to say. Anything is possible. Unfortunately, I learned that lesson a long time ago. People who I would have bet my life on being innocent weren't. People who seemed guilty to me weren't involved. "Let's go see if we can find Jeanette at home. She might be able to tell us something that will take care of all of this."

We make our way back to the campground. Most people are out by the track or out shopping. A few are sitting around their campsites, cooking steaks or snoozing in the sun. The all-night poker game that started the first night we got here is still going on. I think the five men involved are still wearing the same clothes.

The RVs are side by side, crammed into the small area on the infield like sardines. Actually, more like sardine cans. It would be hard to sneeze without blowing out someone's scented candle. One bathroom looks into another guy's bedroom, and one kitchen looks into another guy's bathroom. It reminds me of where I grew up in Cicero, Illinois. The houses were so close together, we always knew what the family next door was having for supper.

The infield is a great place to really get into the heart of the race. You're right where the action is. But I think the campgrounds on the outside of the speedway are more comfortable. I'm happy I didn't pay the extra money to be here. Well, not exactly anyway. I don't want to think about how much money I've put into the pot down through the years.

A helicopter sets down across the field. Jeff Gordon hurries to it with his hat in his hand. I've heard some of the big-money drivers, owners, and sponsors go back and forth to their hotels like that. Nice life, I suppose. A little isolated, but not bad. I'm happy with my RV, hanging out with the people I see at almost every race. Sometimes I don't know their names, but I know their faces, and we always speak to each other as we go by. It's usually easier for me to tell you which one of them pulls for Joe, Junior, Jeff, or Jimmie than to remember their names.

Ruby and I have to ask three different people before we find out that Jeanette Almond is in the huge Vantaré Featherlight motor home with the orange sunset painted on the side. The name TRAVEL BISCUIT is emblazoned across the silver and black body. I'm not sure why anyone would want to be known by that name, but I guess she likes it.

"Weren't we here the first night?" I ask Ruby. "Didn't she have a big party going on?"

"That's right. She had it catered, I think." Ruby knocks on the door and winks at me. "Watch me take care of this, darlin'."

A tall, shapely blond who looks remarkably like my wife leans out the door. The green satin bathrobe she's wearing falls slightly off her shoulders. She glances at Ruby and then levels her attention at me. "Can I help you?"

Ruby pipes up. "Hey, Jeanette! We met some friends of yours over by the pits a little while ago. They said we should come over and introduce ourselves. We were at your party the other night."

As an opening gambit, it's pretty good. Ruby is a fast learner. Unfortunately, Jeanette leans forward, takes my arm, and pulls me into the RV, leaving Ruby to follow behind. What can I say? Not every bit of sweet talk is gonna work on every person. Jeanette must be the kind of woman who doesn't like to make conversation with other women.

I wonder, as her bathrobe slides down a little farther, if Ricky was still infatuated with Ruby when he dated Jeanette or if every woman he went around with looked exactly the same. Some police psychologists say we all run in patterns like that, although my ex-wife looked nothing like Ruby.

"What's your name?" Jeanette preens in a mirror near the door. "I don't think we've met before. I think I would remember that. You say you were at the party?"

I hear a little growl in Ruby's throat and smile at Jeanette (anything for the pursuit of the truth) as I introduce myself. Jeanette offers Cokes that I accept for both of us. As she turns away to get them, I put my hand on Ruby's arm. She's already getting up like there's a string running from Jeanette to her, pulling her off the chair.

She mutters, "Glad—"

"Not *now*!"

"So where'd you say you're from, Glad?" Jeanette's petulant voice slides back to us from the kitchen in the middle of the forty-two-foot land yacht.

"Chicago. This is a great RV. Where'd you find it?"

"I had it custom-made in Florida." She comes back, hands me a Coke, and sets Ruby's drink on the table between us. "My third husband died and left me a *very* wealthy woman."

"We heard you threatened to kill Ricky Sanders," Ruby blurts out, then takes a deep breath like she didn't know if she could breathe until she said it.

So much for practice. "You know how talk is." I try to sweeten the pot, but it's too late. The damage is done.

"Ricky? We dated. He was a little too poor for my tastes." Jeanette squeezes my arm and smiles, but her eyes are wary. The smell of some perfume on her is so strong it's nearly sickening. "And a little too scrawny. I like my men with some muscle."

Ruby gets up from her place on the sofa and forcibly removes Jeanette's hand from my arm. "Never mind that. Everyone knows you scratched Ricky's face and threatened to kill him."

Jeanette, surprisingly, backs away from Ruby. "We had a fight. That's all. It was never serious between us. Ricky was never serious about a girl in his whole life."

"So you thought you'd kill him?" Ruby pursues her mercilessly, one step at a time, across the deep blue carpet.

"I never got close to him last night. I was with someone else."

"Who?"

"I don't have to tell you that." Jeanette looks across the room at me like I'm going to tell her she doesn't have to answer Ruby.

"You do if you want me to go away. See, right now they're looking at my brother for what happened to Ricky. I'm not happy about that, or the fact that you touched my husband. So you better tell me who you were with and where you were when Ricky was killed."

I shrug and admire the scenery outside the RV window. It's another RV, green with yellow stripes and Junior's face on the side. Ruby seems to have everything in hand. There's no point in me doing anything. I'd just be in the way.

Jeanette relents under Ruby's fury. "I was with Paul Massey last night. We were here. Ask him, if you don't believe me."

"I will." Ruby glares at her one last time for good measure, then stalks out of the RV.

I walk out quickly behind her and put on my sunglasses. The sun is bright outside after being in the dimly lit motor home. I follow her, trying to catch up. Ruby walks pretty fast when she's mad.

"Don't you think it's a little strange that her alibi is Paul Massey?" She struts down the narrow passage between the RVs, full of herself. "I mean, either of them could be a suspect, but they might be each other's alibis? I think that's a little strange."

I can't hold it in any longer. Maybe I should, but I can't. "I can't believe how much she looks like you! Maybe Ricky was still in love with you when he dated her."

Ruby stops dead. "What are you talking about?"

"Jeanette Almond. She could be your sister. Older, of course, but you two look a lot alike."

I really don't realize until the last words are out of my mouth that Ruby is taking offense at what I'm saying. Jeanette is a good-looking woman. I said Ruby's obviously younger. What's wrong with it?

"I don't look *anything* like that harpy!"

"Ruby—"

"My *sister*? I can't even believe you'd put me in that category!"

"Ruby—"

"Never mind, Glad. I guess some of that *muscle* she was talking about must be in your brain."

I let her walk ahead. It will do her good to get some of that energy out of her system. I swear, I'll never understand what makes her tick. Just when I think we're on the same page, she's off the chart and in another racetrack. And my little Volkswagen just can't keep up.

Detective Frishburn appears out of nowhere at the end of the RV alley, his suit looking even worse after a day at the track than it did that morning. "Have you talked to your brother lately, Ruby?"

She stops short and puts her hands on her hips. "Not since last night. But I think you're missing a good suspect while you're chasing him."

He smiles. "Who would that be?"

She explains about Jeanette Almond and how she thinks Jeanette might be guilty of killing Ricky. "I think you should investigate that lead instead of my brother."

"I've already heard that story," he replies calmly. "I checked her alibi. She was with Paul Massey during the time the medical examiner thinks Sanders was killed, about five a.m."

Ruby narrows her eyes and purses her lips. "Don't you think that's a little too pat? Both possible suspects are with each other while Ricky was killed? That seems like obvious police work to me."

Frishburn looks at me. "Is she for real?"

"Dangerously so," I answer, despite Ruby's look of warning.

"It's against the law to impede an investigation, Mrs. Wycznewski." He gives her his best stalwart-cop routine. "You'd best find your brother and tell him it won't do any good to run away and hide. He needs to come forward and talk to me. We'll see if he has an alibi even a fraction as good as Massey's."

"If I see him, I'll be sure to tell him, Detective." She stalks away, leaving me alone with Frishburn.

"You'd better keep a better leash on her," he recommends with a wink.

"She's within her legal right to ask questions and to not be so quick to blame her brother," I advise him. "And don't talk about her again like that, huh? I got this slow-burn Polish temper that takes exception to anyone badmouthing my wife."

He shrugs, backing away. "Just a friendly word of warning."

"Thanks anyway."

Frishburn bothers me. I think he knows something he's not telling us about Ricky. He's too bulldog stubborn about wanting to get him. Swapping a little paint isn't good enough. That happens at every race. Even if he knows about Bobby and the shooting, that was years ago. There has to be something else. But I don't have any way to find out what it is unless Bobby wants to come clean.

Ruby is standing next to our RV when I see her again. She's leaning down like she's adjusting something, and I wonder if one of the levelers is off. If one goes out, it's like being on the Titanic. "You got a problem?" I ask her, hoping she isn't mad so we don't have to make up. Unless she *wants* to make up, and in that case, we should step inside. I'm not a public person.

She keeps smiling too wide, not separating her teeth, eyes glued on the back end of the RV ahead of ours. "Am caulghing a hobby."

"What?"

"Hobby ih unna er RV."

"What?" I'm beginning to think she's had a stroke or something. Then I see Bobby's hand waving at me on the other side of the drain, under the motor home. "What the hell is he doing under there?"

"He's hiding." She stops smiling long enough to whisper, "Look natural. Here comes Frishburn!"

I'm not really sure how to look natural. I know that what Ruby is doing doesn't come anywhere near what I would term "natural." So I step in to give her a hand, putting my arms around her and kissing her without looking up as Frishburn walks by us.

"That was close," Bobby hisses from under the RV. "I'm glad you all were here. I don't know what I would've done without you."

Ruby and I both look up at each other. She wipes the pearly red lipstick off my lips and smiles at me. I twirl a blond curl around one of my fingers.

Bobby demands attention. "What are you two doing? I'm in a world of hurt here, and you two are making out!"

"Do they still call it that?" I ask my wife.

"Guess so." She shrugs. "I like it, whatever you call it."

"Oh, for Pete's sake!" Bobby glares at us from underneath the RV. "You two aren't newlyweds anymore. And I think you might be too old to be kissing someone outside in the sunlight, Glad."

"And I think I might have to call Frishburn back over here to show him my drain." Bobby is definitely starting to annoy me.

"Hush." Ruby rubs my cheek with her soft hand. "Just ignore him."

"Ignore me?" Bobby squeaks. "Ruby, they're about to put your only brother in jail!"

"You probably deserve it," she replies.

"I didn't kill anyone."

I crouch down beside Bobby. "Then what *did* you do? I mean besides shooting Ricky years ago and swapping paint yesterday. Why does Frishburn like you so much for this?"

"I don't know," Bobby whines. "He's just got it out for me."

"I was a cop, son. He wants you. Did you steal his car or seduce his daughter?"

"I didn't do anything. Well, almost nothing."

I sigh. "Nothing like what?"

"Aw hell, Glad, it ain't nothin'."

"Tell me if you want our help."

Bobby lays his head back on the ground and takes a deep breath. "I might have been the last person to see Ricky alive."

Ruby bends down beside me. "What are you saying?"

"Ricky and I were playing a friendly little game of poker last night. Well, this morning."

"What happened to going to look at your car and think about winning?" Ruby asks him.

"I did that. Then I got bored and went to look for something to do. Ricky was feeling the same way. We found a little place we could play, and hung out for a while."

"What time was that?" I ask.

He winces. "I'm not sure. After I left your place. I fell asleep and then I heard the screaming. When I heard everybody saying Ricky was dead, I got out of there."

"Did anyone see you two together?"

Bobby shrugs. "Massey came and told him he better get some rest before the race. He said maybe if Ricky paid attention to what he was here for instead of everything else, maybe he could start being a winner."

Ruby looks up at me. "So Massey was with the harpy all night, huh? I think there might be a little problem with his alibi."

"Was anyone else with Massey when he found you?" I ask Bobby.

"I didn't see anyone. It was just me and Ricky in that old shed over behind the Bojangles. We figured nobody would look for us in there."

"Did you fall asleep in the shed?" I try to imagine how this whole thing could come together. I agree with Ruby that Massey is starting to sound suspicious.

"Yeah. I heard the screaming and came out. Everybody said Ricky was dead in his car."

"But you don't know what time that was or when Ricky left you?" Ruby asked, and when Bobby said no, she slapped the side of his head. "Mama is gonna hear about this."

"Oh, Ruby!"

"Never mind. That's why Frishburn wants you, you idiot! Somebody else, maybe Massey, saw you together."

"You have to talk to him and clear this up," I tell Bobby.

"No, sir! That man is out for my blood!"

"You might be able to help him with this investigation by telling him what you just told us."

"Or he might lock me up and forget where he put the key. Never confess. That's what Uncle Danny always said. You just stick to your story."

Ruby got to her feet and brushed the dust off her tight denim shorts. "You stay here, Bobby. Keep your head down. Glad and I will go look in the shed to see if there's anything that might help find out who did this."

"We will?" I'm sure we shouldn't, but it sounds like we're going to anyway.

"Come on." She hauls me up by one arm. "We have to do this while Frishburn is on the other side looking for Bobby."

We walk through the camping area, occasionally looking up as the PA system announces races or other events. The cars are loud and the sun is hot. The smell of food, especially onions, is almost as strong as the smell of gasoline and oil.

"When we were kids"—Ruby leans her head close to mine so I can hear her—"Daddy used to say he was gonna put us in this little shed if we were bad. We always thought there was monsters out here."

The shed behind the Bojangles is hardly even that. It looks as though a strong gust of back breeze could blow it down. The door is wired on, and some of the boards are gaping. It probably goes unnoticed behind here because it's between the race-car-driving school and the restaurants. The drivers know it, and Ruby knows it because she grew up here with her daddy working on race cars. I would never look twice at it except to wonder why it hasn't been torn down.

"They used to store stuff out here. Car batteries and that kind of thing," Ruby explains. "They just kind of built the track around it but never bothered to rebuild it."

I untwist the wire that's holding the door closed. Ruby keeps watch, although it seems to me Frishburn would already have looked here. Bobby is in more trouble than I imagined, and he doesn't seem to realize it. Maybe the infamous threat of a good pop aside the head might come in handy right now.

The door squeaks open, barely noticeable in all the noise and confusion around us. Inside are two barrels that look like they've been used for chairs and an old cable reel that could've been used for a table. The sunlight through the cracks shows us a blue driver's uniform that looks like Bobby's colors to me. A greasy, dark substance is pooled on the floor near it. The light glints off a lethal-looking knife in the middle of the blood.

"Is that . . . ?" Ruby whispers.

"Blood?" Frishburn asks from behind us. "Yes. I think so."

SIX

I HAVE TO GIVE Frishburn credit. He's outfoxed us. We led him here and possibly set up his case against Bobby, if he didn't really have one to begin with. He may have done it on purpose. Good police work, but bad luck for Bobby.

"Don't touch a thing." He moves past us, putting on latex gloves. The sunlight spilling in tells its own grisly story. There's blood on the spool table and on one of the crude chairs.

"Are you saying you only found out about this place now?" I ask in surprise. It seems like Massey would've told him this was where he found Bobby and Ricky. "Didn't Massey tell you they were playing cards here?"

Frishburn looks at me. "Massey and Ricky?"

"No." Looks like I stepped into this one. "Bobby and Ricky."

"You must have another source of information that I don't have," Frishburn returns. "I think you better tell that source that if he doesn't hightail it over and share some of that information with me, we're going to go round and round."

I glance at Ruby, who has been extraordinarily quiet. The look of seeing a murder scene for the first time shows on her pretty face. "Are you okay, sweetie?"

"It doesn't seem like one person has that much blood," she whispers.

I've felt like that before. But I know a messy crime scene looks like this. Some are much worse. This is what I was looking for, how I knew the killing didn't happen in or near the car. Ricky was killed right here, then dragged to his car. Did Bobby sleep through that? He said Ricky left and he fell asleep, waking up when he heard people yelling about Ricky being dead. If that was the truth, when did this happen?

Another thing that bothers me is Bobby's uniform. Nobody lays out a dirty uniform like that, neatly spread out across the top of the spool table. But if Bobby was in the shed the whole time, how did someone do this without getting blood all over him too?

"Convinced now?" Frishburn asks me in a smug way. "I didn't know Bobby was playing cards with Ricky last night. Mr. Massey didn't mention that to me. I'll have to ask him about that. But I think this crime scene speaks for itself. This is Bobby's jumpsuit. That's his name and Team Hamilton logo, right? If that knife turns out to be his knife or a knife he had access to, we'll be set."

"Bobby didn't do this," Ruby insists uselessly.

"I know things look bad for him," I argue. "But look at this too, Frishburn. His jumpsuit. Bobby never lays a clean jumpsuit out like this. He sure wouldn't spread out a dirty one." I can't tell him about Bobby not being covered in blood. That will sound too much like I know what happened, and I'm already on his list for that.

Frishburn nods. "And maybe there's some good excuse for all this." He looks around the blood-covered shed. "But I need to talk to Bobby. Have him come in on his own and we'll do what we can for him. If he makes me keep looking for him, it's not gonna be so good. You know what I mean, Wycznewski."

I do know what he means, but I'm not sure Bobby coming in on this is such a good idea. The evidence is pretty strong against him. I know Bobby is harmless. He wouldn't kill Ricky, and he'd probably pass out from seeing all this blood. But me knowing that and proving it is two different things. From a cop's point of view, Bobby looks guilty as all hell. I'd take him in for less.

Ruby is looking a little paler, and I take her outside without assuring Frishburn that I'll see to Bobby coming in. "You okay?" I ask her once we're away from the shed.

"I'm fine," she replies in her usual stalwart manner. Then she vomits all over the ground. There are people around us, but no one pays much attention. It would be surprising if someone *wasn't* vomiting from indulging in something too much here. And not just beer either. There was a hot-dog-eating contest that almost made me feel like spewing just watching it. One man ate 150 hot dogs.

I grab a handful of napkins from the Bojangles and give them to Ruby. Her color is better already. "Don't feel bad. I did the same thing the first time I saw blood like that."

"Really?" She wipes her lips and finds a Tic Tac to put in her mouth. "I hope I don't *ever* see anything like that again."

"Bobby didn't do it," I assure her.

"Of course not! He'd be more of a baby than me about it! He'd still be out here hurling if he saw that!"

Sirens are coming toward the area. People are making way for the police vehicles and crime scene crew. We don't need to see the crime scene people go through the shed. "Let's get out of here."

People look up, noticing the sirens and flashing lights, although that happens plenty of times too. The drivers don't get hurt so much as fans do. Broken toes from walking into things, sprained wrists from doing too much. A paramedic told me once that every year they have to take more fans to the hospital, mostly from overdoing it. But when the drivers *do* get hurt, it's a lot worse.

"Glad, this looks really bad for Bobby."

"I know, sweetheart. We'll keep looking into it."

"Think there's a chance that blood wasn't Ricky's?"

"No. Someone set Bobby up for Ricky's death, and they went through a lot of trouble to do it. I think there might still be something Bobby isn't telling us. He obviously wasn't in that building when Ricky was killed. Otherwise I think he might be dead too. The question is, where was he?"

Ruby bites her lip. "Should he turn himself in?"

"I don't think so. I think we should get him away from here before Frishburn finds him under our RV. We need to figure some things out before they arrest him."

Startled, she asks, "You think they *will* arrest him?"

"Massey saw Bobby with Ricky before he died, even though he was unwilling to share that with Frishburn for some reason. Bobby's uniform was in that shed with Ricky's blood. I'd arrest him. The swapping paint thing was loose, but with everything else it makes a nice little case against him."

"Mama is gonna beat his butt!"

The image of Ruby's tiny mother doing just that makes me smile, because I think Ruby is right. But for now, the important thing is getting Bobby out of the speedway. I don't want to take the RV back out through the gates. The chances are really good Frishburn will have thought about that. Besides, we might lose our place, and it took me a long time to become a member of the Infield Club to get this space. Who knows when it will come up again? It hasn't been my favorite place to camp, but I won it, and I intend to keep it through the race.

We'll have to sneak him out in the Ranger. But we better be smart about it. They'll probably be checking every car and truck going out. Frishburn knows Bobby is still here somewhere, and Ruby and I are bound to be on his number one suspect list for finding him.

When we get back to the RV and tell Bobby about the plan we've developed, he isn't too happy about it. "I'll have to miss qualifying."

"You'll have to miss it if they take you to jail too," Ruby reminds him.

"Okay. But how are we gonna do it?"

"Trust me." I smile, thinking about the plan.

"I don't like that look," Bobby whines, still under the RV.

"I don't blame you." My smile gets bigger. I don't want to seem cruel, but Bobby has ruined some prime race time for me. I should be able to get some amusement out of what he has to go through right now.

Our Ford Ranger pickup has a toolbox on the back big enough to put Bobby in, but I figure since that's the first place I'd look, it's the first place Frishburn will look too. Instead, we hustle Bobby into the RV when the coast is clear, and Ruby works on him.

"What if this—ouch!—doesn't work?" He glares at his sister as she covers his newly shaved face with makeup and hunts for the wig he can wear. "What if I get caught like this? They might take my mug shot with me dressed like a woman!"

Ruby brings back a short sundress and some sandals for him, then looks at his legs. "We don't have time enough to do the kind of work that would take." She goes back into the bedroom and Ricky stares at me.

"I'm sorry. There's nowhere else to hide you but in plain sight," I tell him, not one bit sympathetic. "If we can make you look good enough, we should be able to get through the checkpoint I know is waiting for us at the security station going out."

"I respect you, Glad," he says. "I really do. But if I get caught like this—"

There's a knock at the front door, and we all go completely still.

"What do we do?" Ruby clutches the green slacks and top to her chest.

"Ignore it," I suggest. "No one knows for sure we're in here."

"I don't think the door is locked," Ruby says.

"Frishburn won't just walk in," I assure her.

But none of us are prepared for who's at the door. "Yoo hoo! Is anyone here?"

"It's Jeanette!" Ruby whispers.

"Let's hide Bobby and get rid of her."

Ruby and I hide Bobby under a bed and then answer the door.

"Hi, Jeanette." I hope I sound happy enough that Jeanette isn't suspicious, but not *too* happy to see her again, so that Ruby doesn't do something bad to me later.

"Hello, Glad." She smiles back at me and glances at the sofa. "I brought by some cookies I had specially brought in from this cute little bakery in Chicago. They make the most divine almond cookies."

She glances at the sofa again, and I feel obliged to ask her to sit down even though I can feel my wife's elbow in my side.

"Yes," Ruby adds in the most artificial tone possible. "Won't you sit down?"

"Why, thank you." Jeanette puts the cookies on the coffee table and smiles. "Go ahead. Try a cookie."

"What brings you by?" I ask around a mouthful of cookie. They *are* pretty good.

"Yes," Ruby says. "What *does* bring you by, Jeanette?"

"I felt so bad about our talk yesterday, especially with Bobby about to be arrested for murder and all. I know this must be a terrible time for you."

"Where did you hear about it?" My tone is still friendly, dumb male.

"I overheard that police detective talking to Paul Massey," she whispers, like there are other people who might hear. "The police know Bobby killed Ricky Sanders."

"Bobby didn't have any reason to kill Ricky," I argue, just to see where this leads and what she overheard.

"Paul said he heard them arguing over a poker game just before the police say Ricky was killed." Jeanette leans close to confide in me. "I heard they found blood in the old shed. Somebody said Bobby had blood on his jumpsuit."

"No!" I manage to look amazed. I do a mean look of amazement. It's all in the eyes and eyebrows.

"That's what I heard." Jeanette nods with a smug look on her face. She turns to offer Ruby her condolences. "Bobby is such a good boy. Ricky too. Such a shame."

"Bobby didn't kill anyone!" There is blood in Ruby's eyes.

"I know you're right, honey. I hope they find out who did it, if Bobby didn't." Jeanette gets up and sneaks toward the door. "It's hard to believe something like that could happen right here."

"Don't worry," Ruby tells her. "We'll find out who did it."

"That's fine. I wish you all the luck in the world. Enjoy those cookies."

Ruby barely waits until the door closes behind Jeanette before she launches into, "That woman knows something, Glad! We have to find a way to make her talk. I'll bet Massey is responsible for what happened to Ricky."

"At least now we know what Massey is saying about Ricky and Bobby," I remind her.

"It's not true either." Bobby joins us in full makeup and the blond Dolly Parton wig Ruby wore last Halloween. "We weren't arguing."

"Never mind," I tell him. "Let's just get you out of here before the next knock is Frishburn with a search warrant."

Bobby agrees and drops his greasy jeans for the green slacks Ruby hands him. It's a tight fit, even with his scrawny ass. She touches up his makeup and pads his bra.

Bobby is dressed in the lime green outfit I dislike so much when Ruby wears it. The color reminds me of Jell-O. Maybe she'll let him keep it. But he doesn't look too bad. Ruby gives him an overshirt to wear that will cover his hairy arms and shoulders. She adjusts the wig and puts on his lipstick. "What do you think?"

"I think he'll do." I look him over. "Let's go."

We put Bobby between us in the front seat of the Ranger and drive slowly away from the RV after setting the alarm. Traffic is heavy, with people going in and out of the speedway to shop, eat, or see the events scheduled in the area. The long line is especially slow, and we see why as we get closer to the guard shack. They're checking every car and truck, probably looking for Bobby.

"I hope this works." Bobby's voice is desperate. Sweat is starting to drip down the side of his face, smearing his makeup. We close the windows and turn on the air conditioning. "How do you wear this stuff?" he asks Ruby.

"Just hush and try to look pretty. Think pretty thoughts," she tells him. "Pretty thoughts make a pretty girl."

"Thanks." He whispers like the guards can hear him through the three cars in front of us.

"Just smile and think you're a girl like you think about winning the race," Ruby insists, then glances at me and sighs. "Only do a better job."

We're the third vehicle now. The line is backed up far into the infield. People are starting to get impatient, probably wondering what's going on. We're coming out of the tunnel and sitting on the hill as the security guards look through the tan minivan in front of us. There are four guards instead of the usual two, along with two deputy sheriffs.

"They're gonna know it's me," Bobby says as the security guards let the van go through and the Chevy Tahoe in front of us moves up in line.

"No, they aren't." Ruby's voice is defiant. "I did a good job on your makeup, and that hair hides a lot of problems. It has lift and good color. It detracts the eye from seeing any flaws in the face."

"If Dad sees me like this, he'll disown me," Bobby insists.

"If you get arrested, he might disown you too," she says. "Now quit whining and pretend you're a girl, like we used to when we were growing up."

Bobby looks at me with fear in his eyes, which are so much like Ruby's. "She made me dress up so she could play with makeup and such."

"I understand."

"Tell him, Ruby."

"He said he understands!" she fires back.

"She hit really hard back then," Bobby defends. "If I didn't do what she wanted, she used to wallop me."

I shrug, trying to keep from laughing while I watch the guards search the back of the Tahoe. "I didn't say anything. I didn't have a sister, but I've heard they're mean as hell. Especially the older ones."

"But you're thinking it," Bobby insists. "You just don't know the pressure."

"Never mind." I glance at him as the guards let the Tahoe leave. "For once in your life, keep your mouth shut. Hold your head down like you're sick. Let us do the talking."

Bobby does as he's told for once. He leans forward and holds a tissue to his mouth. I put the truck in gear and slowly pull forward to the guard shack while Ruby lowers her window.

"Afternoon." The security guard glances into the truck. "Sorry to keep you, but there's been some trouble on the track. The police are looking for someone."

Bobby makes the best darn imitation of someone nearly vomiting that I've ever heard. I can see the look of disgust on the guard's face.

"She sick?" He backs away from the window a little.

"Yes," Ruby answers. "I think she might have dog flu."

"Dog flu?" The guard's eyes widen, and his eyebrows disappear into the hat that matches his uniform. "I never heard of that."

"She's my sister," Ruby explains, "and she keeps dogs. Sleeps with them and all. We think that might be how she got it."

The guard takes another step back and explains the situation to the second guard, who looks like a bulldog. He has to be the head security guard.

He doesn't move from his place near the steps coming down from the shack, but he yells out, "Get that girl to the hospital!"

"We trying to do that," Ruby yells back. "You stopped us!"

"You should have called an ambulance."

"We tried," she improvises brilliantly. "They said there was a big emergency on the interstate and there are none available."

Both guards are clearly unsure what to do. One of them talks to one of the deputy sheriffs. The deputy glances at Bobby, who is still pretending to vomit. Honest to God, I *hope* he's pretending and not about to do it in my truck. He sounds real to me. It must be one of his hidden talents.

They call someone on the radio and then nod at the other guard, who is closest to the truck. I wouldn't want to be in their situation either. A mistake either way could cost them their jobs. It's always hard trying to do your job and keep the public welfare in mind at the same time. I feel for them, but I wish they'd let us go.

Finally, the front guard nods, lifts his clipboard, and waves us through the gate. I put the truck in gear. Ruby smiles and waves, and then we start to inch forward.

I figure half an hour, tops, and the Furr family can decide what to do with their only son. This is nerve-wracking, and I don't like deceiving people I normally work hard to help out. I respect these men and the job they do, but I don't want to be the one who has to tell Ruby's family Bobby has been arrested.

The clutch lets the truck roll back a little before we start forward. We don't move more than a foot when a car horn starts blaring. Cars, trucks, motor homes, and delivery vehicles move aside behind us to allow a security guard's Jeep through the line of traffic that has built up in the heat, waiting impatiently to get where they're going.

"Wait a minute!" Frishburn hangs out of the side of the blue Jeep, waving his arms. "Don't let them through the gate!"

Ruby bites delicately on her thumbnail, a habit I know she gave up when she was twelve, according to her mother. She only does it now when she's so nervous she can't think of anything else to do. She does the same thing when she has a good hand of poker, which makes her easy to beat.

"Damn," Bobby swears softly from behind his tissue and the plastic Wal-Mart bag he's pretending to throw up in. "I thought we were home free."

SEVEN

"DON'T PANIC YET!" I roll down my window too.

"How can you say that? He's right here on top of us!"

"Just calm down and shut up." I smile at Detective Frishburn. "Is there a problem?"

"I think there might be, yes." He looks at Ruby and her "sister" and nods. "Ladies." Then he looks back at me. "I need you to open the toolbox in the back of your truck, Mr. Wycznewski."

"My toolbox?" I hesitate, possibly giving him the impression that I have something to hide. "All right."

He nods and steps back from the door so I can get out with the key to open the lock on the box. I take my time about it. There's no reason to rush. If you move too fast, you make mistakes. If you panic, you have the same problem. I'm confident Bobby can use that pretty-boy face of his to carry this off as long as we need him to.

"I know you aren't stupid enough to try to hide Bobby Furr in here," Frishburn says as I look through my keys one at a time.

"Then why are we looking in my toolbox? Do you need a wrench or something?"

He glares at me. "Look, you of all people should know I'm trying to do my job here. If your brother-in-law would come forward like a man, we wouldn't have to go through this."

"I agree." I watch the astonishment on his face. "But I'm not my brother-in-law's keeper, Detective. If it's any consolation, I advised him to do exactly that. What he decides to do is up to him."

"Then why are you helping him?" He glances at the toolbox and shrugs. "Never mind. Just open the box, if you please."

He motions to the security guards and the deputy sheriffs who post themselves on each side of the box. Frishburn draws his gun while I hop up in the truck and crouch down beside the toolbox.

"I understand if that wife of yours made you do this." Frishburn nods at the back of Ruby's head. "She's a looker."

"Detective," I say as I insert the key into the padlock, "you and I are going to have serious issues if you don't stop hitting on my wife."

"Wycznewski," he drawls, keeping his eyes on the toolbox, "you and I are going to have serious issues when I arrest you for hindering my investigation by trying to sneak out a man I need to question."

I grin at him and open the top of the toolbox slowly. Frishburn and the two guards stare into the toolbox in disbelief when they can see there is clearly no one hiding in it. It's only partially filled with some tools I use on the motor home and the truck.

"Where is he?" Frishburn demands with a snarl.

"I told you before. I don't know. He's probably hiding out somewhere, but I don't know where."

"Are you asking me to believe no one knows where Bobby Furr is?"

"No. I'm telling you *I* don't know where he is. He hasn't been in contact with me, my wife, or her sister. Everyone in his family told him the same thing I did. I think no one wants to talk to him until he's settled this."

"That's crazy." He glares at me for another few minutes, the hot sun reflecting on both of us off the wide chrome bumper of the truck behind us. "But I guess it must be true. The one thing I've always heard about Zeke and Louise Furr is how honest they are."

He nods, and the guards shrug and move away from the truck. I climb down from the bed after closing and locking the lid on the toolbox.

Frishburn's eyes narrow when he looks at me. "I hope I don't find out you lied to me."

I fold my arms across my chest and look right back. "Level with me about why you want Bobby so bad."

"All right." He shifts his stance to be less confrontational. "Because he obviously knows something about Sanders's death. He might not be the one who used the knife on him, but he knows something he's not telling me. I want to know what that is."

I nod in understanding. "Knowing Bobby, if he *does* know something, he doesn't realize it. But if I see him again, I'll tell him he needs to find you."

"See that you do." He slaps the back of the truck as I climb behind the wheel. "Let 'em through!"

"You need to talk to the man, Bobby," I say in an undertone, even though I know Frishburn, who is still watching the truck, can't hear me.

"What can I tell him, Glad?" Bobby doesn't look up from his tissue. "I told you what I know. That's it."

"You said that before and there was more."

"But not this time."

I pull the truck out on the highway and turn left to head toward Midland, where I will happily dump Bobby's carcass with his family. "I hope you really don't know anything else, or he's going to catch you and fry you like a catfish."

Midland is a short drive from the speedway. It's an old town, but not a developed one. It once had a nice train station and stores built up for farmers who came there to sell their goods when the train came through. But now the area is deserted except for a feed and seed store and a funeral home. All the other development has happened at the four-lane crossroad that runs through what might become a town one day.

At the corner is a bank, a gas station, and a Subway sub shop. A small ice cream shop is open, and cars are lined up outside to wait for some relief from the hot day. Ruby's family owns about twenty acres here that her grandfather used to farm. Her father wasn't interested in all that, though. Zeke's only love, besides his family, is cars—fast cars. He's worked with almost every race car driver in the business.

There are checkered flags on his mailbox at the foot of his driveway and car bodies outside the barn when you pull into the yard. I've never been there when there wasn't someone working on an engine, even though Zeke got out of the business after he broke his back five years ago.

He and Louise don't go to races anymore, because he doesn't want people to see him this way, but the man is a legend in the business. They say he helped Richard Petty's father build his first car. I believe it. He has old photos of Fireball Roberts in the kitchen, where Louise always has a pot of something simmering on the stove and a banana pudding in a chipped dish in the fridge.

"Ruby!" Louise yells her daughter's name before we even get out of the truck. A cloud of dust and a few squawking chickens accompanies our drive up from the road to their yard. She looks cautiously at the "woman" with us. "Who's your friend?"

"It's me, Mama." Bobby whips off the wig in a dramatic fashion. Louise shrieks and puts her hand to her throat.

Zeke looks down at him from his wheelchair on the porch. "There better be a good explanation for this, young man!"

"Daddy, there's a police detective who wants me for murdering Ricky." Bobby catches his lime green shirt on the truck as he walks by and has to jerk it free. "Really. I had to dress like this to get away from him at the speedway. He wants to lock me up."

"And why did you have to get away from him?" Zeke demands. "Did you hurt Ricky in any way?"

"No, sir!" Bobby tries to wipe some of the makeup off with his sleeve. "I didn't have any reason to hurt him."

"Then why didn't you talk to this detective if you didn't do anything wrong?"

"Maybe we should come inside," Louise suggests, wiping her hands on her apron. "Hey there." She looks at me. "How are you?"

"I'm fine, ma'am, thank you."

"Glad." Zeke stares at me, his long nose as sharply pointed as his chin. "Did you help Bobby with this?"

"Yes, sir."

He nods. "All right. I want to hear the reason real quick, before I kick both your asses!"

Bobby starts mumbling and whining, as usual. Zeke is an impressive figure, even in a wheelchair. He's not big, but he has a commanding presence. Kind of like my first partner on the job. Only a little over five feet tall, but nobody ever looked twice at him. Zeke's not that much older than me, and while I respect him, I'm not really afraid of him kicking anything. Not that I want to get into anything with him, but I'm not going to back down either.

"I'd like to explain," I offer, interrupting Bobby's sniveling.

Zeke nods and sits back in his chair after we get in the house. "Well, don't just stand there waiting for an invitation, son. Let's have it!"

I explain the circumstances that led to us sneaking Bobby out of the speedway campground, with Ruby chipping in where she can. Zeke doesn't look very impressed. Danny, Zeke's brother, walks in wiping motor oil from his hands, and we have to start all over again with the story.

Danny doesn't look impressed either when he hears the story again as Louise and Ruby dip beans and rice from huge pots on the stove and put them on the blue earthenware plates stacked on the table. There is plenty of hot sauce and vinegar, some corn bread, and a pitcher of sweet tea to go around.

One amazing thing is how quickly meals pop up here. One minute you're talking, and the next minute there's food spread all over the table. It's almost seamless. It goes from pot to table faster than cars on the last lap of a race.

"Sounds to me like you ran when you should have told the truth and stayed your ground," Zeke says to his son. Bobby hangs his head. "And go get that stuff off your face! I don't want anyone else to see you that way."

Louise shouts from the porch that supper is ready as she wipes her hands on her huge white apron. The constant sound of the air compressor in the barn comes to a stop. "Let's not talk about it anymore right now," she decides. "No reason to lay out our dirty laundry for everyone to see."

"All right," Zeke agrees. "But we'll talk about it later, after supper."

A couple of rookie drivers I've seen but can't name come in through the screen door, followed by Fred Lorenzen, who is wiping his perspiring face with a cloth.

"Uncle Fred!" Ruby squeals, and throws herself at him, hugging him tight.

"All right! All right!" He says, hugging her. "It's good to see you too, young'un. I gotta go, Zeke. They're having some trouble down at the track."

"Stay and eat," Louise tries to persuade him.

"Save me some and I'll be back." He nods my way and holds out his hand to me. "I don't think I know you."

"Glad Wycznewski, sir." I shake his hand, probably a little too much. "You're Fearless Freddie. You're a legend on the circuit. I never thought I'd get to meet you."

Fred Lorenzen was the "Golden Boy" of NASCAR Grand National racing. He was good looking and well spoken, and he drove like the devil was after him. In the late fifties and early sixties, the "superspeedways" were just developing in NASCAR. Freddie raced to twenty-six wins on the big tracks. His biggest season was in 1963, when he won a record $113,570. In 1965, he took the Daytona 500 and the National 500 at Charlotte.

Freddie retired in 1967 but returned in 1970 and almost won at Charlotte again. Later that year, though, he and his father were in an off-track wreck that seriously injured his father. People started to say that Fred was dead. But the next year, Fearless Freddie was back again. He raced fifteen times that year and made eight starts the next before hanging it up once and for all.

"Thank you, son," Freddie says. "Zeke, talk to you later."

"Are you okay, Glad?" Ruby asks with a worried expression on her face.

I guess I must look as starstruck as I feel.

"Do you want ketchup with your beans?" she asks.

"Of course he doesn't!" Louise assures her. "Nobody eats like that! Sit down, Ruby. You're so tall, it feels like you're hovering over me, child!"

After Zeke says grace, everybody tucks into the food. I *do* want ketchup, but I don't dare ask for it now. There's a ton of little white beans, I'm not sure what kind, on my plate. Everyone else at the table is scarfing theirs down and talking about restrictor plates. I don't look down. That way I can eat mine too.

"Heard about Ricky being killed at the track," one of the rookies—I think his name is Hambone or something like that—says between bites. "He was a good boy."

The other one smiles at Bobby. "Heard they might be looking for you, old son."

"I don't know what you mean," Bobby mumbles, and looks down at his food.

"Never mind," Louise says with authority. "We don't come to the table and talk of such things. That isn't polite table talk."

No one disputes what Louise says, not if they ever want to come back to her table again, anyway. The rookies finish eating and hurry out the door with talk of what they're going to do to get that extra five miles of gas out of their car.

Bobby starts to stand up, and Zeke thunders, "Sit down!"

I can't even imagine what this man was like when he was younger and could walk. Ruby never mentions him being a holy terror. She loves him and won't hear anything bad about him. But I think he must've been pretty scary.

"Daddy—"

"Here's what we're gonna do," Zeke tells his son. "We're gonna call Deputy Pressler and tell him what happened and see what we can do to make you not look so guilty. Only men who have done something wrong hide, son."

"But even Glad said I should hide." Bobby looks at me appealingly.

I clear my throat. The look on Ruby's face tells me I shouldn't jump in here, but I *did* tell Bobby it might be better if he didn't go to the police right away. I can't back down on that either. "Sir, the police might not look so hard for anyone else to be guilty if they think they have the best suspect."

Zeke's silver-flecked head swivels my way, and his dark eyes impale me right here at the table. "I realize you aren't from here, Glad, and you don't understand the way we do things down here. I've lived here all my life, and I thought I taught my son respect for the police and for himself. This way isn't either of those things. Even if they put him in jail, it would be better than running."

Louise frowns. "Maybe you should hear Ruby's husband out, Zeke. He was a police officer himself in Chicago."

Louise has never called me Glad. I know we haven't known each other for twenty years or anything, but she never calls me anything except "Ruby's husband."

"I've made up my mind." Zeke wheels away from the table toward the phone. He's a stubborn, proud man, and essentially, I suppose he's right. If I were in Bobby's position, I would have gone to talk to Frishburn from the beginning. He held back, and no policeman likes that.

"Daddy, if they arrest me, how will I ever find out who really killed Ricky?" Bobby pleads one last time.

But it's too late. Zeke is on the phone with Deputy Pressler, who is the county sheriff's deputy for Midland. It won't take him more than a minute to hook in with Frishburn and figure out what's going on.

"We might as well all sit down," Zeke says when he's finished. "I'm sure we'll find a way to get you out of this trouble, Bobby. But you have to be a man about it."

"Yes, sir."

"Ruby's husband should be able to figure it all out." Louise huffs up from the table, picking up plates as she goes. "He was a policeman in Chicago."

Zeke nods at me. "You're welcome to do that for Bobby if you can."

"We're already working on it," Ruby assures them with a smile.

"Good." Zeke nods as we all sit waiting for Deputy Pressler to get there.

What happened to my plan? They were supposed to convince Ruby not to investigate what happened to Ricky. Why are they all looking at me like I should be at the speedway asking questions? Where did this go wrong?

Deputy Pressler slides up in the driveway about ten minutes later. He gets out of his late-model Lincoln Town Car with the brown county insignia on the door and hails the rookies who are working in the yard by the barn.

"Come on in, Jerry," Zeke says as he comes to the screen door. "Louise is about to take some banana pudding out. Have a seat. Did you eat yet?"

"Yeah." Pressler glances at Bobby before he adjusts his gun belt and sits down. "I had one of those new chicken teriyaki subs. Pretty good."

Zeke nods. "Bobby has something he wants to tell you."

Bobby knows he's been defeated. He tells the whole story to the deputy while Louise and Ruby finish cleaning off the table and serve the banana pudding.

"You're in some trouble here, Bobby," Pressler tells him, digging in. "I talked to the Mecklenburg County detective who's investigating this thing. He's not too happy about you sneaking out of the speedway."

"I didn't sneak," Bobby disagrees. "I walked out and caught a ride over here."

To his credit, Bobby has thought about saving me and Ruby from possibly getting into trouble too. I'm amazed. I'll have to re-evaluate my theories about Bobby. "The detective only wanted to question him," I add for Bobby's sake. "He doesn't have an arrest warrant."

Deputy Pressler looks my way for the first time as his spoonful of banana pudding stops halfway to his mouth. "Who are you?"

Before I can tell him he's already met me, Louise chimes in with, "He's Ruby's husband from Chicago."

I can see from his face that what she said is enough. There are still some places in the South with large signs that say "Go Home Yankees." And they don't mean the baseball team.

Deputy Pressler humphs like he understands all there is to understand and puts the cool banana pudding into his mouth. "Well, Bobby shoulda stayed put. He's gonna have to come with me now."

"Where to?" Ruby asks.

"I told that detective fella I'd save him a trip down here and bring Bobby to Concord for questioning."

"You know Bobby didn't kill Ricky," Ruby persists. "He's just a big, dumb scapegoat."

"Hey!" Bobby objects.

"You been over to see Ricky's daddy yet?" Pressler asks Zeke.

"Not yet," Ruby's father responds. "I know he's taking it hard."

"He is. Ricky wasn't his only boy, but he was proud of him being a driver and all."

"I know he was." Zeke shakes his head. "It's a terrible thing."

Bobby still isn't telling the truth. He had to leave the shed before Ricky was killed in there. That's the only way it makes sense. But why would Bobby lie about it? He could have a legitimate alibi if someone saw him away from the shed at about the time Ricky was killed.

I sit forward and smile at Bobby. "There's just one little thing you're forgetting to tell us."

"What?" He looks at me like he can't believe I'm saying anything else about it.

"You had to leave the shed after Ricky left."

"I told you, I fell asleep."

"I know you did, but Ricky was killed in there. If you didn't do it, then you witnessed it."

"I didn't see anything!"

"Because you weren't in the shed the whole time after Ricky left."

He shrugs and looks down at his hands. "I might have left for a while."

"Bobby!" Ruby smacks him in the shoulder. "Are you *still* lying?"

"I don't want to get in more trouble."

"You're in deep enough already, son," Pressler encourages him. "If you've got something else to say, I'd say it."

Bobby sits back in the chair and folds his arms across his chest. "I was drinking down at Angel's."

"What?" Zeke almost rises from his chair. "You know that place is off-limits to drivers. They'll probably kick you off the team!"

"And that's why I'm not telling anyone else," Bobby mutters stubbornly. "Ricky left. I went to Angel's. I didn't stay long. When I got back, everyone was carrying on about Ricky being dead. That's the truth."

"That might be your alibi," I tell him. "Someone had to see you at Angel's. It was during the same time Ricky was killed."

"It doesn't matter," Bobby tells me again. "I'm not telling anyone else I was there. Better to go to jail than to be kicked off the team!"

EIGHT

"IDIOT!" RUBY STARTS TO smack him again, but he ducks. "If you go to jail you'll get kicked off the team too!"

"You don't understand," Bobby assures her. "You've never driven for a team."

"Are you telling me the boys down there will respect you more for being arrested for Ricky's murder than if you broke a rule and were drinking at Angel's?" she demands. "How many other drivers were there when you were there?"

"A few," he responds.

She rolls her eyes. "You deserve to go to jail, Bobby. You're such a moron."

"Hush, Ruby," her mother scolds. "Don't talk to your brother like that!"

"Where's Betsy?" Ruby asks her mother, done with Bobby.

"She's out walking with Davy Sanders," Zeke says with a smile. "Just because it didn't work out between you and Ricky doesn't mean it won't work between Betsy and Davy."

"Daddy, marrying someone to take down a fence isn't right."

Bobby snorts. "Especially a Sanders."

"Quiet!" Zeke snaps at him.

"If she likes him, where's the harm?" Louise asks.

"*If* she likes him," Ruby agrees, "but not if she's doing it to make Daddy happy. That's the only reason I dated Ricky."

"I never told you to date him," her father denies.

"You didn't have to. I knew it was something you wanted."

The real Betsy (not the one we sneaked home in my truck, but she *does* look amazingly like Bobby, and all three of them look a lot like Louise) comes in the house with a worried look on her face. Her blond hair is full of hay, and her T-shirt and shorts are messed up. I don't have to wonder where she and Davy were "walking."

"You have to go, Bobby!" she yells at her brother. "Old Man Sanders found out you were here, and he's coming after you for killing Ricky. He wants to kill you!"

Pressler gets ponderously to his feet. "There won't be any killing while I'm here."

Ruby puts her arm around her sister. "Do you want to date Davy, or are you doing it for Daddy?"

Betsy looks at her father. "For Daddy, I suppose. It's the only way we're ever gonna get that fence pulled down."

Zeke smacks his hand on the table. "I never told either one of you to date those Sanders boys!"

"Not in so many words," Louise joins in, "but they knew what you wanted since they were babies."

"Never mind that now." Betsy reminds them of the immediate problem: "Davy and Old Man Sanders are going to come here and shoot Bobby."

Pressler takes hold of Bobby's arm and moves toward the door, suddenly seeming to take the threat seriously. "I think we should go now. I'll let you know what happens with this, Zeke. Thanks for calling." He smiles and nods at Louise. "And thanks for that pudding, ma'am. It was delicious."

Louise smacks him with her dishtowel. "Didn't you hear what she just said? The two of you need to get out of here!"

The look on the deputy's face is priceless. I can tell he doesn't know whether to be affronted or think it's funny. He's stuck with this goofy look caught somewhere between the two. He ends up not saying anything, nodding as he puts on his flat-brimmed hat, and pushing open the screen door.

I never liked those hats. They look too much like the one Mr. Ranger Sir wore on *Yogi Bear*. Even the beat cop's cap looks better than that. I guess they made them flat like that for getting in and out of the car, but I'd rather wear a ball cap on duty than one of those.

We follow them out to the porch. The rookies are gone from the yard. My first impression says something is wrong, since the car is still running in the barn but they're nowhere to be seen. "We should go back in the house," I murmur to Ruby.

She looks around the deserted yard. "Why? What's wrong?"

No sooner are the words out of her mouth than we hear the distinct clunk of a shotgun being closed after it's loaded. I still urge her toward the door, but she pushes against me, straining to see what's going on.

"I just want Bobby." Sanders stands in the driveway near the county sheriff's car.

"You can't have him," Pressler yells back. "You know better than this, Dale. Put that gun away and go home before I have to arrest you too."

"He killed my boy, Deputy! Let him down here with me, and I'll save the state a trial."

"That's not gonna happen." Pressler stands his ground as he adjusts his gun belt around what's left of his waist. "Put that gun away!"

I'm in the back row, so to speak, on the porch. Zeke, Pressler, Bobby, and Louise are all in front of me. Betsy and Ruby are on either side of me. My back is against the door when I suddenly get a brainstorm. Maybe it's years of seeing situations turn ugly that make me do it. Maybe I just want to get back to the speedway.

I sneak back into the house and go out through the back door while Pressler and then Zeke argue with Sanders about not shooting Bobby. Bobby looks like he's going to cry, but he's not saying anything. Another young man, who I assume must be Davy, is crying as he stands next to his father.

Sanders is a burly old man with most of the weight in his belly now, but he looks like he was a football player once. He's got broad shoulders and a beefy neck, his overalls covered with dirt and grease.

He's holding the shotgun on the group standing on the porch, particularly Bobby. As usual, the man with the gun is concentrating so hard on his target, he doesn't see anything else going on around him.

I slide up next to him carefully and put two fingers in his back. Crazy, I know, but it's all I can think of at the moment. I figure the man isn't a criminal and doesn't really want to hurt anyone. He's just a desperately sad old man who wants revenge for his son's death.

"Put the weapon down." I use the old cop voice I knew was still there in me somewhere. "Nice and easy now."

He does what I say, bending down with the gun and laying it on the grass. He comes up with his hands out, eyes wide as he realizes how much trouble he could be in, maybe for the first time in his life.

I drop my "weapon" and nod at the family on the porch. Sanders realizes that I tricked him and comes up with a punch that makes me see stars for a few seconds. The old man packs a wallop.

Pressler jogs down the porch steps with Bobby in tow, leans over Sanders, and shakes his head. "God almighty, Dale! What the hell did you think you were doing?"

Sanders sobs. "I just want my boy back. That's all."

"Killing my boy won't bring Ricky back," Zeke says from the porch.

Sanders gets another idea in his head and tackles Bobby, taking him down to the soft grass under his weight and rolling across the yard. He's nearly two times bigger than Bobby, who flails helplessly against his hammy punches. The rookies reappear from the barn for this, grinning and egging them on.

I look at Pressler, who doesn't seem to be trying to break the fight up. When he doesn't move forward, I take the initiative and separate Sanders from Bobby's thin body. "This isn't going to help either," I tell the old man. "And Bobby didn't kill Ricky. That's just a rumor."

"How do you know?" He abruptly pushes away from me. "Everyone is saying Bobby killed him over a poker game."

"They're all lying." Bobby sniffs, a little blood on his nose, but he stays on the ground. "I didn't hurt Ricky."

"Let the law handle this," Pressler says to Sanders. "We'll decide if Bobby is guilty or not when we see all the evidence."

"Yeah, like you saw all the evidence and let that fella go who killed those two babies last year," Sanders says. "You all don't know your heads from a rat's ass!"

Ruby read me details from the Midland murder case all through last year. A man was accused of killing two little girls, but the grand jury said there wasn't enough evidence to bind him over for trial. People are still upset about it. Not many murders happen in Midland. For the most part, it's a quiet little community. Emotions ran high with someone being accused of the crime, but rumor and innuendo don't make facts that stand up in court.

"Never mind that," Pressler says. "I'm taking Bobby in for questioning right now. If his story isn't straight, they'll arrest him. If it is, they'll let him go. Now get on home, Dale, before I have to arrest *you*."

"No!" Louise steps up. "Come in and have some coffee. We have to stick together through this, Dale. Maybe we aren't exactly kin, but we're neighbors."

Sanders brushes the dirt and grass from his plaid shirt. "I can't do that right now, Louise. But thank you." He nods to Zeke, avoids looking at Bobby, and then walks across the yard toward his property. Davy picks up the shotgun and runs after him.

Betsy bursts out crying when they're gone. "Bobby, you've ruined my life!

"I thought you didn't like Davy." Ruby puts an arm around her little sister.

"I didn't mean that. I just meant . . . oh, what difference does it make?" Betsy runs into the house, and Ruby follows her.

Bobby gets up and dusts himself off. He shakes my hand solemnly. "Thanks, Glad. We both know Frishburn is going to arrest me. I may never see you again. I just want you to know how much I appreciate what you've done for me. Take care of my family."

Did I mention there's a streak of melodrama twelve miles wide in Ruby's family? I know Bobby means to be sincere, but as usual he overdoes it. "The truth will come out," I say. I hope that's a good thing and that he's told the truth. I can't believe I'm saying it, but I promise him, "Ruby and I will do what we can for you."

"Thanks."

Pressler glances at me and starts to speak but obviously thinks better of it. He helps Bobby into the back seat of his car and then drives off down the dusty driveway. I assume that was *Thanks for your help* in county sheriff sign language. Or *Next time, let me handle it.* He was probably confused too.

Ruby comes back out on the porch and shrugs. "I guess Betsy really likes Davy. She thinks he'll hate her now because Bobby killed Ricky."

"Doesn't anyone think Bobby's innocent?" Excuse me for being frustrated.

"I don't believe my boy could kill another man." Zeke looks up at me, eyes narrowed. "I hope you can prove that, Glad."

Is now a good time to mention that I'm not a private detective? Maybe not. Everyone is looking at me like I'm almost as good as Sunday's fried chicken. Not quite Rusty Wallace, but not quite General Sherman either.

Louise puts her hands on her husband's shoulders and nods at me. "Ruby's husband can do it if anyone can."

After giving her mother a hug, Ruby comes down the porch steps and puts her arm through mine. "We'll do it. You'll see."

We get in the truck, no calling out goodbyes or promising to see them later like usual. It's very solemn and quiet. Louise and Zeke stay on the porch to see us off, and then they go back into the house. I don't think I'll ever forget the look on Zeke's face. I've seen it before, but not from him. He's afraid. Afraid he'll lose his son just like Sanders did.

Ruby sits close to me and lays her head on my shoulder as we drive toward the speedway. I can't see her face, but I think the reality of what's happened has really sunk in. It was fun thinking about helping Bobby to begin with, but now it's not a game anymore.

"It's okay." I kiss her hand. "He'll be fine."

She sniffs. "I hope so. But I can't help but worry. He sounds tough, but he's really not, Glad. You know that. He's still a little boy in a lot of ways."

I hate that tone in her voice, and I wish there were something I could do to make it better. But I'm stumped right now. Someone killed Ricky and wants it to look like Bobby did it. Unless maybe Bobby being out with Ricky was just a good opportunity. Maybe Ricky would have been killed no matter what.

Instead of going right back to the speedway, I take a turn to get on North Tryon and head toward Angel's. Someone must recall Bobby being there late last night. Whether Bobby likes it or not, being in jail is worse than losing his place on the team. It's hard for rookies to get a second chance, but it's harder to get out of jail.

The problem is going to be that it will have to be Angel's staff, not speedway staff or drivers, who could testify to Bobby being at the bar. No one admits to going to the sleazy place, but almost everyone from the speedway does. I think it's possible most of the bar's staff might be wanted for one thing or another. I doubt that Angel asks too many questions.

But I have an ace in the hole. I know Angel. He ran numbers in Chicago before he moved down here a few years ago after getting out of a short stay in Joliet prison. Even if no one else can answer my questions, Angel might be able to. He may even have some insight into Ricky's death. I know he will have heard rumors.

I park at Angel's and turn to Ruby. "I'd appreciate it if you stayed in the car."

She blinks and smiles. "No."

"Ruby, it would be better for you to wait out here." I take my 9-mm Glock from the glove box and stash it in the back of my belt. Old habits again. "It might be dangerous."

"All the more reason for me to go in with you." She jumps out and slams the truck door with finality. "You know I'm a better shot than you. I don't know how you stayed alive on the streets of Chicago all those years. I'm happy you did, but I don't know how you did it."

I have to smile. She *is* a catch. "All right. You can come in. But you can't hold the gun."

"Fine." She walks in front of me. "Like you could keep me from coming in anyway."

"Ruby—"

"And you should probably let *me* carry that thing." She glances at my back. "You're likely to shoot your butt off like that. I could put it right here in my pocketbook."

"No." I open the door for her. "You might be a better shot than me, but you have to get your own gun."

"All right." She sighs as we step into the dark interior of Angel's. "I don't know what we're going to find here that will help Bobby."

"Maybe his alibi for when Ricky was killed."

"Maybe. If he'll talk to us."

"Angel is a friend of mine from Chicago. He'll talk."

The interior of Angel's is worse than the exterior. It's little more than a shack. I'm not sure how it stays open. There are obviously no building inspectors in this area between Cabarrus and Mecklenburg counties. Maybe they've just agreed not to get too close to this dump. Probably afraid of catching something.

There are a few tables and a bar. Angel is standing back behind the bar, talking to one of the bikers whose motorcycles we passed outside. He's still wearing his black hair greased back on his head and that little pencil mustache above his lip. Some things never change.

I can't describe what this smells like. I've been in Dumpsters that smelled better. Ruby sniffs and then puts her hand up to her nose, but she keeps on walking on the spongy carpet that seems to be wet with something neither of us wants to know about.

"Get you somethin'?" Angel asks when he sees us.

"We're looking for some information."

He smiles and walks closer, then stops dead. "Is that you, Wyczewski? Get out of here! Did you follow me all the way down here to torment me?"

Ruby glances at me and whispers, "I thought you said he was your friend?"

I smile. "Maybe 'associate' would be a better word."

"You arrested me and sent me to prison for two years! You got a lot of nerve comin' into my place!" Angel slams down the glass he's holding.

Ruby rolls her eyes toward heaven. "He's not going to help us."

"Excuse me." I smile at her and nod at Angel. "Could I have a word with you in private? I have a proposition for you."

Angel backs farther away from me until he's almost stuck between the wall and the big, dirty bar. "No way! You roughed me up good when you arrested me. Anything you got to say, you can say it in front of my patrons."

Ruby looks at the barstool next to her, probably trying to decide if she should sit on it. I guess one look is enough. She doesn't sit.

I take a deep breath, not so worried about looking bad in front of Ruby as I am about coming away with some answers for Bobby. This thing with Ricky's death is escalating and threatening to ruin race week—and send Bobby to prison for a crime he didn't commit, of course. "Angel, I'm just looking for some answers."

"Yeah?" He wipes his nose on his shirt sleeve. "Like what? And why would I help you?"

"Because you're on parole and I doubt if anyone from Chicago knows you're down here." I pause and smile as he squirms. Hit that right on the head. "And I doubt if any of the police around here know you skipped on parole either."

"Dude!" The biker at the bar shakes his head and moves away from Angel. "You're gonna get locked up for that."

Angel comes closer to me, but his whole body is twitching. Funny, I don't recall actually breaking any part of him when I arrested him, but it has been a while. "All right, Wyz, you don't have to tell everyone in the bar!"

"Wyz?" Ruby smiles. "Is that a nickname?"

Angel laughs. "Yeah. Short for his name and what I saw him doing the first time we met."

Ruby laughs with him. "That's funny!"

"Never mind that." I interrupt them both. Damn, I forgot about that stupid name he used to call me. He was my snitch for a few years before he got caught running numbers. "I'm looking for information about Ricky Sanders's death."

"You mean the guy at the speedway, right? The rookie?" Angel strokes his chin.

"Yep. The guy they like for the killing says he was in here drinking when Sanders was killed. Show him the picture, Ruby."

She takes out her wallet with the photo of Bobby in his jumpsuit. "He's my brother," she tells him, holding it out.

Angel studies the photo. "Yeah, I've seen him and every other rookie in here, including that Sanders boy."

"Were they here?"

"This one was." He points to Bobby. "I don't remember what time. He met a few other drivers here, but Sanders wasn't one of them."

"You remember when he left?"

"Nope. Before it got light outside. Maybe after midnight. Otherwise, I'm not sure. He didn't drink much, though. Said he was racing the next day."

Ruby puts her photo away. It isn't much help unless we can get a close time for him being there. Bobby could still have been at the track killing Ricky according to Angel's time frame.

"Thanks anyway." I take Ruby's arm and we start to leave before something in this hole makes us sick.

"Wyz?" Angel calls me back. "I've heard something that might be interesting to you."

"Okay."

He looks at me, and Ruby makes a clicking noise in her throat. "You have to grease his palm," she whispers. "You know, 'Give me money.' That's the way it works, Glad."

I take out a five, but Ruby slaps down a twenty. She bends in closer. "What do you know, Angel?"

He glances around the almost-empty bar. "I heard he saw something he shouldn't have seen."

"Like what?" Ruby wonders.

Angel shrugs his thin shoulders. "I hear more than car parts run in those big trucks sometimes. Maybe he saw something besides a car part being unloaded. That's just what I hear."

NINE

"What else could Bobby have seen?" Ruby asks as we walk out of the bar. "And that stuff about what else they deliver in trucks at racetracks? That's stupid. What *don't* they deliver?"

"I don't know yet. But I think we should talk to Massey again. All of this seems to lead right back to him."

"I just hope they don't arrest Bobby until we can get some solid information." She shudders and takes my hand. "They aren't very nice in prison."

"He wouldn't be going to prison, honey," I tell her, trying to cheer her up. "At least not right away. He'll be in the county jail."

She glances at me. We're almost eye to eye. My Ruby is no slight force to be reckoned with. "Remind me not to have you cheer anyone up, Glad! They might be likely to kill themselves when you're through!"

I'm not sure what I said wrong. I've been in prisons before, and I've been in county lockups. County is like a picnic. But she doesn't know that. Maybe I'll stick to what we're doing, focus on trying to find out what happened to Ricky. She seems to do all right with that.

We get back to the speedway and ask around about Massey. Apparently there's some big event up at Concord Mills Mall and he's there with Team Massey, which probably means him and Spencer. Not that I blame him. Spencer is his top driver. He's won a few races and has a good point average. He's Massey's best opportunity to win the Chase this year.

Ruby and I run into Andy Anderson as we're getting ready to leave, and he wants to go to the mall too. Round that out with his wife, June, and we're a full payload. I wouldn't have included them, but Ruby invites them before I can stop her

Concord Mills is exactly the kind of mall I normally hate, except for the Bass Pro Shop. I could spend all day in there. I don't fish much, but I like looking at all the gizmos. They have camping gear and rifles, a huge fish tank with real game fish, and anything a sportsman could use. No NASCAR items, but no one's perfect. There are a couple of NASCAR shops in the mall too. I'm sure we can manage to hit them either before or after we talk to Massey.

Not that I plan to do much walking around and looking. If we don't wrap up this thing with Bobby, it could go on through the Coca-Cola 600, and no one wants that. I don't want to be thinking about Bobby when I'm watching Joe win the race.

"I love this place," June sighs as we get through the traffic on Speedway Boulevard and are close enough to the mall to see it.

"They've done a lot of building out here since last year," Andy remarks.

"That's right," I say with a laugh, "you weren't here last October."

"Stuff it, Glad." He's angry he had to miss the October race. He had to stay home and spend that weekend with June's parents, who came out from Arizona. Andy still has a stationary house in Florida. He's nervous about living full time in a motor home.

But he's right. The area around the speedway is pretty heavily developed, considering that when we used to come here, the closest place to get anything was Charlotte or Concord, a good half-hour ride away. There are some decent restaurants now within only a short drive. Although I don't know who'd want to eat in them when they could be cooking on the grill by their RV.

"They said Massey and the others are by the NASCAR track." Ruby points toward the little kart track as we come in sight of it.

"Wow!" Andy says. "I want to do that!"

"If you got into one of those death traps," June objects, "you'd never get back out again and we'd miss the race."

Andy backs down. "Or I could go and look at the fish in the Bass Pro Shop."

June nods. "That's more your speed."

She and Ruby laugh at that. I'm not sure why. I feel sorry for Andy. June tells him what to do, and he hops to it.

"Quit daydreaming, Glad," Ruby says, "and park this thing!"

I don't hop to it. I leisurely pull the truck close to the NASCAR theme park and stop. Ruby and I don't have that kind of relationship. I don't tell her what to do. She doesn't tell me what to do. Kind of like how Russia and the United States used to be when Russia was still the Soviet Union.

"Where will you guys be?" Andy asks us.

I shrug. "Looking for Massey."

"Are you really going to try to find out who killed Ricky?" June obviously can't believe it. "Isn't that something best left for the police?"

"It would be if Bobby wasn't involved," Ruby reminds her.

"I'm sure they'll sort out the truth anyway." June pats her arm and smiles.

I look at Andy, hoping he's not about to do the same to me. He can smile sympathetically, I guess, but I really don't want him to pat my arm. The idea gives me the creeps, and it has nothing to do with him being another man. Why do women pat people at all? That's one basic difference between men and women. I don't know what caused it or who the first woman was to pat an arm or a baby's butt. Men just aren't made like that.

We split up, making sure we have each other's cell phone numbers. This mall is huge. I don't know if you could get lost, as it goes in a big circle like the track, but you could get really tired of looking for someone, and I'm not good at waiting.

We leave each other at the mall entrance with June carefully guiding Andy away from the little NASCAR minicars. Ruby and I head in that direction. A loudspeaker is blaring, and drivers are talking about the race and their teams.

I stop and stare when I see Joe up there in his jumpsuit. Can I be this lucky? The NASCAR theme park is having an outdrive-your-favorite-driver contest, all money going to charity, of course. "We have to do this!"

Ruby stares at me. "We're trying to find Ricky's killer."

"There's Massey and Spencer over there." I point them out as I move us closer to the long lines of fans who want to race against their favorite drivers. I can't believe that I'm here and so is Joe. What are the odds?

Jimmie Johnson isn't here, or I know Ruby would feel the same way. Yes, Bobby is in trouble, but a short ride isn't going to change anything. We might even learn something else.

"Don't try to fool me that you don't just want to drive with Joe," she argues.

"Okay. I admit it. I want to drive with Joe. It won't take that long, and then we can talk to Massey and Spencer."

"If *your* brother was facing a murder charge, I wouldn't be asking about something as silly as a minicar race!"

"You would if Jimmie was up there! I'm staying! That's that."

Ruby looks at her fingernails and doesn't say anything else about it. I can tell she's ticked.

After about thirty minutes, my line is finally moving forward. We're closer to Joe, who is waving and smiling for some tourists to take his picture. Jeff Burton is up there too and has a long line of fans waiting to drive with him. Spencer is taking the first group out on the track. That's good. It gets rid of some dead weight that doesn't care who they drive with.

"Glad, we're moving away from Massey." Ruby taps her sandaled foot impatiently.

She's right. Massey has finished answering reporters' questions, and he's standing off by himself, watching Spencer wave as he gets into a car. But Joe is standing almost close enough for me to touch him. Not that I would.

I know. Compared to Bobby's predicament and Ruby's unhappiness about it, I shouldn't even consider how important it is for me to race with Joe Nemechek. I know.

I look at her sad blue eyes and her sweet lips and I know I have to do the right thing. Joe will be there again some other time, if I'm not too old to get into a minicar. I think Joe would help his wife first too.

I take Ruby's hand, look away from Joe's eyes (not an easy thing to do), and tug her away from the people who immediately move up to take our spot. But that doesn't matter. "Let's go."

"Thanks, sugar." She kisses my knuckles and smiles at me.

We make our way through the people at the back of the crowd, where they're only dreaming of racing with one of the drivers because they'll never get to the front of any of the lines before the drivers leave. Massey is still watching his boy, Spencer, as he races along the small track with dozens of screaming fans yelling his name.

I concentrate on how he looks, trying to decide if he's a man who looks like he has something to hide. He does, of course, but everyone looks like that to me. Everyone is guilty of something. I learned that a long time ago. It's mostly how bad that something is that is up for question.

"Mr. Massey." I approach him politely.

I recall my first partner always telling me to approach a suspect politely if I wanted to stay alive to see retirement. A man is less likely to shoot you in the stomach if you're sounding nice and polite, he used to say. And he was right, I suppose. He stayed alive until retirement, and he kept me alive.

Massey immediately looks guarded. He definitely knows something about what happened to Bobby. He remembers me and Ruby from the pit-road run-in. He knows why we're here. "I don't know anything else about Ricky Sanders's death. I'm sorry he's gone. He would have shaped up to be a good driver."

"Why didn't you tell the police where you saw Ricky and Bobby playing poker?" It's just something I'm curious about. It took me and Ruby to show Frishburn where to look for the evidence that would completely incriminate Bobby.

"I didn't think about it," he answers, his hand twitching. "If you're thinking I knew what they'd find in that old shed, you're crazy!"

"I didn't say that. But it seems like you'd remember to tell the detective so he could look there first." I smile lazily. It always throws people off. "Unless you were setting up the whole thing after Bobby went to Angel's. Maybe you weren't really sure they wouldn't find anything of yours there."

Massey looks around and wets his lips. "I don't know what you're talking about."

Ruby pitches in with, "We heard you got in a shipment of car parts for Team Massey last night. What else was in there that Ricky wasn't supposed to see when he was with you?"

It was a good try. Really. Ruby intimidated Jeanette, but Massey is made of stronger stuff.

He straightens his tie and smiles back at us. "I hope you're enjoying race week. I see Spencer coming this way. Would you two like an autograph?"

Spencer is still combing his hair back to its usual heightened grandeur when he gets there. I don't know what women see in him. He's got big teeth and too much hair besides looking a little wormy to me.

"Thanks, Mr. Massey." I smile and start to move away. "We'll see you around."

Ruby moves with me, and we get through the crowd that is still waiting for their rides with Jeff Burton. I don't want to think about Joe out there on the mini track, where I should be.

"What did we learn from *that*, Glad?" Ruby whispers when we get clear in the crowded mall.

"We learned that you can't always get what you want."

"Glad!"

"Okay. We learned that Massey is hiding something. I don't know if it's something worth killing Ricky for. But there *is* something going on with him."

"Good." Ruby rubs her hands together. "I sure hope it doesn't take Spencer out, though. That man is *hot*!"

"What?"

She fans herself with hand. "All that blond hair and those nice white teeth. He's so pretty it makes me jealous to look at him!"

I stop dead in the mall, and several people walk straight into me. One apologizes, and the other one glares at me. "You think *Spencer* is hot?"

She sidles up next to me and whispers, "He reminds me of you, sweetie."

Now I'm really affronted. How could he remind her of me? That's not possible. I can't imagine—

Then I see the smile in her eyes, that little imp of laughter, and I know what just happened. She laughs. "Got you!"

"Geez, Ruby, you hold a grudge for a long time. I told you I was sorry about Jeanette."

"True. But this was so much more fun."

We get down to Starbucks and then take some iced mochas outside, sitting on a bench and talking about what to do next.

"What could be in a truck like that going from state to state?" Ruby squints in the bright sunset even with her sunglasses on.

"Could be drugs, guns . . ." I shrug. "Almost anything."

"That's what I thought. How do we find out what truck made a delivery?"

"Security guard logs, maybe." I sip my mocha and lean back against the side of a wooden fence. "But I don't know how we'd get our hands on them."

"But we think Angel is reliable enough to base all our theories around Massey?"

"I don't know. Maybe."

"What? You think it could be something else?" She tosses her cup away in the trash.

"I don't know. Bobby and Ricky are playing poker because they're bored but too excited to sleep."

"Right."

"But Massey comes along and tells Ricky he better get some rest. Ricky goes outside and sees something Massey is unloading. Massey waits until Bobby goes to Angel's, then lures Ricky back into the shed and kills him. Something doesn't make sense to me."

"Like what?"

"Like why would Massey do that? Why not unload and then tell Ricky to get some sleep? Didn't he know the truck was coming in? If there was something illegal in the truck, I've got a feeling he'd know exactly when it was coming in."

"So you think Angel didn't know anything? He was just making it up?"

"Maybe. Snitches do that sometimes for money."

Ruby gets to her feet and stretches, a sight that makes me feel a little crazy. Then she gets this determined look on her face. "We have to go back and talk to Angel."

"There's no guarantee he'll tell the truth."

"Maybe not," she agrees. "But I plan to get my twenty bucks back."

"I don't know what to do next. We're back to where we started if Massey didn't do anything."

"But why bother having Jeanette as an alibi if he didn't do anything wrong?"

"Maybe she wasn't an alibi. Maybe they like each other."

"Then who killed Ricky and why?"

"I don't know, sweetie." I squeeze her hand. "But we'll keep asking questions until we find out."

"We only have until the race is over," she reminds me. "After that, everyone leaves."

"And if there *is* any evidence, they take it all with them."

"So now what do we do?" She slips her hands into the back pockets of her shorts.

I look at her and have some ideas, but I'm sure she means "about Bobby," so I keep them to myself. "We start at the beginning. It's what you always do when you hit a dead end. We know how Ricky was killed and where he died. If we can figure out why someone would want to kill him, we might be able to figure out who did it."

There are giant-screen TVs everywhere in the mall when we head back into the air conditioning. Frishburn is on TV, standing behind another man. His tie is dirty and crooked, and he looks like he slept in his clothes. The other man, I'm assuming, must be the police commissioner, or someone else with a title and a six-figure salary behind it.

Behind them all is Humpy Wheeler, the man who powers Lowe's Motor Speedway. He's probably leaning pretty hard on the police to find out what happened and make an arrest before the race on Sunday. That way, the press is all about the race and not what happened before it started.

"We want the public to know that an arrest has been made in the death of rookie driver Richard Sanders. The Concord police have questioned a suspect and feel confident they have the right man." The commissioner-looking figure looks at the TV camera.

"We want to thank the Concord Police Department for all their hard work in resolving this issue and just want to express our condolences to the Sanders family. Ricky was a fine driver and a hard-working young man," Wheeler says carefully.

Ruby grips my arm. We both know what's coming. It's exactly what I was afraid of before Deputy Pressler came for Bobby. Everyone needs this cleaned and spit-polished right away. Bobby is handy and, in all truth, set himself up to be a good murder suspect. He had motive, weak as it might be, and opportunity. Jeff Burton's jumpsuit wasn't in that shed with Ricky's blood on it. And Junior wasn't seen playing cards with Ricky before he died.

"We've arrested Robert Tracey Furr of Midland in the death of Richard Sanders," the commissioner says carefully. "As of this moment, he is in the Cabarrus County Jail awaiting his bond hearing."

Both men take some questions about what happened and how it happened, but of course, the officials aren't at liberty to say. Partly because they don't know and partly because they can't say even if they do know, unless they want a mistrial. The media should know better, probably does know better. But I spent two years working as a media person with the Chicago PD. They have to ask even though they know we can't answer.

TEN

"Let's go." Ruby tugs on my hand.

"Okay." I wish there were something else I could say to make this easier on her. But the best I can do is put my arm around her and let her know that I'm here for her. We start walking and see Andy and June. They have several bags and a box Andy is struggling with. I take the box from Andy and keep walking.

"Oh, Ruby, I'm sorry," June says.

I guess everyone in the mall saw what happened. Even if Bobby gets cleared of this, it will take a long time for people to forget it happened. There will always be those snide remarks, "I thought you were in prison" comments, remember-when stories. But the main thing is to be on the outside so he can get angry over those remarks. I hope something turns up so we can hear Bobby whine about this over lunch.

"What are you going to do, Glad?" Andy asks to one side so the ladies can't hear us.

"I don't know yet. I think we've been looking in the wrong direction so far."

"Maybe you should hire a private detective to help you. I know a good one. I had one investigate June years ago. Thought she was cheating on me."

"Was she?"

"Nope. She was going for laser hair removal and didn't want me to know." He laughs. "It was the darnedest thing! I felt like a fool. I never want her to know."

I agree and keep walking. I like Andy, but he can be a plain stick of wood sometimes. It seems June is only making things worse for Ruby, because they're both crying. I'll be glad to see the end of this expedition.

We pack into the truck again, bags and boxes in the bed behind us. Ruby is wiping her eyes and sniffling. I find her cold hand and squeeze it. "We'll find an answer, sweetie."

"I hope so. June has a friend whose brother went to prison for twelve years for less than what Bobby is accused of. I don't want to see him go to prison, Glad. There has to be some way to prove he didn't do it. You know he didn't kill Ricky."

"I know. We'll find out who did it."

"How? We don't have a clue. We don't even know where to look for a clue."

"There's not much we can do tonight, but early tomorrow morning, we'll walk through what Bobby says happened. Maybe we can find something the police missed. It happens all the time."

"Okay." She blows her nose and wipes her eyes. "As long as there's still something we can do, there's some hope."

I don't want to disillusion her at this point, but I don't really know if there is any real hope. The police have a good case against Bobby. It's going to take some significant evidence to change their minds. I can't imagine the real killer confessing at this point, since he or she has obviously gotten away with it. I wouldn't confess.

The line of red taillights heading back across the bridge toward the racetrack on Speedway Boulevard looks like a never-ending snake barely moving, curling up and away. Yeah, things have changed here. It was always crowded, but it gets worse every year. The sport keeps growing, which is good, but that means more RVs, cars, trucks, and people too.

It starts raining as we show our ID and go back through the tunnel to the infield. It matches our moods when Ruby calls her parents to let them know what happened to Bobby. We drop June and Andy, along with their bags and boxes, at their RV. The sounds of partying don't stop for the miserable weather. The rain comes down harder, making Ruby's wind chimes on the side of the awning ding.

"I wish it would stop raining and we could do something useful," Ruby mourns as I cook two hamburgers on the grill.

"Even if it stopped, there wouldn't be anything to see in the dark. We don't want to try to find out what happened with flashlights. What we're looking for is probably going to be a small detail. We can't risk missing it."

A couple of men in their swimming trunks run by with women in wheelbarrows, racing each other in the rain. They yell at me and Ruby to join in, but we're just not in the mood. We were the winners last year in the greased-pole contest. We both had a few beers too many, and I don't want to go into what all went on. Suffice it to say that Ruby and I are not slackers in the partying department. That's one of the things we love about racing.

"Do you think Bobby will be okay?" Ruby asks in a quiet voice I hardly recognize.

"Sure. He'll be fine." I flip the burgers, the smell of charcoal sizzling into my nose, teasing my stomach. I *hope* Bobby will be fine. He's not a tough guy, but I think he'll manage. He's smart enough to stay out of trouble, anyway.

"I hope so." She sniffs. "Mama and Daddy were really upset. No one has gone to jail in our family since they caught my great uncle running shine. But that was before I was born."

Kim and David stop by with a few beers and some chips. I throw a few more burgers on the grill as Ruby goes inside the RV to get some plates.

"I hope this rain doesn't wash us all away," Kim says with a smile. She's a kind of plain woman with brown hair and eyes. Kim is the type of person you wouldn't notice unless someone pointed her out.

"Yeah." David grins. "It's really raining out there." David is just like his wife. Low-key, kind of shy, brown hair and eyes. When everyone else is cheering their favorite driver, David and Kim stand there and *look* excited.

Before I can add to their scintillating conversation, Kim leans close and says, "Is Ruby okay? We heard about Bobby."

"Stupidest thing I ever heard." David shakes his head. "What are the cops thinking? Bobby couldn't hurt a fly."

"They're thinking they have a viable suspect they can make a case around," I tell them as I flip the burgers again. "When the evidence stacks up against someone, you don't ask too many questions. You just say thank you and move on."

"But they have the wrong person," David protests. "They'll have to find that out, right?"

"I hope so. Do you realize how many unsolved homicides are on most detectives' desks? It could take a lifetime to go through a cold case file. Some detectives work twenty years on one case and never solve it. It's like a blessing from God when you have a suspect and good evidence. You can go home, put your feet up, and watch the Speed Channel without thinking about all those people out there looking for an answer to who killed their loved ones."

Ruby comes out at this point and sees the blank, glazed expressions on her friends' faces. She flaps the paper plates down on the table and puts her hands on her hips. "Glad, have you been talking about being a cop again? You know normal people can't take that."

David blinks and sits back in his chair. "That's okay, Ruby. We're used to it by now."

"As long as he doesn't talk about dead people and what they do to them." Kim shivers. "I don't know how people watch that stuff on TV. I don't want to know what I look like on the inside. Especially if I was dead."

I didn't realize what I was saying. I know Ruby's right. But if someone asks a question about police work, I switch into detective mode. I was on the job for a long time. I can't help it.

The burgers are finally finished as I stay out of the conversation with Ruby, David, and Kim. Sometimes I can't tell you how old I feel when I'm with Ruby and some of her friends from school. I don't watch *American Idol* or *Survivor*. They don't want to hear my street stories. It's not so bad when it's just me and Ruby. We seem to mesh together even though I'm at least one generation older than her. It doesn't seem to matter.

"What do you think, Glad?" Kim intrudes into my slightly depressed world.

"Sorry." I put the burgers on the table. "I was thinking about the race."

"No wonder!" David laughs. "Joe is on the pole. I'd be thinking about it a lot if Jeff was on the pole."

I tell them about meeting the driver David pulls for, Jeff Burton, at the mall, and David wants to know every detail. Now here's a subject I can talk about, regardless of age. Racing gets me through it. That's another thing I love about it. You can be talking to a billionaire from Venezuela or a teenager from Unionville, North Carolina, and not feel a bit out of place.

"But what do you think about going over to the monster-truck race tomorrow?" Kim asks impatiently. "Ruby said she'd like to go. Some of our friends from school are going to be there. One of Ruby's old high school sweethearts is going to be there with his truck, Old Faithful."

"Yeah," David adds. "It's a Dodge Ram with a 565-cubic-inch engine, 2,000-plus horsepower. It has 66-inch-high tires. He's won a bunch of contests with it. I think we'd have a good time."

Just what I was thinking. Going out with Kim and David and Ruby and a bunch of their friends, including one of Ruby's old boyfriends. Wow! Could there be anything more fun than that? "I think I'll let the three of you go. I'm gonna hook up with a few old buddies, and we'll be talking cop stuff all day."

Everyone complains and tells me that I need to go too. We go back and forth for a few minutes until we're all tired of it and move on to another subject. I hope that's the last I hear about it. I'd rather go to the dentist than spend that kind of time with Ruby and her friends.

Kim and David finish their burgers and stay on under the canopy for an hour or so, talking about the race and who they think will win the Chase for the Nextel Cup. An ambulance enters the infield to pick up some poor guy who broke his ankle trying to ride an empty beer keg down a muddy path. A crowd gathers in the rain to watch the paramedics take him away.

The racing crowd is pretty hardy, but a steady, hard rain eventually takes its toll. The night closes in around us, and people go to bed. Or they at least take the party inside.

After David and Kim leave, Ruby and I go to bed. When she lays her head on my shoulder, I can feel that her cheeks are wet. "Are you crying?"

"It's the rain." She snuggles closer. "And Bobby. It's hard to imagine what we can do to help him. I'm not giving up. I just don't know exactly what we can do."

I wrap my arms around her and sniff that fruity perfume she uses. There isn't anything I wouldn't do to make her stop crying. "We'll find something, sweetheart. Don't worry about it. Hey, Ruby's husband was a police officer in Chicago for fifteen years. He's bound to be able to think of something."

She kisses me and I stop thinking about Bobby or anything else but her. The rain patters on the RV roof and we slip into the quiet night.

The next morning I wake up with Ruby sitting on top of me, completely dressed and a cup of coffee in her hand. I can tell this isn't a cuddle-up, stay-in-bed kind of morning.

"Get up, lazybones." She bounces a little. "I have chicken biscuits in the kitchen. The sun is shining, and the clues that will save Bobby are waiting to be found."

Not really awake yet, I take the coffee from her and set it on the tiny side table. I grab her and drag her back on the bed for a good-morning kiss. If I'm going to have to spend my day looking for other people who may have killed Ricky Sanders, I deserve this.

Ruby rubs her face. "It's like kissing a Brillo pad!"

I rub my chin on her cheek and grin. "That's what happens when you wake a man up by sitting on him. Especially when you're already dressed. I mean, sandals and everything. Come on!"

She laughs at me. "I just wanted you to know we weren't going to be doing any fooling around this morning. I have to save my brother."

"No fooling around?" I slide my hand over her rounded butt, and she squeals.

"I offered chicken biscuits and coffee. What else can I do to get you up, darlin'?"

"You've done a helluva good job already, sweetie."

She hits me on the shoulder. "Not like *that*!"

I laugh at her, loving every curve and angle of her face. "All right." I swat her butt. "I'm getting out of bed."

"Thank you, Glad. I love you."

This has taken a serious turn by the sound of her voice. "I love you too, Ruby. It's gonna be okay. And you don't have to thank me for helping Bobby. He's my brother now too."

Without warning, she jumps on me, kissing me a hundred times, despite the beard. "You're the best! How did I ever get so lucky?"

"I was thinking the same thing." There's that big, stupid grin on my face again. "There's never been anyone in my life like you."

She opens those baby blue eyes wide and smiles at me. "Even if I'm already dressed this morning?"

"Dressed or not dressed, honey, you are the only woman for me."

"I kinda like you too." She kisses my chin one last time, then slaps my butt. "Now get up and let's go prove my brother is innocent of this heinous crime."

"Heinous?" I laugh at her. "Is that your word for the day?"

"My word for the day is going to include something about kicking your ass if you don't quit talking and get dressed."

She's humming as she leaves the bedroom. I get out the electric razor, cram myself into the tiny bathroom, and get dressed in record time. I know if I don't, there won't be any chicken biscuits left for me.

I walk out of the bedroom ready to banter with my wife again, but we have a visitor. Dale Sanders, Ricky's father. I don't know if I should get the pistol I keep in the table next to the bed or just tackle the old guy to the floor. There wasn't much to it the first time, and I don't see him holding a gun this time.

"Glad." Ruby reads my mind. "Mr. Sanders is here to help us."

I'm still a little leery. Just because you can't see a gun doesn't mean there isn't one. I don't want to take chances with Ruby's life. "Maybe Dale and I should step outside."

"He isn't here to argue about Ricky and Bobby," she continues. "And you're not stepping outside without me."

"I'm sorry about yesterday," Dale interrupts. "I just kind of went crazy when I heard about Ricky. I've had a chance to think about it awhile. I know Bobby wouldn't kill my boy. At least not on purpose. I know Bobby didn't do what the police are saying he did."

The old man stares straight at me as he's talking. He seems sincere. And I still don't see a gun. "Okay. I accept your apology. I can't imagine what it would be like to lose a son."

Sanders looks at Ruby. "Do you two have kids? I can't believe Zeke and Louise didn't tell me."

"No." I smile at Ruby's blushing cheeks. Would she like to have a baby? We've never really talked about it. It's been good with just the two of us. I don't know what it would be like living in an RV with a baby, but then except for nieces and nephews, I don't know what it would be like living with a kid at all.

Sanders nods, his lined face looking haggard and worn. He raises his gaze to mine again. "I want to help you. I worked security here for thirty years. Bruton and Humpy know me by name. There isn't any part of this track or this facility I haven't seen. Maybe I can help you prove that Bobby didn't kill Ricky."

I understand what he's saying. He might be a big help. He probably knows everyone, like Zeke and Louise. He *did* hold a gun on me, but I can't really say I wouldn't have done the same thing in his position. I hope I never find out.

Ruby smiles. "So that works for everybody? Let's eat and decide on our strategy."

We go outside in the sunshine and sit down around the table with our chicken biscuits and coffee. Ruby starts explaining to Sanders about what we already know. I guess it's probably not easy for him to hear the details of Ricky's death. I wonder if he'll be able to handle investigating it. Maybe anger and the need to find out who really killed him will help.

Out of the corner of my eye, I see a man approaching. Ruby smiles, and Sanders nods at him and says, "Morning!"

"Good morning!" Joe Nemechek waves. "How are you doing, Sandy?"

Sanders shakes his head. "I lost my boy, Joe. We're hoping to find out what happened to him."

Ruby introduces herself. "Would you like some coffee, Mr. Nemechek? There's chicken biscuits too."

"Call me Joe. Mr. Nemechek is my father." He pats his stomach. "I have to pass on the chicken biscuit. I'm trying to cut back, eat healthy. It's not easy getting in and out of a car window."

Ruby laughs. "I know what you mean." She stares at me. "This is my husband, Joe. Your biggest fan."

Joe comes right over and holds out his hand. "Good to meet you, Ruby's husband. I appreciate your support."

I shake his hand, but I can't get my mouth to work. It's Joe Nemechek, for God's sake! The best NASCAR driver in the world. What can I say to him? He's going to think I'm a total loser no matter what I say.

"Well, it's been good seeing you, Sandy." Joe shakes his head. "Sorry about your boy. I hope you find out what happened. If I can do anything to help, please let me know."

Joe looks at me again as Ruby and Sanders tell him goodbye. I suddenly realize that he doesn't know my name. At the same moment, I realize I don't have a camera. I could have a picture of me and Joe to show everyone.

I jump up and run into the RV. It takes me forever, but I finally find the camera. I run back to the door, throw it open, and scream, "Glad Wycznewski!"

But Joe is already gone, and now Ruby is laughing so hard that tears are streaming down her face. Sanders is calmly eating a chicken biscuit, and I feel like a damn fool. I should've told Joe who I was first and *then* gone inside for the camera.

"Thank you, darlin'," she says. "I needed a good laugh."

Sanders shakes his head. "What's wrong with you, boy? Joe's no different from the rest of us. He's a good man."

"I know," I mumble as I sit back down. I eat my cold chicken biscuit and drink my cold coffee. There will be another time for a picture of me and Joe.

"Ruby tells me we're gonna check out that old shed first," Sanders says. "I don't know what we can find there that the police didn't already find."

"No offense to CMPD," I say with my mouth full of biscuit, "but a lot of times things are missed. Especially in heavy-traffic areas like this." I study his face. "Are you sure you're up to doing this?"

Sanders draws up his chest. "I know Ricky was killed there. I can handle it."

I know there won't be anything overt left at the shed. Probably even the blood has been cleaned up. Bobby's jumpsuit and the knife are definitely gone. It's just the idea of dragging this sad old man to the spot where his son was killed.

But he's determined to go. We take a few plastic bags with us in our pockets and cross the muddy infield toward the shack. It looks like there's already a lot going on in that area besides the milling around of fans, drivers, and sponsors. Two men wearing bright yellow hardhats are at work tearing down the old shed. Only a few two-by-four beams are left by the time we get there. Everything else is gone.

Ruby looks at me with stricken eyes. "What now, Glad?"

ELEVEN

SANDERS RUSHES TOWARD THE workers. "Hey, what the hell are you all doing? That shed was evidence in a murder trial!"

"We got orders to take it down," one of the construction workers answers. "We're just doing what we're told."

"Where is it going?" I ask the man.

"I dunno." He takes off his hardhat and wipes his forehead on his sleeve. "They said to stack it on that truck. Maybe the driver knows."

Ruby steps up. "Who told you to do this? Who gave the order?"

The man shrugs. "My boss at the temp office."

The three of us mutually agree that we need to find the driver. We leave the construction workers and skirt around the side of the pickup truck, which is marked TRR with an oval racetrack around the letters. It could be anything from a construction company's logo to one of the racing teams'. It's definitely not a truck that belongs to the speedway.

Ruby states the obvious when we see the empty cab. "There's no driver."

"If one of those boys back there isn't driving it," Sanders observes, "then the driver has to be here somewhere."

Another astute observation. We all stand there and look around as if the truck driver is going to pop up and announce himself.

"Let's take a look in the glove box." Ruby sneaks that way. "Then at least we'll know who owns the truck."

It's a good idea. But there's no registration. Another dead end.

"Well, we can't just let them drive off with the shed," Sanders says, sounding pretty convincing.

"I don't see where we have much choice." I look through the back of the truck around the edges of the shed pieces carefully piled in the bed. There's nothing really there. Wood chips. Some straw. A piece of leather that looks like it could be from a belt of some sort.

There's something else too. Hair. Long, dark, tough pieces of hair.

Ruby is looking around my shoulder. "Horse hair. I think that might be part of a bridle in your hand."

I nod, thinking we might be on to something. "Maybe whoever wants the shed owns horses."

"What are you talking about?" Sanders demands. "Are you saying my boy was killed by a horse?"

Ruby puts her hand on his arm. "No. But maybe by someone who *owns* a horse."

"I don't know anyone who works at the speedway who owns horses." He shakes his head. "And even if you could do that whatchamacallit test they do on those TV shows, it would take you until Bobby is an old man to test every horse."

"Not really." I hope we can get on the same page with this. "This truck could hold some clues. Whoever got the clearance to take down that shed probably knows something about what happened, and they either take care of horses or raise horses. Any idea who that could be?"

Sanders shrugs but has a sudden gleam in his eyes. "No, but I know someone who had to let this truck through."

Ruby snaps her fingers. "Security! They must know who this truck belongs to."

We take my truck up to the nearest security shack and park it on the side, out of the way. We jump out and run toward the shack like detectives on *Miami Vice*. I really liked that show. I never knew a detective, plainclothes or not, who could feasibly be like Crockett and Tubbs, but I sure liked their style.

The woman and two men in blue Lowe's uniforms stare at us like we're either an invading army or we've lost our minds. Probably both. I doubt if many people get out of their cars coming through here.

Then the woman, an older lady with iron gray hair, sees Sanders and almost looks relieved enough to faint. "Dale! What the hell are you up to? You almost gave me a heart attack! What are you doing up here?"

Sanders explains the situation. The other two guards are busy checking passes as vehicles come through toward the infield. "I need your help, Anabelle. That truck has to be registered with you all. I need to know who owns it, who was driving it, and who gave them permission to take down that shed."

Anabelle doesn't look too sure about doing what he's asking her to do. I don't blame her. It could mean her job. She shakes her head and her lips purse. With my superior knowledge of people's facial expressions, I'm betting she's not going for it.

"Okay. I'll do it for you, Dale." She hugs him. "For little Ricky."

Well, you never know. I would've lost good money on that one. She takes Sanders into the guard shack while Ruby and I wait outside, watching the cars go by.

A few minutes later, Sanders runs out with a piece of paper in one hand. "That truck belongs to the Thunder Road Ranch up on Rocky River Road. Shouldn't be too hard to find."

"Who's the driver?" Ruby asks, just in time to see the truck fly by us with the broken-down shed in the back.

Sanders curses, spits, and then looks back at the sheet Anabelle gave him. "It's registered to Thunder Road Ranch. Don't say who the driver is."

"So somebody let that woman in driving that truck without asking who she was or getting ID," Ruby says with conviction.

Sanders and I stare at her. "What woman?" I finally ask. If there was a woman driving that truck, I didn't see her.

"A blond. She looked natural." Ruby shakes a pebble out of her sandal. "She was wearing sunglasses and a pink tank top. What were you two looking at?"

It occurs to me that I was looking at the truck. It was an older Chevy dually, good condition. Those older models were really tough workhorses.

"I was looking at the truck," Sanders agrees with me.

Leave it to Ruby to see the woman's hair color and what she's wearing. I don't want to sound sexist, but who else but a woman would be looking at anything but the truck?

"That leaves us with zip," Ruby reminds us. "Except now, the shed is gone. All we know is that some blond with expensive sunglasses went in there and grabbed the shed and no one stopped her. Anyone else want to know how she did it?"

"I think we have a little more than the fact that she was a natural blond," I reply. "We know the name of the ranch. We can look it up. It's bound to have a phone number and an address."

Sanders nods. "Maybe even a website."

Nothing could have come out of that old man's mouth that would surprise me more. I guess it shows, because his forehead bunches up and he snarls, "What did you think? We don't have Internet or cable out there in Midland? I've been to NASCAR.com a thousand times. Ricky loved Speedtv.com."

He pauses, and it reminds me of his loss. "Sorry. I wasn't thinking," I say. "And you're right. What self-respecting horse ranch wouldn't have a website?"

But an hour later, not only can we not find a website, we can't find a phone number. No phone number. No address. Ruby has Googled the name and the logo's acronym but has come up with no good hits for either one. She sits back in her chair as I hand her a glass of iced tea. "Thanks. I can't believe we can't find this place."

"Maybe it's not a ranch." I sit opposite her at the kitchen counter and pop the top off a Bud. "Maybe it's just someone who raises horses. If they don't buy and sell, there's no reason to have their name out there."

"That makes sense." Sanders's voice floats over the top of the sofa to us. He took a small nap while Ruby was on the Internet. "But Rocky River Road ain't that big. We can drive up and down and look for it."

"That's true," Ruby agrees with him. "But what will we say when we find it?"

"We'll worry about that when we get there," I decide. "If we can find out who owns this TRR place, we might get a new lead on Ricky's killer."

We try to convince Sanders to go home. He won't listen. I wouldn't either. It's kind of scary to think about how many things I have in common with this old man. Maybe it's just a father thing that I can relate to. I really hate to think I'm turning into an old redneck.

We pile in the truck and head out of the speedway, probably missing all sorts of great events. I am *never* staying on the infield again. I can blame it on that one thing. None of this would've happened if we were camping outside the speedway like normal. People can keep their million-dollar RVs if they have to go through things like this all the time.

We pass Frishburn at the security gate. From the look on his face, he just found out about his murder scene being destroyed and hauled away. I'd like to help him out, but he's made it clear that we aren't going to cooperate with each other. Maybe once we figure out who really killed Ricky, I'll share what I know.

In the meantime, we'll be cruising Rocky River Road. The road makes you think of driving in the mountains. Every other curve is a switchback turn with a little sign that says SLOW CURVE. Some of them are so overgrown you can't see them at all. The people who live here have no patience for those of us who don't and are looking for horse farms. They pass us going seventy or eighty miles an hour on every turn.

"Glad, you could speed up some," Ruby says as another car passes us, honking its horn. "You drive slower than Mama."

"Maybe you can see up these long driveways, behind kudzu and through pine trees, but I can't. If we go too fast and miss the place, we'll just have to come back again."

"*Honey*, maybe you should let me drive," she volunteers.

"*Sweetie*, maybe you should sit back and not worry about people passing us."

"Maybe I should drive," Sanders offers. "That way you two could climb in the back and slug it out."

Ruby smiles at me. "That's okay. I'm sure we'll get there."

I pretend not to hear the word "someday" muttered beneath her breath. I could teach my beautiful wife a thing or two about driving fast. I've been involved in police chases going over a hundred miles an hour. I can drive fast. There's just no point. We're looking for something. This is different. "Where the hell are the addresses?"

"I saw one back there," Sanders answers from the back seat. "It's out here. We just have to find it."

Kim calls Ruby to remind her that she already purchased tickets for us to go to the monster-truck race today at noon. Ruby thanks her, then reminds me, "We have to wrap this up, Glad. Those tickets were expensive."

"You should've told me you wanted to go to the dirt-track race," Sanders says. "I could've got you in for free."

I try to bring them both back to the reality of our present situation. "First of all, we have to find this horse place. Chances are whoever took that shed down is in the process of burning it. I don't know what else was inside of it, but someone went to a lot of trouble to get it out of there."

"We know that, sweetie," Ruby answers. "I was just telling you about the race."

I suddenly see a small sign tucked away behind some kudzu in the middle of a turn. I point it out for Ruby and Sanders. "Horses for sale. Maybe that's our place."

Ruby looks around. "But there's no driveway. Where is it?"

As we swing through the turn, a large, green pasture opens up on the right. The gently sloping hills are the background for a gracious white house with two-story porches and a circle drive surrounding a fountain. Behind it is set a picturesque red barn and a low, flat stable. There's no sign, but I get the feeling we've come to the right place.

"Look there on the mailbox." Sanders points. "Thunder Road Ranch."

I swerve into the drive, a truckload of manure coming up behind us. "I think the best way to play this might be that we're here to see the horses. Our mysterious lady in the pink tank top doesn't need to know why we're really here."

There's no sign of the truck from the speedway. I wouldn't stop at home before I did something with evidence from a police investigation either. The chances are too good that Frishburn could be right behind us. He probably isn't, but I wouldn't take any chances.

We park in the empty drive and stroll toward the house, looking at the horses in the pasture. "Do you know anything about horses?" I ask Ruby.

"Of course I do." She slides her arm through mine and smiles up at me. "I've been riding since I was two. Almost as long as I've been driving a car."

"That's a tall tale." I can't help but smile back at her. It doesn't matter where we are or what we're doing. She always touches my heart.

"Maybe. But you know my daddy. He wanted us kids to be able to take care of ourselves. I could shoot the tail feathers off a crow before I could walk."

"All right, it's getting a little deep now." I kiss her cheek. Not that I doubt Ruby is accomplished. She's always surprising me.

Sanders pushes by us and heads for the wide front door. He rings the bell and then knocks several times. A woman in a pink uniform answers, looking at us with frightened eyes. "We want to look at horses," he tells her. "Who owns this place, anyway?"

"No one home. Come back later." She starts to close the door.

"Wait a minute." I put my hand on the door to stop her. "We need to talk to the owner. Where is she?"

"She not home. You come back later." She tries to close the door despite my hand.

"Let me try this." Ruby pushes past me. "Hello. My name is Ruby. I'm looking for a horse. Is the owner home?"

"No one home," the other woman insists. "You go now. Come back later."

It's obvious we're not going to get in that door unless we're willing to push the housekeeper, or whoever she is, out of the way. And I'm not willing to do that. The blond in the dually has to come back sometime. We can wait for her.

Ruby glances at her Jimmie Johnson watch. "The race starts in twenty minutes. It'll take us about fifteen minutes to get back to the dirt track."

"We have to stay here," I tell her. "We have to find out what happened to the shed."

"Nobody is more devoted to finding out what happened to Ricky than I am," she answers. "But we have to give Kim seventy dollars for those tickets whether we go or not. I think we should go and come back."

Have I mentioned that Ruby is a little frugal with pennies? We don't have a name-brand item in our RV. I think her daddy taught her how to squeeze Lincoln before she could shoot the tail feathers off a crow.

"I'll stay here," Sanders offers. "It makes sense. I'm the one who should be here. You two go on. I'll call you if the owner gets home."

Despite my misgivings about leaving Sanders, I agree to go with Ruby. It seems to me we're abandoning the stakeout. What if something important happens? What if we lose valuable evidence while we're gone?

I tell Ruby about my concerns. She looks at me like she can't believe I said anything. "You know, this isn't a police action. I think we could watch the monster-truck race and still come back here to look for evidence. We *are* here to have a good time."

"Are you saying I'm not any fun?" I glance at her as we follow Rocky River Road back toward the speedway. The dirt track is right across the street from Lowe's, a newer addition to the track area. "You were the one who insisted we solve Ricky's murder. I just wanted to have a few beers and watch the race. Now when I'm trying to help, you shoot me down."

"Don't be silly." She puts on some lipstick as she looks in the mirror on the visor. "I'm still concerned about Bobby. But we did tell Kim we'd be there. She bought us tickets."

"It's all about the money." I shake my head. "Is it worth seventy dollars if we lose this trail to Ricky's killer?"

"Glad, I love you. Don't worry so much. These things have a way of working out."

On that note, I give up the argument. Bobby is her brother. If Sanders can't figure out what happened to the blond in the dually or misses her somehow, I guess it will be her fault. Apparently, we *have* to go to the monster-truck race.

The traffic gets pretty heavy as we approach the track. There are smaller races around the area, like in Mooresville, where they hold mostly dirt-track races. When you're waiting for the big race, any race will do. You want to hear the roar of the engines and smell the exhaust.

When we finally get into the parking lot, I'm glad I have my little Ranger. I maneuver it between two big Ford trucks and turn off the engine.

Ruby snakes her arm around my neck and looks into my face. "You aren't mad, are you?"

I don't take my hands off the steering wheel. "Of course not."

She kisses my cheek. "You *are* mad."

"No, I'm not."

"Yes, you are." She slides close to me. "I can tell. Your eyes get all scrunched up and you get this terrible frown between your eyebrows. If you'd looked at me like that when we first met, I would never have married you."

I look closer into her big blue eyes. "Would you like to have a baby? Not now, but maybe someday?"

"What made you think about that?"

"What Sanders said earlier. You're a young woman, Ruby. It's natural for you to want to be a mother." I can't look at her as I say this. My gaze falls away from her face and ends up on my wedding band.

She turns my face toward hers. "I love you, Glad. Maybe someday we'll want to have a baby."

"Someday may be longer than I have for that process."

Ruby shrugs and smiles. "Then we won't have a baby." She puts her forehead against mine. "But it was a great choice for a diversion. Now let's get back to why you're mad at me."

I don't get to answer, as Kim and David knock on the window, urging us to get out and walk over to the track. Without saying anything, Ruby and I agree to disagree for the moment. Ruby gets out of the truck and takes the tickets from Kim while I grab a couple of lawn chairs and walk through the gate with David telling me about his new business repairing aquariums. We only see them a few times a year, but every time it means a new endeavor for him. I always wonder what happened to the last sure-fire money maker.

By the time we're comfortably seated in our chairs on the grass, the truck race is already under way. The monster trucks growl and sling dirt, lurching from side to side as they take each other on. The trucks are normal-sized vehicles, but the tires are huge. It makes for quite a spectacle as they dive over old cars and pull wheelies and doughnuts around the dirt track.

One of the trucks is driven by Ruby's ex-boyfriend from high school. She and Kim squeal and point when they see him in his bright red Dodge Ram with the name Old Faithful painted on the side. The two women are giggling and whispering, which always makes me nervous. I can't really tell what Old Faithful looks like, but he's sure to be younger and have more hair than me.

Old Faithful is challenged by a Chevy Silverado named Black Widow, black with a red underbelly. Black Widow is clearly a better driver. She pushes Old Faithful to take more and more risks until the Dodge flips over, huge wheels spinning uselessly in the air.

People rush out to make sure Old Faithful is all right. They drag him out of the truck and he waves to the crowd. When he takes off his helmet, he has a head full of frizzy copper-colored hair. I think I'll be happy with my meager amount of hair after this moment. I don't feel jealous anymore.

Ruby jumps up and grabs my arm as Black Widow jumps down from her truck and throws off her black helmet. "Glad, that's her! The blond in the pink tank top from the speedway!"

TWELVE

"OKAY, WE'RE GOING TO have to be cool about this." I try to keep up with Ruby as she elbows her way through the crowd toward the Black Widow. "She may be the same person you saw in the truck. She may not be. Whether she is or not, we have to be careful. If we scare her off, we may never find out what happened to that shed."

Ruby totally ignores me. We get into the large group of people surrounding the blond. She's autographing their T-shirts, bare backs, and arms with a marker. I have an idea of how we can find out who she is. I suppose I could ask her to sign her *real* name instead of signing Black Widow like she is on all the other guys. Once we find out what her name is, we can find out other things about her. Maybe we'll understand her involvement with what happened to Ricky.

I start to tell Ruby my plan when she tugs on my shirt to pull me closer. "Glad, I think we should let her sign your T-shirt. I mean, it just won't make sense to pretend that *I* think she's cool or something. Besides, I don't see any other women who want her to sign a shirt or a body part. And I like this shirt. I don't want her name permanently etched on it."

"I agree and—"

"—and we could have her sign her real name!" Ruby looks at me. "What do you think?"

Since this is my original plan and just happens to come out of Ruby's mouth, I think it's brilliant. "Good idea. I'll see what I can do."

Ruby isn't completely sure about the idea after another look at the Black Widow. "But you can't go by yourself. You may need backup. I'll go with you."

"I don't think that would be a good idea. Like you said, this is a bunch of men. If you stay with me, she might get suspicious."

"But you might need me."

"I think I can manage. You can go back and wait with Kim and David."

I love it when Ruby gets jealous. Her eyebrows go up like a couple of surprised birds, and her eyes get big. She has this way of twisting her mouth and putting her hands on her hips that kind of drives me wild.

She's doing it right now. Not that she has anything to be jealous about. The blond driver is good looking, but I'm a one-woman man. I'd tell her all of this, but we don't have that much time. She's going to have to trust me. I'm sure I'd trust her in similar circumstances.

Well, maybe not. Not that I wouldn't trust *her*—it would be the man I'd be worried about.

"Okay," she finally agrees. The word is short and unhappy.

I kiss her cheek and send her away before it's my turn with the Black Widow. I weigh my options: my best Go Army T-shirt with Joe's actual signature on it, or I strip and let her sign my back.

Since I *really* like my shirt and don't particularly care how many people see my bare chest, I take off my shirt as she smiles at me.

"Could you sign your real name on my back and Black Widow under it?" I ask innocently.

She eyes me from head to toes and tosses her head. "How about if I sign my real name on your back and my initials on your head? I think there's enough skin showing to do that."

Before I can protest, she grabs me by the neck and puts her initials on my head. The cool, smooth tip of the marker feels really strange. I turn around when she's done, the picture of a fascinated male who can't get enough of her. The marker runs across my back and she's finished. I can't tell what she wrote, but Ruby should be able to read it.

The Black Widow looks at me again as I turn around, trying not to stare at the deep V of her cleavage, trying to keep my gaze on her eyes. She leans her head forward and kisses me. I can only imagine what the bright red lipstick looks like all over my mouth. I don't want to imagine what Ruby's response to that will be. With any luck, she didn't see it. My misgivings about my T-shirt are quickly over as I use it to wipe away the lipstick as I walk away.

Keeping my cool, I retrace my footsteps back to where we're sitting. The program announcer tells everyone it's time to clear the track for the next event. The Black Widow gets in her truck and drives off the track.

I see Kim and David, but Ruby is gone. When I ask where she went, Kim shrugs. "Are you sure you care? You kissed that blond slut right on the mouth. No telling how many diseases you got. Now you want to share them with Ruby. You boys from the North have a strange way of showing you care."

"Which way did she go, Kim? And I didn't kiss the Black Widow. She kissed me."

"Yeah. We saw you fighting her off. If Ruby knows what's good for her, she'll leave you like yesterday's garbage." Kim turns away from me to illustrate her point.

David laughs and slaps me on the back. "You still got some lipstick on your mouth. I don't think I'd go any further with that I-didn't-kiss-her stuff. Your best bet is to get down on your knees and beg."

I think he's exaggerating. Ruby knows me better than that, and she knows I was only up there to help Bobby and find Ricky's killer. Sometimes people make things worse than they really are.

But I don't see Ruby anywhere. The next event, a tug of war between two other monster trucks, begins on the field. The Black Widow's truck is gone. I take our chairs back to the Ranger, hoping Ruby is there. I know she didn't leave, even if she is mad, which I know she isn't.

But Ruby isn't at the Ranger either. There's no sign of her anywhere. Where is that mind link, like the one we had before, when I need it? I see Ruby's old boyfriend across the way and think about her going over there to make me jealous. That seems possible if Kim is right and Ruby is mad about that kiss.

But I see his frizzy red hair with his head bent close to a short girl with black hair. Definitely not Ruby. Ruby could use this girl for a shot put. So where is she?

My cell phone rings. The number that comes up is Ruby's cell. I answer it quickly. "Where the hell are you?"

"I'm in the Black Widow's truck."

For a minute I can't take this in. It's not possible. "Where?" Then I realize she's not kidding.

"I told you. I am in the Black Widow's truck. I saw what she wrote on your back. She wrote 'Black Widow,' not her real name. The plan wasn't working, even though you gave it your all."

She's upset. I can tell from the tone of her voice. "I can't believe you're mad about her kissing me."

"Really? Why *not*?"

"I'm sorry, okay? I did the best I could." And I really botched *that* up. Best to change the subject. "Where are you in her truck, and where is she?"

"I climbed into the truck to take a look and see what I could find. I thought she might have some ID. Then she got in before I could get out. I'm in the back seat under a tarp."

I close my eyes and try to be patient and calm instead of annoyed and frantic. "Where is she?"

"She's in the office, I think, but I can't tell for sure. Come over that way and see if you can find her truck. I can get out by myself, but I need a diversion to make sure she doesn't see me."

"A diversion?" My eyes feel like they might roll out of my head. "What kind of diversion?"

"The kind where you make her look away while I climb out of the truck. Maybe you could get her to kiss you again. That worked pretty well."

I'm not even going there. "All right. I'll think of something. Then we're going to have a little talk about putting yourself in dangerous situations. Trying to help Bobby is one thing. Getting in trouble is another."

"Could you save the lecture for later, sweetie? I think they might be putting the truck on a trailer. If I get hauled out of here, things might get a lot more complicated."

I agree and put my cell phone in my pocket. The office is only a short walk away. But at that moment, Kim and David decide to interfere in my life. I'm sure they mean well, but I don't have time for it.

"Glad," Kim approaches me. "We can't find Ruby anywhere. Did she leave?"

"Not exactly." I keep walking toward the office. The Black Widow's truck comes into sight. Ruby's right. Two men are pulling it up on a trailer.

"Well, where is she?" Kim demands, trying to get David to help her. "What did you do with her?"

I mean to keep my eyes on the truck, but the question surprises me so much that I glance at Kim. She's walking fast beside me, tiny little legs barely able to keep up. David is walking behind her, nodding and looking stressed. "*Do* with her? What do you mean?"

"We've heard you and Ruby can have some pretty rowdy fights." Kim motions to David, trying to engage him in the conversation. "It's okay. Everybody has trouble sometimes."

David finally takes the cue. "Just let us take her home, Glad. Nobody has to say anything. Kim just wants to make sure she's safe."

I'm not sure at this point exactly what they're talking about. I'm not saying Ruby and I don't argue once in a while, but no one has ever called the sheriff, and neither one of us are dish breakers. I look for the Black Widow's truck again. The two men are tying it down. I can see the Black Widow talking to a man behind it. How in the world am I going to cause enough of a diversion for Ruby to get out of there?

"Glad? Are you listening to me?" Kim grabs my arm and pulls on me.

We're rapidly approaching the truck on the trailer. The driver is getting into the cab of the Peterbilt, and the Black Widow is taking a check from the man she was talking to.

At this point, I'd rather walk around and pull Ruby out of the truck and deal with the consequences later. We don't even know if the Black Widow was the woman driving the dually from the speedway. The monster truck might be headed for Myrtle Beach, for all we know. I don't want to drive that far looking for Ruby if I can help it.

Sometimes there's a moment when a really strange idea comes into your head and you immediately pounce on it because you're desperate and you can't think of anything else. It doesn't mean it's a good idea. It doesn't mean it's a bad idea either. It's just something you grab out of the air and act on. The consequences always come later.

In this case, I know Ruby is sitting under a tarp in the back seat of the Black Widow's truck, waiting for a moment that I have to make happen. One of my goals in life is to try not to ever let her down.

So I bend down and pick Kim up in my arms. It's easy to do. If she weighs ninety pounds, it's a lot. I've had pastrami sandwiches that have weighed more than her. And it's such a surprise to her when I pick her up, her hand is still attached to my arm.

She looks up at me with what I can only describe as terror in her brown eyes. She glances back at David, who actually steps away from us. I'm not sure about his thinking on that, but when this is over, he'll have a lot of explaining to do.

With David out of the picture, I sprint the few yards between the Black Widow and the man with the check. I'm guessing he's the manager of the dirt track. That would help me out. But my brainstorm works either way.

With Kim in my arms beginning to struggle and scream, I start yelling too. "Help me! Help me! Someone help me! This woman is having a seizure. She needs medical attention. Is there a doctor?"

Kim certainly continues to aid in my diversion. Out of the corner of my eye, I see David beginning to run toward us. The Black Widow stuffs her check into her bra and then comes toward me, looking upset but intent on helping. The man who is possibly the manager runs toward me too, shouting for a doctor.

I'm hoping that Ruby notices I've brought everyone to the driver's side of the monster truck. That should leave the passenger side clear for her to get out. Kim is so worked up, she keeps screaming even after I lay her down on the ground. Maybe she understands. Maybe she's just being helpful.

"Someone get something in her mouth so she doesn't bite her tongue," the Black Widow yells as she climbs on top of Kim and holds her down.

"Will this work?" The man who is possibly the manager offers her a fat cigar.

She nods and shoves the cigar sideways in Kim's mouth. Immediately the screaming stops. Kim is still thrashing on the ground, probably trying to get away from the Black Widow. We're attracting a crowd. David is trying to push his way through to his wife, probably realizing the error of his ways. Too late, of course. No doubt he'll be sleeping in the shower for the next few nights.

I glance around and slowly make my way toward the passenger side of the truck on the trailer. I hope Ruby has noticed what's going on. I don't see her yet. If she got out, surely she'd come around where I could see her. What else could go wrong?

I start to take out my cell phone and call her again when I see the back passenger door cautiously open. Ruby sticks her head out and waves to me. I slip around until I'm under the door and she slides down to me. She's no lightweight like Kim, but I pick her up anyway and walk around the front of the big rig like I do it twice a day, every day.

"Took you long enough," she complains, even as she kisses the side of my neck and snuggles her head into my shoulder. "But thanks, darlin'."

"Don't mention it." I put her on her feet when we're clear of the Peterbilt. "Especially don't mention it to Kim." I glance back at the crowd that continues to grow with no sign of Kim or David. I hear the sound of an ambulance coming into the park. Like I said, sometimes you have these desperate ideas that work, but you have to pay for them later. I have no doubt I'll pay for this one somewhere up the road.

But in the meantime, Ruby is safe.

"What's going on back there?" She glances back at the crowd.

I explain about my diversion, and Ruby stops walking. "What's wrong?" I ask.

"We can't go away and leave Kim and David! You started this, you have to make it better."

“What do you want me to do? I’m not a doctor.”

“Kim doesn’t need a doctor,” she argues. “She needs someone to rescue her from the mess you put her in.”

“*You* told me to create a diversion. I had to work with what I had.”

“I understand that. But we can’t leave Kim there like that. Find David. I have an idea.”

We wade back through the crowd toward the center of the scene, where Kim is still laying on the ground with the Black Widow on top of her. The ambulance is trying to find some place to park. We only have a few minutes before they come to take Kim away.

I see David off in the crowd, looking lost. Probably trying to figure out what to do. I feel sorry for him, and I suppose Ruby’s right. The least we can do is save them.

Ruby moves like a force of nature, pushing her way through the crowd until she reaches Kim’s side. I see her approach the Black Widow as I get David’s attention. As usual, she takes the tough-guy stance.

“What are you doing?” she demands. “Get off of my sister!”

“I was trying to help,” the Black Widow offers. “We were afraid she’d hurt herself.”

“She’ll be fine. I have her medicine.” Ruby kneels down and shoves what is probably a Tic Tac into Kim’s mouth.

The Black Widow gets to her feet, and Ruby pulls Kim up off the ground. Kim spits the cigar out of her mouth and slugs the Black Widow as she spits out pieces of tobacco.

“Where’s Glad?” Kim demands, looking more animated than I’ve ever seen her. “Where the hell is David?”

I'm happy I don't have to go home with her. I start to walk away, but David grabs my arm.

"You can't leave me like this," he pleads. "We have to do something. Kim will never forgive me. We don't have a sofa to sleep on, just two chairs."

"I feel for you, buddy. But what can I do?"

He nods. "I have a plan. As soon as the girls are clear, we meet up with them and you let me punch you for doing that to Kim."

As plans go, I don't think much of this one. I'm sorry about what happened to Kim and I know David is sorry he didn't do more to prevent it, but I'm not a punching bag. "I think you should come up with something better. I'm willing to help you, but I'm not willing to stand still and let you hit me."

Before either of us can say anything else, David erupts in pent-up fury. "You shouldn't have done that, Glad! You'll have to pay for what you did to my wife!"

With those gallant words, David punches me in the jaw. I can only assume Kim and Ruby are behind me. I can't imagine what other insanity could have taken David to this extreme. My first thought, of course, is to punch him back. Then I realize things could really get ugly, so I back off. Ruby won't want me to punch her friend anyway, and if it helps him out, I suppose I deserve the punch. It just better not happen again.

I'm right. Kim runs past me and throws herself into David's arms. They are laughing together, giving me dirty looks. David picks Kim up, and they start to walk away, with him bow-kneed under her weight.

Kim glares at me one last time. "That will teach you not to abuse women!" She glances at Ruby. "You either need to get him therapy or get rid of him."

Ruby smiles and nods. When Kim and David are gone, she touches the spot on my jaw where David hit me. "It's red. Does it hurt?"

"A little. But I did the only thing I could think to do to save you."

She kisses the red spot. "Is that better?"

"Maybe. You could do it again just to be sure."

"I could," she agrees, "but we have to get going."

I'm hoping this means we'd better get going home for that kiss, but my gut feeling is she's not talking about what I'm talking about.

"I have it." She furtively moves away from the crowd at that end of the park. "I know who she is. Oh my God!"

Ruby holds up a driver's license with the Black Widow's picture on it. "I found it in her jacket on the floor. She's Frances Massey. I can't believe she's Frances. I haven't seen her in a long time. Who knew she'd changed so much? She killed Ricky."

"I don't think we can say that until we know something about her," I remind her as I mourn the loss of what I was thinking about doing when I got home with her. "We don't even know if she had a motive to kill Ricky. Or if she knew him, for that matter."

"You know how racing is, Glad," Ruby reminds me as we get back in the truck. "Everyone knows everyone else. Frances is Paul Massey's daughter. She's the one who fooled around with Ricky while he was dating me and got pregnant."

"We still can't make that jump of accusing her without proof. What's her address?"

Ruby shows me the Thunder Road Ranch business card. "At least it would make sense why she was taking down the old shed. She was protecting her daddy."

I'm not sure I understand why Paul Massey needs protecting. If Ricky got Frances pregnant, she looks like the kind of woman who could take him out herself and not rely on her father for help. If Frances is protecting anyone, it's probably Frances.

Ruby takes out her cell phone to tell her mother that she just saw the woman who got together with Ricky behind her back, and they launch into a ten-minute tirade about Frances and Ricky.

When she gets off the phone, Ruby looks at me. "Glad, we have to go out there and find out if it was Frances, Paul, or both of them who killed Ricky. It's the least we can do for him, bless his soul."

I don't stop to ask why she wants to do anything for Ricky. I guess it must be more about what she can do to her ex-rival, Frances. In any case, we are heading that way. I hope Ruby can be objective when it comes to dealing with the woman who stole her man.

THIRTEEN

"YOU JUST JUMPED FROM Paul Massey being the killer to his daughter being the killer," I remind Ruby. "We can't run crazy out here. We have to have proof."

"What about her moving the shed Ricky was killed in?" she argues. "I think she had motive as well. Ricky got her pregnant. Everyone knew he wasn't fit to be a father."

"But we don't have any proof. The shed is missing. The only things that would be proof belong to Bobby. We can't go and knock on Massey's door and demand that he tell us why he killed Ricky."

"True," she agrees. "Especially since his daughter did it."

It's hard to get Ruby off of a tangent once she gets going. Unless someone confesses, she'll always think Frances Massey killed Ricky.

The motive for killing him seems a little lame to me. If this were a crime of passion because Ricky got Frances pregnant and deserted her, I think she would've killed him a few years ago. She looks like she could've picked Ricky up and shoved him through the car window, but that's only circumstantial. We're going to have to find a lot more than an old shed and an old relationship.

"I can't get Mr. Sanders on the phone." Ruby turns off her cell phone.

"Maybe he's in a dead zone." I put my foot down a little harder on the gas. Maybe it's nothing, but we left Ricky's dad in enemy territory so we could go to the race. I can't really throw this back at Ruby, since we did find Frances Massey there.

"I hope so." She looks out at the passing scenery. "We probably shouldn't have left him."

"We probably should've thought of that a while ago." I press my foot a little harder on the gas again. Sanders is a tough old bird. I'm sure he can take care of himself. But just the same, I'd rather be there than sorry.

I turn the Ranger into the long driveway that leads to the Massey place, which we now know is Thunder Road Ranch. I can't imagine that Paul Massey, as sharp as he is, can know about his daughter grabbing the shed from the speedway. He'd have to know the police would come after him for it. If we found out where it went, they will too.

It's beginning to rain a little, kind of like the sky is dripping. Ruby always says this is good plant weather. I think she got that from her grandmother. It just feels uncomfortable to me. The rain slides down your back and soaks in. I prefer a good, pounding thunderstorm. It's here and it's gone. The track has a chance to dry out, and life is good again.

I still don't see anyone in front of Massey's house. We really don't know if Paul Massey even lives here. Just because his daughter lives here doesn't mean anything. For that matter, we don't know for sure that the shed is here. Just because the truck that took it from the speedway came from here doesn't prove anything. Nothing seems to be any different than when we left Sanders here. I glance at my watch. It's been three hours since we left for the race.

Ruby tries calling Sanders's cell phone again. There's still no answer. "I have three bars, so he should have a signal too." She shivers in the rain after we get out of the truck. "I think something may have happened to him."

I'm beginning to agree with her when I hear a cell phone ringing. I pick it up from the side of the porch and answer it.

"I think we found Mr. Sanders's cell phone," Ruby says on the phone as I answer it.

"You think?" I ask before I turn it off. The phone has been on the ground for a while. I wipe the rain off it and open it up. There's nothing wrong with the phone except that it's not with its owner. The smell of the rain cooling the pavement on Rocky River Road drifts past the jack pines that line the driveway.

I glance around the front of the house. That's all I can access because of the pasture fence that runs on both sides of the house along the property. The horses have taken shelter from the rain. All of this is making me uncomfortable in a way that has me wishing I could call for backup.

It dawns on me that I *can* call for backup. All I have to do is call Detective Frishburn. He can come in with his police car and take care of it. I can go look at the NASCAR museum. If Sanders is really in trouble, Frishburn can shoot someone.

"What are you doing?" Ruby puts her hand over my cell phone.

"I'm calling the police. I don't want to be responsible for that old man's death."

"If you call the police and they come in with sirens and guns blazing, Massey could hurt Mr. Sanders. We have to take care of this ourselves."

I would laugh, except I can see from the look in her eyes that she's serious. That realization takes me from amusement to fear in less time than it takes a good driver to rack up points in the Chase. "Ruby, we can't go in there and get Sanders out. If the Masseys did grab him, they won't just give him back. We have to call the police."

"You could kill him if you do that," she warns. "My way is best."

I don't know for sure that my heart can take hearing what her way is. I'm afraid we've gone way past trying to figure out who killed Ricky, to becoming an amateur SWAT team. That doesn't suit me at all. But Ruby is already turning away to walk over to the front door. "No, honey, let's think about this. We can't just waltz in there and take him out."

"Glad, we have to save him."

"Ruby, let's think about this *after* we call the police."

"I don't think that's a good idea."

I smile. "And this is why we have police, so people with good ideas, like going into this house and demanding they let Sanders go, don't get killed."

She stares at me, blue eyes clouding like the sky above us. "I don't know how you survived being a cop. You have to take chances sometimes. You have to put yourself out there."

"Would this be a good time to show you the scar from my bullet wound?"

"Probably not, since you let that woman write all over you."

"Only because you said I should."

"I didn't tell you to kiss her, but you managed to get that in too."

"Are you going to beat that to death?"

We're squared off in Massey's potentially dangerous front yard, in the rain with no jackets or an umbrella, arguing about things that don't matter while Sanders could be in big trouble inside. The stupidity quotient has gone beyond the end of the meter.

I see the front door begin to open and push Ruby down on the ground beside me, shielding her with my body. I can't believe I let it go this far. I have too much experience to be so incompetent.

My peripheral vision shows me a large figure approaching from the house, and I wish I had my Glock from the truck. It's too late to wish it, but if it ever comes up again, I'll be better prepared.

"Hey, Glad and Ruby, right?"

I glance up into Paul Massey's smiling face and nod. "That's right."

"I found Ricky's dad wandering around out here. He said you'd be back for him. You two want to come inside and have a bite to eat? We just sat down to a big mess of greens and some new potatoes and rice. You're welcome to join us."

As threats go, this wasn't a serious one. And not what I expected. True, I'm not much of a greens eater, but I'll take it over getting shot any day.

Ruby pushes out from under me, pats her hair, licks her lips, and takes Massey's hand to help her to her feet. "That sounds wonderful. I'm starving. You know, we let Mr. Sanders out to look at the horses. He's thinking about buying one for his grandchildren. Glad and I lost track of time, and we thought something awful might have happened to him because of it."

Massey laughs and tucks her hand into his arm as they stroll toward the front door. "I didn't know what to think when I got here.

I was looking for my daughter and saw Dale out in the yard. Naturally, I thought the worst. He's getting on in age. I thought maybe he wandered off and ended up here."

I'm still on the ground, wondering what just happened. I don't think anyone is interested in whether or not I'm coming in for greens. I drag myself off the wet grass and follow behind my wife and Massey like an old Corvair, sputtering to catch up. Is Massey the bad guy in all this? If he is, you can't tell it by the way Ruby is acting with him right now. She's a good actress, I'll give her that. I know she doesn't really like Massey. You'd never guess she isn't coming on to him. But I know she's not.

"There you are!" Sanders greets us from the foyer. "I was beginning to think you forgot about me."

Ruby hugs him and demands to know where he's been. Sanders laughs and answers, "You know me. I can always find the food. Are you two gonna have something to eat?"

"Now that we know you're okay." She hugs him again.

I give him his cell phone, watching carefully as Massey and Ruby pass through another door into a room beyond. I can't see if this is the dining room, but it had better be something comparable and have food in it. "You might want to hold on to this. We tried to call you. When we found your phone outside, we were worried."

Sanders holds me back from following Ruby and Massey and glances around surreptitiously. "I got in here to take a good look around. No sign of the shed. But I have another lead. When I saw Massey here, I remembered about Frances. That was a damn stupid thing Ricky did. Maybe we've been looking at the wrong member of the family."

"Are you two coming in or what?" Ruby asks from the doorway.

"We're coming," Sanders assures her. "Just save us some of those collards."

The dining room, like the rest of the ranch-style house, is decorated in early Texas chic. Everything is big enough, including the large set of steer horns over the fireplace. All of those cactuses and sombreros remind me of the gift shop at the Alamo. I always wondered, standing there where Davy Crockett died, if he'd like people selling little plastic statues of Santa Anna right there.

Massey helps Ruby to her chair, but I make sure I sit beside her. I've had about enough of him ogling my wife. The little Hispanic woman who answered the door when we were there before is serving lunch on a mahogany dining-room table big enough to seat at least twenty people. The smell of collard greens with vinegar vies with the scent of freshly made corn bread and bacon grease. Another woman, younger, is pouring iced tea into large glasses.

As we start to eat, Massey is rambling on about Spencer getting close to having as many points as Junior, and the French doors open from the patio. The Black Widow, still in her driving gear, looks around the room, smiles at me, and walks toward Massey. She kisses the top of his head and mutters, "You could've told me we had company for lunch, Dad."

Ruby looks at me with her I-told-you-so look, and I realize she may be right. Frances Massey could be involved in Ricky's death. Her motive at this point might be a little shaky. It would have made more sense to kill Ricky right away after he dumped her when he found out she was pregnant. But she's definitely in the running, especially after hauling the shed from the track.

"Hello again. I'm sorry, I don't remember your name." Frances tosses her head and winks at me.

"That's okay." I get to my feet and hold out my hand. "I'm Glad Wycznewski, and this is my wife, Ruby. You're a helluva driver."

"Thanks." She glances at Ruby but doesn't say anything to her. "I'll change and join you for lunch." She saunters out of the room.

Massey takes us on a tour of the house when we finish eating. By now, Frances has joined us again, changing from the black and red Widow outfit into jeans and a pink tank top.

"That's the same one she was wearing this morning," Ruby hisses in my ear as we stand back from the rail on the back deck, which overlooks the horse pasture. Sanders is up front talking to Massey. Frances has wandered down to the other end of the forty-foot deck.

"I thought it might be." I look down at the sloping ground below the house. An Olympic-sized swimming pool is glinting blue in the sun, throwing back the scent of chlorine. White furniture sits beside it on the glaring white concrete. Some kind of red flower is scattered in big pots all around it.

It's a pretty scene. Like something from a movie set. It doesn't look real. It always amazes me how much artificiality a lot of money can buy.

"What are we going to do?" Ruby keeps her eyes on Frances, who seems to have forgotten there are other people here.

"I don't know. I don't think there's anything we can do. We can't just ask them about the shed. We sure can't ask them if they killed Ricky."

Massey turns back toward us and urges us closer to the rail to see a young colt playing in the green grass. Ruby asks where the bathroom is and excuses herself with a meaningful look at me.

I hope she remembers what happened with the truck today. I know she's going to snoop, and maybe it's not a bad idea. At least if she gets caught, she can say she got lost.

I step up to engage Massey in conversation to give Ruby whatever time I can. We talk about racing, of course. He starts outlining everything that has gone into making Spencer in the Chase this season.

"Who do you pull for, Glad?"

I explain my undying loyalty to Joc. "Ruby is a Jimmie Johnson fan."

He nods his head and curls his lip. "Spencer's a better driver. He could run Johnson off the road and never notice the difference."

"That may be." I don't argue the point. "You know how women are, though. They make up their minds and it's hard to change them."

Sanders pipes up with his pick, Jeremy Mayfield, the number 19 car. "Now that boy can drive. Reminds me of Fireball Roberts in his prime."

"Speaking of the ladies,"—I nod toward Frances's back—"what about your daughter?"

"I don't think she pulls for anybody right now," Massey says with a kind of sadness to his tone. "She's had a rough time. We both have. Driving those big trucks is the only thing that seems to take her mind off it."

I'd like to ask what's been rough in her life, but I don't think it's appropriate and I think it would sound too curious. Instead, I ask about the horses. "How long have you been raising them?"

"Not me." He takes another sip of his bourbon. "It's all Frances. She loves those animals."

Massey goes on to tell us more about Spencer and his new car. His modifications sound impressive, but really all the engines are pretty much the same as far as I'm concerned. They might tweak them a little here or there, but NASCAR regulations put them all close to being the same. It's the skill and fearlessness of the driver that make the difference in my book. That's what makes them folk heroes.

Sanders looks around and says, "Where's Ruby? She didn't fall off the deck, did she?"

This is why I hate working with partners. You never know what they're going to say that might get a pool cue busted over the top of your head. Or in this case, ruin Ruby's brilliant plan to do a little snooping.

Massey looks around too, and his brows knit. "I don't know. Frances? I think Ruby might have gotten lost in the house. Could you go and look for her?"

Frances doesn't answer, but her sullen expression says it all. She stalks by us and almost gets to the sliding glass door when Ruby pops out of the house.

"That was scary." Ruby laughs. "I didn't think I was ever going to find my way back out. Your house reminds me of my last visit to Texas. Everything is so big!"

Massey laughs too, but Frances eyes her suspiciously. She's about to brush by her when Ruby takes something out of her pocket. "I meant to tell you, I found this in the front drive when I got out of the truck." She hands Frances her driver's license.

Frances takes it and looks at it for a long time. "Thanks. I didn't miss it yet, but I'm sure I would have. Funny how it got out there."

"I know. It's strange how things happen sometimes." Ruby shrugs and comes back out on the deck to join us again. For a minute it looks like Frances might stop her. Maybe she wants to know exactly where Ruby's been or where she found the license in the drive, but that moment passes and Frances disappears into the house.

I'm not sure about Ruby's strategy, if there is one. This might have been a good time to give the license back, but I think I would've mailed it. I can't be sure, because Frances seems to be such an unhappy person, but giving back her license might have been a mistake.

I mention that we need to go. I don't think we're doing any good standing out here. I hope Ruby found something interesting inside. But we can't discuss it here. It would be best to leave.

"Well, I hate for you to go," Massey says. "I've enjoyed your company. Maybe you'd like to come up and watch the race in my condo. It's a lot more quiet and a lot less dirty."

"That wouldn't be as much fun then, would it?" Ruby asks with a sweet smile.

"Besides," Sanders remarks, "we probably still would be pulling for our own boys."

As he finishes, Sanders's eyes fill with tears. I'm not sure what to expect, hoping he doesn't say anything to give it all away. Ruby makes a better partner. At least I have some idea of what she's going to do next. Sometimes.

"Of course, I would've been pulling for my boy if he'd made it into the race." Sanders wipes the tears from his cheeks and sniffs. "Nobody would've been prouder than me."

Massey puts his hand on Sanders's shoulder. "I know. It's never easy losing a child. It will eat you up if you aren't careful."

"Thanks." Sanders shakes hands with Massey. "I appreciate your sympathy more than others', after what my boy did to your daughter. That was a bad time, and I regret he wasn't man enough to take care of it."

"It was a long time ago," Massey says. "And I blame Frances as much as Ricky. She was always impulsive and reckless. Things have happened that have changed all that. But I don't bear your boy any hard feelings. And I know Frances doesn't either. Hell, it was her idea for Team Massey to take him on as a rookie driver."

This is a gold mine. I realize we've heard more important facts from Sanders's surprise outburst than we have from all of our calculations. I'm not sure what to do with it at this moment, but Ruby may know something more that can add to it.

Massey walks us out to the Ranger and closes Ruby's door. We thank him again for a great afternoon. I start the engine and put my foot on the gas pedal.

Sanders is still sniffling in the back seat, wiping his nose on his sleeve. "I don't know how we ever thought that man could be Ricky's killer. What that family has gone through and still stays together. He even had a good enough heart to forgive Ricky. That takes a big man."

I'm not sure about Sanders's turnaround. Maybe he heard something I didn't that made him feel like he could trust Massey. I glance at Ruby and see that she's so excited she can hardly sit still. I don't really need to ask, but I might as well help her out. "So, what did you find?"

"I'm not sure," she admits. "Maybe it's nothing, but I walked through most of that house. You both walked through it too. Frances and Ricky's baby would be about three by now. It's hard to keep a three-year-old quiet. And there were no toys."

I shrug, not really feeling like this is much of a clue about how the Masseys could be involved with Ricky's death. "Maybe the multiple housekeepers take care of that. Or maybe the kid is already at a boarding school. These people don't live like normal people, honey. Not seeing any kid paraphernalia doesn't really help us out."

"It's more than that. I saw his little room. Well, his big room, but it was set up for a little boy. Glad, not a thing was out of place. It was like a museum."

Sanders's mournful cry comes up from the back seat like a warning from a bad horror movie. It raises the hair on the back of my neck and makes me look at him in the rearview mirror. "Are you okay back there?"

"Don't you understand? Don't you see the heavy burden God put on this poor family?"

Ruby turns back to face him and takes his hand. "What are you talking about, Mr. Sanders? What burden?"

"Massey told me before you got here. Ricky's son, my grandbaby that I never saw, died last year. God help me, but I didn't know."

FOURTEEN

We drive Sanders back to Midland. He's a basket case. Ruby promises to bring his truck back from the speedway later. We stop in to see Zeke and Louise and find them talking to a reporter from the *Weekly Post*, a local newspaper.

I'm not sure if this is a good idea, but Zeke is determined to make his point to the public about Bobby being wrongfully imprisoned. Betsy is there with Davy, Ricky's brother, holding hands. I guess the families decided it's okay for them to be together.

"And what are the police saying about your son's arrest?" the reporter, a tall, thin young woman with a serious expression, asks Zeke.

"That's the problem." Zeke points at her. "They aren't sayin' nothing. My boy hasn't seen a lawyer. He hasn't been told any information about a hearing. I just want to know when justice will be served."

Louise waves me and Ruby over to the far side of the big kitchen. "Would you all like something to eat?" And when we say no, "What about a cup of coffee?"

"No thanks, Mama." Ruby hugs her. "Have you heard from Bobby?"

"He called earlier. We're trying to find him a good lawyer. Franklin Marshal was the best lawyer around until he died last year. He would've taken this case and told the police what's really going on."

Zeke catches on to our conversation. "Too bad Bobby's not a veteran. Old Eldeon Percy would've helped him."

"But he's in Montgomery County," Louise reminds him. "Besides, he's the district attorney now."

Zeke shakes his head. "All the good ones are gone."

"So what are you planning to do to help your son?" the reporter from the newspaper asks.

"Whatever I have to do," Zeke answers. "Gene over at Gene's Bar-B-Q is gonna have a fundraising dinner for him. A couple of Bobby's NASCAR friends are going to help out too. We've got that local band—what's their name, Louise?"

"Right Turn Fred," she says. "Don't forget, Mr. Massey promised to have Derek Spencer bring his car down too. Isn't that nice of him?"

"Mama, we have to talk about the Massey family," Ruby tells her.

"So this is your daughter?" the reporter asks, writing quickly in her notebook.

"Betsy over there with Dale's boy is my daughter," Louise explains. "And this is Ruby, my oldest daughter, with her husband, the police detective from Chicago."

"So you're a police detective?" the reporter asks me.

"Not anymore. I retired a couple of years ago, before I met Ruby." I can see the crestfallen look on the girl's face. She hardly looks old enough to be a reporter, or anything else. I'm sure she was hoping I could give her some interesting spin on the case. I could, I suppose, but it's more important to keep everything quiet until we figure this out.

I'd like to talk about the Masseys with Zeke, but the reporter doesn't seem to be in any hurry to leave. It smells like Louise has a pie in the oven, so I don't blame her. There's probably not a person alive in Midland who doesn't know Louise will feed you while you're at her house.

Zeke finishes the interview with a flourish, defying the Mecklenburg County Sheriff's Office to find any shred of proof that Bobby's guilty. I don't go into the amount of circumstantial evidence, not to mention the knife of Bobby's that apparently killed Ricky. Men have gone to prison for less.

Louise and Ruby take the reporter to see Louise's great-grandmother's quilt in the hope that she might want to write about it. Besides Rusty's old license plate, it's the Furrs' most valued possession.

Ruby gives me a wink and a nod. She knows I really want to talk to Zeke alone, and that's why she brought up that old quilt. Smart girl.

"How about we go out on the porch for a few minutes, Zeke?" I suggest.

"That would be okay. I'm so riled up right now, a breath of cool air might calm my nerves."

I hold the door for him because I know he'd rather die than admit he needs me to push his wheelchair. He's a proud old man. I think he's wrong to let his pride come between him and the sport he loves, but that's just me. I hope if I'm ever crippled I'm not too proud to ask for help. I want somebody to push me right up there by pit road where I can get the best view. If somebody doesn't like seeing an old man in a wheelchair, they'd better look the other way.

The day is starting to cool down. It's almost six. There's a wonderful flower smell that Zeke explains is wisteria as he points out the lazy purple flowers covered with bees hanging off one of the jack pines.

"Sit down, Glad." Zeke points to one of the old rocking chairs on the porch. "What's geared up your gizzard to want to talk to me?"

From the barn across the way, the sound of someone working on an engine that's loud and choking makes us raise our voices. The engine finally backfires and then sputters and dies. The strong smell of gasoline hangs heavy on the evening air.

"I want to ask you about the Masseys," I begin carefully. I don't really want to tell Zeke what we suspect. He gets a little crazy sometimes. I don't want him trying to help like Sanders did.

"You mean Team Massey?" he asks. "Or the family?"

"Whatever you know about them."

He stares at me like he's trying to dissect my face. "This is about Bobby, isn't it?"

I pause, not answering, but I know he's looking for any sign of hesitation. "In a way. I know you know racing better than almost anybody else. Ninety percent of all the drivers live close by. Everybody knows everybody's secrets."

"*Almost* better than anybody else?" He squints up at me. "That's not a good start to buttering up an old ear of corn like me. You gotta slather it on."

"Zeke, you're something else." I laugh. "Okay, *nobody* knows racing like you."

"Damn straight." He nods and grins. "Now what was it you wanted to know?"

"Whatever you know about the Massey family."

He takes out a small white paper and pours a little tobacco from a box he maneuvers out of his pocket. He licks the paper and then rolls it into a cigarette, sticks it in his mouth, and lights it with a match. The smell of tobacco joins the other aromas, including a little skunk that might be left over from the night before. "Sam Massey was a good ol' boy. He liked to drive hard and fast. I used to help my daddy work on his cars. We tinkered with the engine some, trying to get more speed. I sat listening to the two of them talk for hours in that old barn. I think that's where I started loving racing. It gets in your blood."

"I thought your daddy was a farmer."

"He was. Wouldn't do anything else. But he loved to tinker. He'd take apart the tractor and put it back together. One time he took apart Mama's stove. It never worked again. She told him she'd fill him full of buckshot if he ever came near her kitchen again."

I laugh with him over the story, but there's one question I'd like to ask. "Why didn't you ever drive? You love it so much. I can't imagine anything better than actually being out on the track."

"No. That wasn't for me," he answers. "I drove around a dirt track a few times when I was a boy. I didn't have the stomach for it. I like to watch it, love to mess with the cars, but I couldn't be a professional driver. Like Ricky, I just didn't have the nerve to really push the limit. You gotta do that."

There it was again. If everyone knew Ricky was afraid to go fast, why did Massey hire him? I ask Zeke his opinion.

"We were all surprised when Massey took Ricky on. Maybe he thought he'd get over it. But if there's one thing I know, a driver is born, not made. They can polish him up, but the best ones want to go fast. Sometimes too fast, like Sam Massey. Back then there weren't any safety seats or much of anything else to protect the driver. Sam hit one ninety-five and lost control of his car. There wasn't much left of him by the time we got him out. I hated it too, with his boy there and all."

"So Paul Massey watched his father die, but he still built himself a team?"

"Racing was in his blood." Zeke shakes his head. "There was no way to get away from it."

"What's Paul Massey like?"

"He seems to be fair, open minded." He grins at me. "He'd have to be to hire the boy who got Frances pregnant."

"What was that like? Did Ricky help out at all? Did he pay child support?"

"What for? Frances lives with her daddy, and they have more than Ricky could ever give her. Half the time since that happened, he was out of work."

"And that didn't make Massey angry?" I ask. "Most men wouldn't hire a man who got their daughter pregnant and then wouldn't marry her or support the baby."

"I don't think it was that way. I don't think Frances wanted to marry Ricky. It was just something that happened. Bad luck. There was some talk of her giving the baby up for adoption. I don't know what happened to that. I think she had a boy. He must be three or four years old by now. Frances is making quite a name for herself in Super Trucks. She might turn pro one day, who knows?"

I tell him what Sanders said about Frances and Ricky's baby. I don't see what it can hurt. "He said the baby died last year."

"Well, I'll be. How do you think the Masseys kept that quiet? They must've had to go out of state, maybe out of the country. What did the boy die from?"

"I don't know yet. But I'm going to find out."

Betsy remembers a friend of Ruby's from high school who was also friends with Frances Massey. Before we leave Zeke and Louise, Ruby calls Donna Tucker's parents, who live a few miles away. Donna is playing with a band that just happens to be performing at Speed Street in Charlotte. I was afraid we were going to miss it this year.

Speed Street is a major event set up in the Center City area of Charlotte for all of the people attending race week, as well as anyone else who wants to have a good time. Last year there were more than 500,000 people pressed into about eight city blocks.

There is plenty of music and a lot of street vendors with T-shirts, food, arts and crafts, and NASCAR souvenirs. It's well populated with drivers who give away free autographed pictures and programs. Kasey Kahne, Dale Junior, Bobby Labonte, Jimmie Johnson, Kurt Busch, and Jeff Gordon were all there last year. I'm hoping Joe will be there this year.

Ruby and I decide to park and ride the bus down to the event. It's a lot easier than trying to park in Charlotte. The buses are running a few minutes apart, every bus packed. Ruby and I squeeze into one of the back seats. It's impossible to talk for the sound of laughter and someone bursting into some version of a NASCAR theme song. The smell of suntan lotion dominates the bus.

Ruby sits close to me, joining in the singing. The man on the other side of me is wearing a pink T-shirt with little pictures of Greg Biffle all over it. He sings louder than Ruby and doesn't smell as good. I figure with the right bump in the road, I could probably push him on the floor. As a product of fifty-cent beer night, he probably wouldn't get up again until we were ready to get off the bus. Not nice, I know. But I don't really push him down there anyway. You can't act on every crazy impulse.

The first thing that hits you when you get off the bus is the smell of onions, peppers, and sausages cooking on open grills in the street. The bands are loud and so are the cars. There are show cars parked up and down the streets, glossy red, black, and yellow paint jobs gleaming in the lights. A couple of the NASCAR drivers brought their cars.

Ruby sees the Lowe's car, number 48, and runs toward the line waiting for Jimmie Johnson autographs. I follow behind her, glancing around for any sign of Joe, but I don't think he's down here. They're giving away some Army T-shirts for his number 01 car. Ruby has her cell phone, so I'm not worried about losing her. It's worth it to me to wait in line for a T-shirt.

Imagine my surprise when I get to the front of the line about twenty minutes later and see Joe's crew chief, Gary Putnam. He's not Joe, but he's almost as good. "You sound just like you do talking to Joe." I'm obviously a starstruck fan. I don't care.

"Well, I guess that's a good thing, so Joe knows who's talking." He shakes my hand and gives me a T-shirt. "I hope you'll be there Sunday to cheer Joe on."

"You know it." Then, since I have the opportunity to ask, I wonder what the problem is with the overheating brakes Joe has experienced in the last few races. "Is that a design problem or something else?"

"Why don't you come and take a look at it yourself and tell me what you think?"

I'm pretty sure I misunderstand him. I stand there for a minute while he walks away. He looks back at me and motions for me to come behind the long table where at least thirty people are giving away T-shirts for one driver or another who can't be there.

I finally manage to make my feet follow him through the crowd. I duck under a red cord keeping people back from the car. Then I just stand there again. I can't believe he really means for me to look that closely at Joe's car.

But he motions me on again and says, "Come on. Tell me what you think."

I can't even find words to tell him what I think. There's Joe's number 01 Army car before me. The only thing missing is Joe. Putnam shows me around the car, telling me about the improvements they've made for this season with airflow and design modification.

"Now the brakes," he explains, "have been a pain in the ass since we made some of those modifications. But we've been working on them, and we think we got it right now."

I nod and try not to look too dazed by celebrity, although I suppose my actions up until now have already given me away.

"Would you like to sit in it?"

I can't believe he even has to ask. I'm sure this is some kind of joke. But there's Putnam, and there's Joe's car. Do I want to sit in it? Hell yes!

It's not as easy as the drivers make it look to hop in and out of the windows. Fortunately, I've been in Bobby's car and a few NASCAR models, so I don't look like a complete idiot. I even manage to slide in without getting caught on the window or falling on the street.

All I need is a picture to prove it to other people. I look around, but I don't see Ruby. She has the camera. I'm about to call her on the cell phone when someone offers to take my picture. I look up and there's Joe. The streetlight above his head is bathing him in an unearthly glow. I could die now and be a happy man.

"I figure since you must be taking my job, I'd brush up my picture-taking skills," Joe tells me. "Hey, I know you. Glad, right? Ruby's husband."

"Uh—that's right. How did you know?"

"I met you at Sonoma when you got married. And I saw you again this morning. Don't you remember?"

"Sure." I wish I could find something funny or smart to say, but the words aren't coming. All I can do is stare at him.

"So you want me to take your picture?" he asks again.

"That would be great."

Joe Nemechek takes my picture, then he takes a picture with me and Putnam. Then Putnam takes a picture of me and Joe. Then someone else takes a picture of me, Joe, and Putnam.

I can't believe Ruby missed this for a chance to see Jimmie Johnson. She's never going to believe this happened. I shake hands with Joe and Putnam, then I leave probably as stupid looking as I feel. I see Ruby coming toward me and can't wait to tell her what happened. I don't care if I can't prove it.

"Glad! I've been looking for you everywhere! Look what I got!" She holds up a Jimmie Johnson T-shirt and shows me where he autographed it. "He's the best."

"You won't believe what happened to me." I hold up my own T-shirt. "I had my picture taken with Joe and Gary Putnam. I was inside Joe's car."

Ruby's eyes narrow. "Where? I didn't see Joe or his car. Are you sure it wasn't a cardboard poster of it?"

"I think I can tell the difference between a poster and the real thing."

She opens her mouth to say something else, but something behind me catches her attention. I glance around and see Joe walking toward me through the crowd. For a minute, it's like those slow-motion TV commercials where the person is bouncing through a field.

"Hey, Ruby," Joe says when he reaches us. "I meant for Glad to have this camera. It's disposable. I thought he might like to have the pictures."

"Was he *really* in your car?" she demands.

"You'll have to take a look at the pictures." Joe smiles and salutes before he walks away. "See you all later."

I can't say it until Joe is gone, but a few seconds later I burst out with, "Thanks, Joe!"

Ruby slaps me on the back as she tucks the disposable camera into her purse. "I wish I'd been in Jimmie's car. You got lucky, Glad."

"I know." I grin and then kiss her right there on the street. "Now let's go find your friend."

Lucky for us we have a program and a map. We're able to find Donna's band despite there being so many people you can hardly move up the street. Donna's band is called the Slow Death Angels. Their music is a little bit punk and a little bit country. Donna plays the guitar and sings. All five band members are dressed in black. Nothing terribly original, but they sound pretty good.

We stand there and listen, eating Polish sausage and drinking beer between eating elephant ears. The crowd gets bigger as the night comes down. So does the police presence. All in all, though, it's a pretty quiet crowd. Everyone seems happy to be here. I know I am. I'd like to strip off my T-shirt and put on my Army shirt. I almost forget that we're here to talk to Donna.

Then the band takes a break and I remember why we came. Donna sees Ruby and they start kissing, hugging, and talking at the same time. Ruby asks Donna about Frances and Ricky's baby.

Donna shakes her head, dark red hair with purple highlights flying out around her. "That was a bad time for her, Ruby. It's like she had to become a different person just to survive, you know? I wish I could've helped her, but I was gone a lot."

"What happened to the baby?" Ruby asks her.

"He died from leukemia last year. Frances did everything she could to save him. She even took him to Mexico for some kind of treatments that aren't legal here. Poor little boy died down there."

"That's terrible." Ruby shakes her head. "I guess that's why she got into driving those big trucks. She's really good at it."

"Yeah, she is," Donna agrees. "I hope it takes some of the pain away. She was so full of anger against everyone and everything for taking Justin away from her. She really hated Ricky right then, even though it wasn't any more his fault than hers."

"You heard about Ricky dying," Ruby says. "They say he was murdered."

Donna's pretty young face gets hard. "Serves him right. He never lifted a finger to help them. Always let Frances get by on her daddy's money. What kind of man does that?" She looks up at the stage. "Looks like I have to get back. It was good to see you. We'll have to do something sometime."

"Exactly!" Ruby agrees with her noncommittal date setting. She takes my arm as she waves to Donna. "This is starting to make sense now, Glad. I think I understand what happened."

We're walking away from the lights and sounds of the festival, heading for one of the buses in the distance by mutual consent before the midnight rush when Speed Street closes. This end of North Tryon Street is dark and deserted in comparison to the festival at the other side.

I hear a screech of wheels on pavement and look down a black side street to see headlights shining at us from a large vehicle, almost on top of us. We quickly step to the side, but the truck spins around and comes back at us.

FIFTEEN

"Run, Ruby!" I veer her toward the left, where part of a building juts out into the street. I run to the right to draw the truck away. The truck may be fast and big, but it doesn't have human maneuverability. I duck around as soon as the driver sees me and starts heading in my direction. To throw him off further, I throw trash cans down behind me.

"Glad!" Ruby yells and waves from her vantage point on top of the building addition.

I wish she'd stayed put, where the driver couldn't see her. It's obvious the person driving is after us. I don't have much time to think about it with the big engine breathing down my neck, but I always assume where there's one weapon, there could be another. The driver might be trying to run me down right now, but in a minute or two, he or she might be trying to shoot me.

With that cheerful thought in mind, I squeeze into a recessed doorway. The truck possibly could crash into the doorway enough to pin me in place, but it screeches by me, the smell of diesel lingering in the night air.

"Stay put and get down!" I yell to Ruby. "He may be coming back."

We both stay where we are for a few minutes. I'm focusing so hard on the side street where the truck disappeared that Ruby's tug on my arm makes me jump about two feet.

"I think she's gone now," Ruby says. "Sorry. I didn't mean to scare you."

"I wasn't scared. I just didn't see you."

"That had to be Frances."

"It could have been. Or it could've been Paul. At this point, there's no way of knowing. But I think we must've rattled somebody's chain."

Ruby walks alongside me as we start back toward the waiting area for the bus. I wish now we'd driven down.

"Come on, honey." She's still trying to convince me that the crazy truck driver was Frances. "You know that woman is pure evil. Did you see the way she looked at me? She wanted to rip my face off right there."

"Or her Daddy is taking care of things for her. I still think Paul is behind all of this."

We run for the last two seats on the bus going back to the speedway. It's so loud with singing and chanting that we can't talk any further about the incident. When I think about how perfect my time was with Joe, I realize I should be singing too. But I feel cold and sober. Ruby could've been killed back there. That fact makes me more aware of what we're doing and less aware that I should be having a good time.

Up until that moment when I saw that truck coming down on us, the investigation into Ricky's murder has been like some weird game. Now I realize whoever killed Ricky knows what we're doing and doesn't like it. Our lives are at stake. That puts a different spin on things.

When we get to the parking lot where we left the Ranger to ride the bus, two things become apparent. First of all, whoever came after us looked for us here first. Second, he or she knows our vehicle. All four tires on the Ranger are slashed.

"Oh, Glad." Ruby puts her hand on my arm. "Those were new tires too. This just proves I'm right. I can see Frances doing this. Paul wouldn't stoop so low."

"Whatever." I dial the police and the AAA auto club. "I wonder why they're trying to scare us off."

"We must be getting close to something. It seems pretty strange to me that we saw Frances earlier and now this happens. And did you see that truck? She drives trucks professionally."

"We were with Paul too. I'd say either one of them could be responsible. But you're right about the truck. It was diesel too."

The police arrive a few minutes later to take our statements. We tell them about the truck trying to kill us at Speed Street and show them the tires on the Ranger. The two officers who respond write it all down and take pictures of the tires.

"This could be gang related." One of the officers, who barely looks old enough to drive, nods at the other, who doesn't look much older.

"Could be," is the cryptic response from the partner.

"Haven't you been listening?" Ruby demands. "Someone tried to kill us because we've been investigating a murder. The truck tires are just another part."

Both young men look at her, appreciating her obvious assets in shorts and a tank top. This makes my neck start to feel a little hot, but I remind myself of what's important. That includes staying alive.

"Well, don't worry about it, ma'am," one of the officers drawls. "Nothing will happen to you while we're here."

"Yeah," the other officer agrees. "We'll take good care of you and your daddy."

That's it. A person can only take so much abuse in one night. I open my mouth to say what needs to be said. Ruby grabs my arm and kisses me on the mouth, and then the AAA guy comes up in his truck.

"I think we can take it from here, officers." Ruby smiles. "Thanks so much for your help."

Both men shrug and head back for their car. I close my mouth and glare at them. Then I glare at Ruby. "I could've handled that."

"You could've."

"You didn't have to do that."

"I didn't. I just wanted to."

How can I stay mad at her? It's a curse in some ways being married to a woman who has an answer for everything. It's just that I really like her answers most of the time. Especially the ones that involve her kissing me. Those are particularly sweet.

The AAA guy, Max, tells us that because he only has one tire, the truck will have to be towed. Like that's news to me. He offers to take us back to the campground and have the Ranger brought to us. Not bad service for what we pay each month. I've only had to call them a few times. Last time was in New York at Pocono. We had a stone go through the RV's radiator.

I'm a little uneasy about leaving my truck here. But I suppose no one is likely to steal it with four flat tires. I hope the stereo is still in there when we get it back.

We are about to squeeze into the truck with Max when Jeanette Almond drives by, stops, and comes back. "Hey, you two have a problem?"

"You could say that." I nod toward the bad tires.

She shakes her head, blond hair spreading out around her face. "Bad luck. I'm going back to the infield if you'd like a lift."

Jeanette's whole car doesn't look too much bigger than the front seat of Max's truck. It's one of those Mini Cooper cars like they used in the movie. The name of the movie always escapes me, but I remember the Mini Coopers. Ruby thinks they're cute. They remind me of my first go-kart.

But if we go with her, Max can go ahead and take care of my truck. "Thanks, Jeanette. We appreciate it."

Of course, I have to wedge myself into the back seat. There's not enough room to turn my shoulders, but there's no way Ruby is going to let me ride in the front seat with Jeanette. I wouldn't want to anyway. I don't particularly feel like being groped at the moment. Fortunately, Jeanette drives the Cooper like a driver on the track—fast. It shouldn't take us long to get to the infield.

I try to tune out the barbed conversation from the front seat. Jeanette is trying to impress Ruby by telling her where she's been and what it's like to fly around with sponsors and team owners. She doesn't really have anything that Ruby would want, but she's the kind of person who has to try to make herself sound more important than she is.

"Jeremy might have taken the pole," Jeanette says, switching to racing, "but Team Massey has the fastest car. Everybody's said that since they saw Derek Spencer run in practice. He's bound to win this time. Did I mention my brother helped design his engine?"

"Spencer was in with a pack of five or six other cars all going the same speed," Ruby points out. "He has a shot at the 600 just like Junior, Jimmie, Kurt, and Greg. Practice was good for everyone except Jeff Burton."

"Yeah. That was hard luck losing that oil line. He'll have to start at the back."

"He'll probably make it up. He was doing pretty good until that happened."

"Spencer has a few tricks up his sleeves," Jeanette tells her. "They're gonna have to do better than pretty good to catch him."

"Too bad about his teammate," I manage to add to the conversation.

"Teammate?" Jeanette glances back at me in the mirror.

"You know. Ricky Sanders." I guess out of sight really is out of Jeanette's mind.

"Oh yeah. Him. He was a good kid. I'm sure he would've been okay."

"Did you know Ricky dated Frances Massey between me and you?" Ruby asks. "They were pretty hot for a while."

"Really? I didn't know that." Jeanette finally turns the Cooper off U.S. Highway 29 into the speedway property.

"She had a baby with him," I say. I'm not really expecting much of a result, just thinking she might know something that we don't.

"I didn't know that," she says again. "But I don't know Frances that well."

The guard at the infield gate waves her on, recognizing the car. Jeanette pulls down into the campground area and stops.

"Thanks for the ride." Ruby gets out of the car.

"Yeah, thanks." I start pushing myself out of the back seat.

"You're welcome. Sorry about your truck."

"We'll see you around." Most of my body is out at this point. If I can get my legs to unfold, I'll be fine.

"Yeah, see you." Then she adds, "Sometimes it's better not to dredge up the past."

I look across at her, wondering if this is some enigmatic way of saying goodbye. Then I realize she's talking about Frances and Ricky. It strikes me as an odd thing to say for someone who supposedly doesn't know Frances all that well. But maybe I'm paranoid now. I nod at her and close the Cooper's passenger-side door.

Ruby and I watch the little car speed off across the infield. "You know, I really don't like her. And not just because she came on to you."

"Me too."

As we walk to our RV, we pass several poker games beginning, a few outside on the ground and a few in lawn chairs under awnings. Several people are singing as they strum guitars, and an impromptu gospel chorus is getting louder in the distance.

The smell of grilling meat is everywhere, reminding me that it's been a while since we got a bite at Speed Street and I need a midnight snack. I pass on offers to play poker. I'm tired and hungry. It's been a long day, and not exactly the fun-filled one I had in mind.

“I’m getting hungry.” Ruby’s words echo my thoughts, like they so often do.

“Why don’t we grab some chicken and take it home. That way, I don’t have to fire up the grill and you don’t have to plug in the microwave.”

She kisses my cheek as she takes my arm. “Sounds good.”

Over a bucket of chicken, coleslaw, and mashed potatoes, we try to talk through everything that’s happened. Ruby gets a phone call from her mother and goes inside the RV to take it since a rock band has just started up and the noise on the infield has reached new decibel levels.

I’m listening to the wail from the various kinds of music that are mixed together with the sound of loud engines from garages and out on pit road under the lights. Practice showed a few problems from drivers who need to correct them. Everyone wants to be perfect for the big race.

“Mind if I sit down?”

I look up into Detective Frishburn’s tired face and realize how many times I must’ve looked exactly the same. Just because Bobby is tucked away in the county jail for now doesn’t mean the investigation doesn’t continue. A detective works long hours for not a lot of money. I know that too well. Looking at him makes me sorry we played games with him.

“Sure. There’s no chicken left, but I think there might be some ham in the fridge and a biscuit or two. I won’t offer you a beer.” As apologies go, this is one of my best.

Frishburn sits down heavily in the chair opposite me, which Ruby recently vacated. “Thanks. I’ll take you up on that offer.”

Ruby is still inside talking to her mother and is likely to be on the phone for another hour or so. I put some ham on a plate, pull out a few Diet Cokes, and head back outside. I don't see any point in dragging Ruby away from her mother unless Frishburn has something interesting to say.

"You can tell it's getting closer to race day," Frishburn says as I put the food and drink in front of him. "It gets louder, ever notice that?"

"Yeah." I pop the top off another Bud. "I think it gets crazier too. There are a lot of people not sleeping and drinking too much."

He laughs. "I'd like to think that. I agree with the too-many-people idea. The rest just doesn't seem to matter. I see it every day. I know you did too."

"It's part of the job." I shrug and sit back in my chair. It feels like Frishburn didn't just drop in to chat. But what does he want?

"I know we got off on the wrong foot." He chews up the ham sandwich he made with one of the last biscuits. "I'm sorry that happened. Truth is, I could use somebody on the inside right now. Everybody sees me and they know why I'm here. You've got experience in this. I checked your record. You only left because you wanted to."

"I suppose that's true."

"It was the last shooting, right? The kid. It wasn't your chest that didn't get better. It was your head."

He's right. It's not something I like to talk about. It's not something I like to think about. When I killed that kid, it was like something went flat in me. I knew I couldn't keep doing the job. But I have a rule. The only one who hears my nightmares is Ruby. She's the only one I talk to about what happened.

"You're not here to talk about what made me quit being a detective."

He holds up one finger while he finishes chewing and sucks down a big swig of Coke. He belches and smiles. "You're a damn fine detective, Wycznewski. I know your captain hated to lose you."

"Flattery will get you another biscuit. But it won't get you the story of my life."

"I understand." He leans across the table toward me. "I want to talk to you about this case. There are too many things that just don't add up. And I think you and your wife might know something, even if you don't realize it. I heard about what happened to you at Speed Street."

"Good. I'm glad someone is taking us seriously." I'm a little wary of showing him mine without seeing his. I want him to give me something up front.

"I believe someone might have tried to kill you. And maybe it's because you've been snooping around. Don't try to deny it."

Not exactly what I wanted. I take a sip of beer and wonder what cards he's holding that he doesn't want to show. "I don't know what you're talking about."

"What do you want? I said I need you. What else can I give you?"

I don't mess around. "You can tell me what you have so far. You have forensics backing you up. While I wouldn't trade that for Ruby, I'd like to know what you've found out."

"I can see that. I'm pretty sure you've got something I need too. What do you say we put them together? I can't promise it will mean your wife's brother will go free, but maybe it will show what really happened to Sanders."

"Okay. Let's put our heads together. But before we do, I need some assurances from you that this is all off the record. Whatever Ruby and I have done checking into this isn't valid evidence anyway. I just don't want to get burned for it."

He nods, knowing what I mean. "Okay."

Ruby comes out of the RV at that moment. She looks at the two of us hunched over the plastic table and swoops down like a mother hen protecting her chicks. "Not out here! Are the two of you crazy, or just plain stupid? If you're going to talk business, you'd better get inside."

I know she's right. I'm anxious to hear what Frishburn has to say. It's been gnawing at me since I watched Ruby running from that crazy truck driver in Charlotte. We have to find out who killed Ricky, and quickly. I'd leave the race right now rather than take a chance on Ruby's life. I know that's saying a lot considering Joe qualified for the twenty-first position, but I love Ruby more than Joe.

"After you, Detective." I grab my beer and follow Frishburn.

He nods at Ruby and smiles as he passes her to go inside. "Evening, Ruby. I'm sorry about your brother. I hope it turns out in his favor."

"Thank you," she says. "I'm sure it will."

Leaving the noise of the parties outside, we sit in our little living area set up in the front of the RV, behind the driver and passenger seats. Ruby is uncharacteristically quiet. Maybe she understands I'm waiting to get information from Frishburn before I give out what we know. Maybe she even brought us inside because she's been eavesdropping. Either way works for me.

Frishburn looks at both of us with such a deadpan serious look on his face that I almost laugh out loud and ruin the moment. "I can tell you this: we don't really believe Ricky Sanders was killed because he swapped paint with your brother, Ruby. I'm not completely convinced Bobby was involved at all. In fact, I took him into custody for his own good as well as the weight of the circumstantial evidence against him."

Ruby sits forward with a terrible, vengeful expression on her pretty face. "What are you saying? My brother is locked up with people who did awful things because you want to *protect* him? Couldn't you have put him up at the Marriot instead?"

"You don't understand," Frishburn says, and tries to make it right. "The captain doesn't agree with me on this. There's a lot against Bobby. His uniform was in that shed where Ricky was killed. Preliminary forensic tests show his knife, the one we found with his jumpsuit, killed Ricky. He had motive, however puny, and opportunity. I'm telling you that I don't believe he did it."

Ruby looks at me. I try to help Frishburn explain. "He couldn't prevent Bobby from being arrested because of the evidence he had to turn in. That doesn't stop the investigation."

"That's right." He picks up on it with a grateful smile. "It may be for the best in lots of ways, Ruby."

"Pardon me if I can't see any of them." She crosses her arms across her chest.

"He could be in danger if he were free right now," Frishburn says. "We think Sanders was killed for something much bigger than swapping paint or any of those other possible ideas. We think he was in the wrong place at the wrong time. I think it's possible Bobby may have seen something too. Maybe he doesn't realize it. But the killer might not believe that. The safest place for him right now is in jail."

Ruby starts to speak, but right then the door to the RV opens and Bobby sticks his head inside with a big, stupid grin on it.

"I was about to tell you," Ruby says. "Bobby made bail."

SIXTEEN

"BOBBY!" RUBY SHAKES HER head. "What are you doing *here*?"

"What? I thought you'd be happy to see me." He sneers at Frishburn with a near imitation of the King's curled lip (Elvis, not Richard) and asks, "What's *he* doing here?"

"We're trying to work together on proving who killed Ricky," I tell him.

"Like he thinks anybody besides *me* did it," Bobby scoffs.

Frishburn gets to his feet beside Ruby. "Son, I'm only doing my job. I don't have anything to gain no matter who's guilty. I wish it didn't have to be this way. But if your sister were dead, you'd want me to arrest someone too."

"Someone *guilty*, maybe," Bobby says. "I didn't do anything."

"For someone who's innocent," Frishburn comes back, "you do a damn good job of looking guilty."

Before they really square off, I get between them and close the door to the RV. "Come in and sit down, Bobby. We were just talking about you."

"I can't discuss this with him." Frishburn gets up. "No offense, but he could still be the killer."

"I'd like to say none taken." Bobby saunters farther into the room. "But I'd rather knock your lights out."

Again, I get between them. Ruby grabs Bobby's hand and hauls him into the back of the RV. "You can't expect us to be so open-minded that we'll think Bobby might have killed Ricky," I tell Frishburn. "You might be right about wanting to know the truth. But the truth for us is that Bobby was framed for this."

Frishburn scratches his head. "That puts me in an awkward position, Glad. I'd like to trade information with you, but there's no way I can let him know what we're talking about. It could compromise the case, if it comes down to that."

"I guess this is as far as our partnership can go then." I put out my hand. "Good luck to you."

He shakes my hand. "You too. Just consider what I said about Bobby. Now might be a good time for him to go home. You and Ruby be careful too. I can't stop you from nosing around, but it might be dangerous."

It's frustrating for me to watch Frishburn leave. We were so close to finding out everything he knows about the case. It could've meant cracking it tonight. I'm worried about Ruby after being attacked by the truck. I wish I could send Bobby and Ruby home for a few days, but I know Ruby won't go. Maybe we can convince Bobby it might be dangerous.

Ruby pokes her head around the pocket door that separates the front from the sleeping quarters in the back. She glances around and then looks at me. "Is he gone?"

"He's gone. And so is our chance to end this."

"What do you mean?" Bobby pushes by her. "Are you saying you think I'm guilty too?"

"No, he isn't." Ruby slaps him in the head, kind of playfully, but with a resounding smack. "Don't be so stupid, Bobby. We were almost killed tonight trying to help you."

"Ow! You don't have to hit so hard!" He rubs his head where she hit him. "How was I supposed to know? I was sitting in that stinking jail. Mama and Daddy come up with a way to get me out and all I get is grief from you two for being here."

"You need to go home," I tell him. "And as soon as the auto club gets here, that's where you're going."

"Aw, Glad. What about the race? Mr. Hamilton says I can't race until this is cleared up, but I want to watch."

"Never mind that," Ruby says. "Do you have your car here?"

"No, Uncle Foyle brought me over after Daddy told him I was getting out."

"Well, you'll just have to stay holed up here until we can get you home," she answers. "Are you hungry? Did they feed you in prison? You look kind of puny to me."

"I haven't lost any weight, and I'm fine." Bobby slumps into a chair and sulks. "Exactly why is it that it's not safe for me to be here?"

Ruby quickly relates what little we know. "It might be Massey who was driving that truck tonight. Or it could be his daughter."

"Frances wouldn't try to kill me. She might have killed Ricky. She hates him. But she wouldn't kill me."

"Detective Frishburn thinks whoever killed Ricky might come after you." I try to make him understand. "He thinks Ricky might have been killed because of something he saw. He thinks whoever killed Ricky might think you saw it too."

"Saw what?" He looks at us. "I only saw the inside of Angel's and my eyelids. If there was something else going on, it passed me by."

"I don't think the killer is going to ask you if you saw anything or not," Ruby argues. "He or she will kill you and ask questions later."

"What could Ricky have seen that would be so bad?" Bobby pushes the Hamilton Team ball cap back on his head. "What could have been going on out there when Massey called him out? The most I ever knew of is maybe tinkering with the engine or airflow on the cars. But everybody does that. They'd have to kill all of us."

"Think about it, Bobby," Ruby encourages him. "Who was outside the shed when you went out? Was Ricky out there with Massey?"

"No. I didn't see either one of them. There were a few mechanics out working on the cars. I saw a few drivers and a few fans. I hitched a ride over to Angel's and then I came back and came by your place. I didn't see anything unusual."

Ruby leans her elbows on the table and thinks about what he said. "There had to be something. You probably didn't even notice it. For that matter, Ricky might not have noticed it either. It had to be something pretty important to kill him for. I agree with you, Bobby. No one would kill somebody for tinkering."

"What drivers did you see?" I ask him.

"Let me see." He counts on his fingers and says, "David Stremme was out with his crew chief looking at his car. John Staple was out there talking to Derek Spencer. There was another rookie, but I can't remember his name right now. Ruby, is there a beer for me?"

"It's in the fridge, but I don't think that will improve your memory."

"You can't expect me to have noticed everything. It was mostly dark, and I was tired. I don't really remember anything."

"Isn't John Staple the crew chief from hell over at the pit-crew school?" I ask him.

"I think so. Staple used to be Massey's crew chief," Bobby explains. "He was fired for something a couple of years back. I guess they're still friendly. He's always over there."

Maybe I'm jumping at shadows, but after Jeanette's remark as we were getting out of her car, I'm thinking that maybe we're wrong about both Masseys. What if Paul and Frances weren't involved at all? I try this theory out on Ruby. She's not too fond of it.

"Don't forget we saw Frances drive away with the shed," she reminds me. "She has to be guilty of something."

"Or she's trying to protect someone."

"Frances isn't involved with Spencer." Bobby takes a long pull off his Bud. "She hasn't been seeing anyone. Spencer told Massey he has a steady girlfriend and is thinking about getting married. You know how they like drivers to be married."

"That doesn't make any sense." Ruby shakes her head, blond curls dancing.

"Maybe I should find Staple and ask him a few questions." I'm not thinking about what I'm saying before I say it.

"You mean *we* should find him and question him, right?" Ruby arches a slender blond brow above her right eye.

That's not what I mean at all, but I realize, having made the first mistake of sounding like I wasn't going to include her, that I have to tread very carefully. "I was thinking I could talk to Staple while you take Bobby home."

"I was thinking Bobby could get a ride with someone and you and I could continue investigating."

"I was thinking I should go with both of you." Bobby takes a gulp of beer and grins at us. "I could be a big help. You need me."

"We need you to stay alive," Ruby tells him. "You have to go home if I have to call Uncle Foyle to come and get you. I'm sure he's out here somewhere."

"It's not safe for you either, Ruby," I try to reason with her. "Look what happened earlier."

"It's not safe for you either then, honey," she concludes. "We both need to go and watch each other's backs."

"Who's going to watch my back if I don't go with you?" Bobby sounds as pathetic as he looks.

"Fine," I give in. "We'll all go."

"Maybe we should all dress in black and put guns in our pockets." Bobby rubs his hands together.

"Don't be ridiculous," Ruby says. "It would look strange for all three of us to be dressed in black at the same time. People would think we were trying to make a statement or something. But the guns aren't a bad idea."

They both look at me and I shake my head. Maybe the two of them should go, and I'll go hide out at Zeke and Louise's.

The number 112 car has smoke coming out from under it as we walk by pit road. Spencer is in the driver's seat, arguing with the crew chief. Massey is down there too, pacing back and forth as he listens to the two men arguing. The pit crew and a few mechanics are standing there waiting to find out what's going on. Eager fans are eating hot dogs and nachos and watching them.

"Looks like a good time to find Staple." Ruby nods toward the melodrama.

"Yeah," Bobby agrees with her. "But where do we look for him?"

"It's not that late. He should be finishing up at pit-crew school." Ruby slides her arm through mine and smiles at me. "What's wrong, darlin'?"

"I feel like the three of us are walking around with a target painted on our backs," I explain.

"That's a little overkill, isn't it? I don't think there are snipers out here looking for us."

A loud backfire echoes through the infield, cracking the air like a gunshot. Ruby ducks down beside me, and Bobby hits the ground.

"I'm glad I'm the only one who's nervous about this." I have to laugh. The two of them have been pretty brave up until this point.

"We have to find out who's behind this." Ruby stands up straight again. "This is ridiculous."

Bobby gets up and dusts himself off, trying to pretend he didn't drop to the ground to protect himself. "I thought I saw some money on the ground. Guess I was wrong."

Everyone is talking about the hot weather. Hot weather means harder driving conditions for the race. The track reacts to hot and cold. It gets slicker, harder to hold on to for the drivers. Bump drafting becomes even more dangerous. Usually it's warm in Charlotte in May, but not as warm as this year. This is more like the July we came down to visit Zeke and Louise.

Anything like that can throw off a race. The leader can become the underdog in a few turns. In some ways, it's an opportunity for rookies to show what they can do. In other ways, it means wrecks and cars that can't race. I hope Joe has taken that into consideration. I'd like to see him win a race this weekend. It's been a while for him.

"I see him!" Ruby points as we approach the pit-crew school.

"Let's get him!" Bobby starts walking faster.

Great. Just what I need, a *pair* of overachievers. "Okay, just a minute. Let's hang back here and talk about this." I snag each of them by the backs of their shirts.

"Glad, he might get away!" Ruby's gaze is on the retired crew chief's back.

Bobby squirms. "Yeah, we have to get him now."

"Ruby, you and I have talked about this," I remind her. "You can't just go in and accuse people of things. You miss the whole point and they don't tell you anything."

"Okay." She's obviously unhappy with the agreement.

"Bobby, that goes for you too." I break his laser-like stare at Staple. "We have to go in undercover. We have to let him think we're just shooting the breeze, talking to him because he's been here forever and knows everybody. Got it?"

"I don't know if I have that much BS in me, Glad." He folds his arms across his chest and sticks his lower lip out.

I roll my eyes impatiently. And this is the future of NASCAR. "Just follow my lead. Don't say anything unless it fits in. If we blow this, we might lose valuable evidence. And you might get killed in your sleep tonight."

I can see from the look on his face that the last part was overkill on my part. That's okay. Maybe I got him to understand. Sometimes talking to him is like beating your head on the wall.

"Okay, Glad. It's your show. I guess you should know what you're doing," he finally concedes.

I nod to my accomplices, and we start forward again. The pit-crew school is closing down for the night. Staple is filling out papers and putting away jumpsuits. It must be hard on a man to take less than he wants, I consider. Maybe he found some way to get even.

"Can we sign up for tomorrow?" I ask him with a friendly smile on my face.

"No. We're full up for tomorrow. You can sign up for the day after. Best I can do." Staple looks at me, and then his eyes narrow as he sees Bobby right behind me.

"That's fine. We've done this before, but my wife liked it so well, I thought we'd come back and try it again."

"I know *he* doesn't want to do it." Staple nods at Bobby. "I thought you were in jail."

Bobby shrugs. "I'm out now. I don't want to miss the race."

"You shouldn't be able to race." Staple's words are accusing. "You killed that boy."

"I didn't kill anybody," Bobby replies.

"Somebody did." The old crew chief's face is red with exertion.

"There's new evidence." I shove the words between them, even though they're lies. "The police think someone else is responsible for Ricky's death. That's why they let Bobby go."

Staple's eyes narrow up even further, until there is barely a slit in the weathered lines of his face. "Yeah? Who do they think did it?"

Ruby leans in close. "Somebody said they saw Derek Spencer with Ricky."

I'm almost convinced the old man is going to have a heart attack. His red face totally loses all color, and his eyes roll back in his head.

"Are you all right?" I ask him. "Do you need to sit down?"

"No. I mean yes. I'm fine." He mops his brow with a dirty handkerchief. "Things are different now than when I started. It used to be a man might tweak something here or there to try to fool the judges. But that was it. We did some drinking, but never anything else. You could make a good living—well, a living anyway."

I'm not sure what he's babbling about or if it pertains to Ricky's death. The one thing I'm sure about is that he knows something. He's kept it to himself, but he feels bad about it. If I could have a few hours in a room with him, I could talk him into telling me what happened.

But that was in another lifetime. He's already recovering from the shock of the information we gave him. "If you know something, you should tell someone." I don't really have any hope he will, but it just seems like I should say that.

"I don't know what you're talking about." He stares through me. "I have to get finished up here. You come back day after tomorrow and I can get you in."

I know there must be something else I can say. I've talked men around dozens of times. It's all in the psychology. Everyone has a need to confess. You find the right buttons and push them and it all spills out. If I had a little more time, I could do it. Like this, I'm standing here with my foot on the brakes when I should be cruising.

Ruby steps toward Staple and puts one hand on his shoulder. "You've probably been a good man all your life. You've worked hard and tried to do the right thing. It's important for you to do the right thing now."

Staple's face crumples. "I wouldn't have done anything without *them* pushing me. I don't know why I let this happen. They'd do anything to get what they want."

Why didn't I think of that? Or was it those gorgeous blue eyes and that sexy Southern drawl? Whatever it is, Ruby should be on the police department staff.

"Who pushed you?" she asks him. "What do they want?"

"Hey, Bobby!" Derek Spencer comes up behind us and slaps Bobby on the back. "Good to see you, man. When did you get out?"

Bobby, unable to pass up any opportunity to talk about himself, responds with a handshake and a five-minute explanation of what happened to him. When I look around, Staple is gone. Ruby shrugs, but her mouth is a little impatient. She thought we were going to get what we needed too.

Was that dumb luck that Spencer appeared? He's talking to Bobby about the trouble he's having with his car. I've never known him to talk to Bobby before about anything. Was Staple in on whatever Ricky saw that got him killed? If so, was Spencer trying to cover his tracks with the old man?

Spencer is there long enough for Staple to get in his pickup and drive away. The minute the old man disappears, Spencer's whole demeanor changes. Bobby's casual "See you around" falls on deaf ears and a rapidly retreating back.

Ruby stares after him. "Now what do you think about *that*?"

Bobby huffs. "Yeah. I was about to tell him what else happened to me and how unfair it is that the officials won't let me race. I guess he had something else to do."

Ruby and I just exchange looks of understanding, because the chances are we won't be able to get Bobby to understand the significance of what just happened. About that time, the PA system calls my name to tell me the AAA driver is here with the Ranger.

Bobby has had his fill of investigating, thankfully, and, thanks to my words about him being murdered in his sleep, has decided to go home. Ruby and I run him out to Midland and spend an hour or so drinking coffee and eating biscuits with sour cream and fig preserves.

On the way home, we talk about what happened with Staple, both of us feeling sure he is involved in some way. It makes sense, since he's been pals with the Masseys for years, except for the part about them firing him. Maybe they offered him a chance to redeem himself.

"If we could get Staple off by himself," Ruby says, "I think I could talk him around."

"You mean sweet-talk him around." I smile at her and take her hand across the seat. "I don't think I ever looked at a man I arrested like you just looked at Staple, or put my hand on him to comfort him."

She sighs. "You know, not every man is flirting with me. He was having problems, Glad. You have to get some confidence where I'm concerned."

"I didn't mean—"

At the side gate to the speedway, a long line of vehicles with flashing blue and red lights are waiting to get inside. Traffic has backed up to Highway 29 and beyond. Drivers are laying on their horns and revving their engines.

"Now what?" Ruby asks. "Someone must've had a baby, like last year at Daytona. Remember, Glad?"

A uniformed officer, looks like a sheriff's deputy, is coming by all the car windows. He stops at ours and shines his flashlight in the window. "License and registration."

I take out my license while Ruby hunts for the registration. "What's the problem, Deputy?"

"There's been an incident," he says. "Security found another man dead."

SEVENTEEN

We're still a day away from the race, and three people have died. It's not unusual for someone to die from a heart attack or stroke, like one of those three people. I guess the excitement gets to be too much. Or when the weather is too hot, like this year. But Ricky's death is the first murder that's happened at a track while I was there. And John Staple's death is questionable.

The word spreads quickly through the infield campers. A lot of people, especially the old timers, knew Staple and can talk for hours about what a great crew chief he was and how unfair it was that Massey replaced him.

No one is really sure why Massey replaced him. Rumors run the gamut from "He was too old" to "He didn't want to get with the new Team Massey program." There didn't seem to be any hard feelings between the two. Staple was a frequent figure in the garage, working on Spencer's car, and in the pits, handing out advice.

Everyone is speculating on what Staple did to kill himself. It's all rumors and hearsay. By midnight, I've heard three different stories.

Bart Macklin from Salt Lake City says Staple hanged himself in the pit-crew-school building. He says a cleaning man found him there and cut him down but couldn't save him. Don Jenkins from Aurora, Illinois, says Staple asphyxiated himself in one of the cars he used to work on for Team Massey. He says one of the mechanics found him and tried to revive him and then called 911.

Barbara Simmons from El Paso, Texas, says Staple ran himself over with a car. I can't listen to the rest of her account of how that happened. The first two could at least be credible—although Ruby seems to understand how it could be possible for a man to run himself down. But the police haven't released any information, so no one knows for sure.

Was Staple murdered? Did he commit suicide? The one thing that strikes me is that whatever happened to him happened right after we talked to him. If he killed himself, it might be because of what we said. Maybe he was a man on the edge of desperation. I feel a little guilty if we compounded his problem, but if he was involved with what happened to Ricky, it was going to come out anyway.

"What now?" Ruby asks me at 3:15 a.m. "Staple was obviously the weak link, whether someone killed him or he killed himself. With him gone, Team Massey closes ranks and we never find out what really happened to Ricky."

We're lying in bed listening to the hard rain pound on the roof of the motor home. I don't have any answers at this point. It seems like each time we find someone who might know something about Ricky's murder, we run into a brick wall. "I don't know what to say. If Bobby hadn't come in last night and we were able to get some fresh information from Frishburn, maybe we'd have some answers now."

She raises her head off my shoulder. "You can't blame Bobby for this. He didn't know what was going on."

That's fair enough, I suppose. But it doesn't give us any more answers. "Maybe we could have Bobby hypnotized," I suggest. "Then he might realize what he saw before Ricky was killed."

"No way. No voodoo or magic spells either. We have to figure this out, Glad. What would you do now if you were trying to solve this in Chicago?"

Ruby has a problem with anything that smacks of the paranormal. For her, that includes hypnotism and discussions about cellulite. It's unusual for someone from the South not to believe in ghosts and devils hopping around in circles. But that's her. Personally, I believe anything is possible. "If this were my case in Chicago, I would've already passed it off to forensics and a junior detective, because my suspect is in jail."

She punches me in the side. "Bobby isn't guilty."

"I didn't say he was. I'm telling you what I'd do if I were still on the job. Frishburn must have some serious reservations about Bobby, or he would've done the same thing by now. I'm sure he has a ton of cases on his desk and a captain or lieutenant breathing down his neck."

"So what makes him think Bobby didn't do it?"

"Who knows? If Bobby wouldn't have come back at that moment—"

She hits me with a pillow. "Quit saying that and think of something. You must be able to detect something."

"I'm retired, sweetie. I only detect the smell of breakfast cooking or if it sounds like the RV engine is having a problem. I don't think much about solving murders anymore."

"We've been through this already. And we decided we could solve this and save Bobby. You just have to get your head in the game."

I kiss her neck and nuzzle her ear. "Maybe my head is in a different game."

She folds her arms to cover her breasts and stares at me. "How can you think of anything else when my brother might have to go to prison for the rest of his life? He could even get the death penalty."

It doesn't matter if she's right or wrong. All that matters is that we're going to lie here until we figure out what happened to Ricky. I sigh and fold one arm under my head to stare at the ceiling. If there is a single thought in my head about how to figure out who killed Ricky, I can't find it.

I did find out that besides Staple's death, Joe Nemechek had to order a new engine for his car. I don't like the sound of that. Usually that means trouble this far along. I don't like my man to have trouble this close to the race. There has been a lot of engine trouble this week. I think it might have started with Ricky losing his engine.

"So?" Ruby asks.

"I don't know," I admit. "Do you have any ideas?"

"Well . . ." She takes a breath. "It occurs to me that we never got a look at that shed Frances Massey hauled away. There has to be a reason she took it. It might be an obvious reason, like covering her own tracks."

She suddenly sits up in bed, and I have no hope that we'll get any sleep or fool around at all this morning. "I mean, think about it. Frances is strong enough to have killed Ricky and stuffed him into his car. Donna said she hates him for what happened to their little boy. She had access to the speedway because of her father. Maybe she left something in the shed she was afraid a continued police search might find."

All in all, not bad reasoning. It's not what I want to hear at this time of the morning when it's pouring down rain, but it does kind of make sense. "That's pretty good. What do you suggest now, Holmes?"

"Well, Watson." She slides across me and kisses me until I'm only thinking about one thing, and that thing doesn't involve racing or Ricky. "I suggest we sneak back out to Thunder Road Ranch, hope there isn't security in place, and try to find that shed. Maybe Frances hasn't had a chance to do anything with it yet. We could still find what she was looking for and turn it over to the police before the race."

I knew it would involve going out in the rain. That was one of the things I hated worst about being a beat cop. I probably wouldn't have taken the detective's test except I knew they didn't stand around in the rain as much. "Why don't we wait until the rain stops?" I suggest.

"She might be looking for someone snooping around by then." Ruby's already up and dressing in the darkness.

"If she's expecting anyone, then she already burned the shed and whatever was in it. If she thinks she's clear, she's not going to expect anyone whether it's raining or dry. So we can wait here until the rain stops."

"It's not supposed to stop raining until the afternoon. If we wait until then, it could be too late. This way, we still have a little darkness left."

I hear the zipper go up on her jeans. It will only take her a quarter of a second to put on shoes and a poncho. If I don't get up, will she go without me? Could I coax her back to bed? "Ruby, it's crazy to go out at this time of the morning and sneak over there. Come back to bed for a while and let's talk some more."

"Darlin'," she whispers, "get your lazy butt out of that bed and let's go get this over with. We aren't gonna do *anything* else until we solve this."

"Sweetie, I'm not going *anywhere* until it stops raining. I'm sorry. But the shed will still be there."

Silence follows my ultimatum. I can almost hear the gears shifting in Ruby's head as she decides what to do. I know she won't do this by herself. She wants to save Bobby, but she'll wait for me.

"Okay. See you later."

The pocket door slides open as I try to get out of bed. My right foot catches in the sheet, and I end up on the floor trying to reach my jeans. "Ruby! Don't go by yourself!"

"I'm not." She laughs, seated by the bedroom window. "I just wanted to see how long it would take you to get up if you thought I was leaving."

I find my jeans and tug them up over my briefs. There's some definite payback coming for this. I don't know when the opportunity will arise. But my beautiful, smart-ass wife has it coming. I just hope I live long enough to see that she gets it.

"If it makes you feel any better, we can stop for coffee and biscuits on the way out. They don't start selling the Krispy Kreme doughnuts until five."

"That cheers me up a lot." I shove my feet into my boots and pull a T-shirt down over my head.

"Oh, Glad, you'll get over it. Once we get through with this, we can enjoy the race. We just have to get Frances Massey in the same jail cell where they were holding Bobby."

She's stubborn, I'll give her that. It doesn't matter to her that someone tried to kill us or that it's raining. Really, it's hard to tell which one is worse right now.

There's a loud party, as usual, at Jeanette's RV. The woman is a party dynamo. She just keeps going. We ignore it and head for the Ranger with the hoods pulled up on our ponchos. The rain slides off, but I still feel wet. The poncho doesn't do anything for my feet and pant legs. I still can't believe this couldn't wait until morning.

To make matters worse, they're delivering Joe's new engine. It comes in a big crate and is being unloaded from a truck. The guys out there are as miserable as I am. Some of them won't be miserable for long, though, because they get to work on the number 01 car. That would make me feel better right away.

But I'm driving out to Concord to look for an old shed that's probably in a dirty barn with rats in it. If I'm lucky, I'll find it and there will be some shred of proof that Frances Massey killed Ricky Sanders. If I'm not lucky, there won't be any proof and I'll walk around smelling like manure for a few days and probably die from pneumonia.

"Oh, poor Glad," Ruby empathizes like she can read my mind. "You have to go out on a rainy night and look for a dismantled shed. How bad can that be?"

"Pretty bad so far," I inform her as we drive out of the speedway. "I'm not taking any odds that it gets better."

"Would you like me to drive?"

"No. That's the only thing that could make this worse."

She swats my wet poncho. "Who was it that ran us off into that ditch outside of Talladega last year? And I think I remember you getting a speeding ticket in Arizona this year."

"Not a ticket," I correct her as we drive down the dark road. "The officer understood why I was speeding. He only stopped me to make sure my speedometer was working."

"Only because you flashed your badge at him. He would've ticketed anyone else. He said so."

The truck hits a stream of water flowing hard and fast across Rocky River Road. For a moment, we zigzag in the swift current coming from the river overflowing its banks. Ruby grabs the door and my arm.

"It's okay," I assure her. "We aren't going to be swept away."

"Don't make fun of it," she warns. "My great aunt Sue was caught in a current like that, and it pushed her Toyota off the road and into the river. She would've drowned, but a volunteer firefighter saw it happen and attached a grappling hook to her car from a big tree."

Ruby's family members have the most outrageous experiences. Or maybe it's that I don't really have a family anymore and I've forgotten what it was like. I don't know. Maybe I'm just feeling a little depressed out here with no lights and the river closing in to take us.

"That was it back there!" She hits my shoulder and bounces up and down a little. "We have to go back."

"Is it on this side or the other side of the flood?" I'm looking for someplace to turn around.

"This side for now. Hurry up and go back. We don't want it creeping up to the end of the ranch's driveway."

I finally find a wide drive and turn the truck in to pull it around. I pull back out and head the way we came. Sometimes it's hard to believe people live out here. There are a few lights here and there, but mostly you can't see the houses or cars of any of Rocky River's inhabitants. It's very different from Chicago, where there is always some light even in the darkest alleys.

"I think it's right around this curve," Ruby tells me, reminding me to slow down.

"I think I see the horse sign." I put my foot down easy on the brake to keep the back end of the truck from fishtailing and swing into the driveway. A small opening in the jack pines looks like a likely place to park for now. We can't risk driving by the house, but on foot, in the rain, we might just make it.

"Here's a flashlight for you." Ruby hands me one. "I wouldn't advise using it until we get past the house. We don't want someone up raiding the refrigerator to see us."

"I think I've been in situations like this more than you have, sweetie. You let me take point. If anything happens, you come back to the truck and get the hell out of here. That way, you can bail me out of jail for trespassing."

Ruby sticks her flashlight in her right pocket. "I think I can handle myself, sugar. You just take care of yourself. And what is 'point,' anyway?"

Without really explaining it, I tell her to follow me. We lock up the truck, and I slip the Glock into my other pocket. Ruby doesn't have to know I'm armed. It would probably just worry her.

"And don't worry," she whispers through the rain and the darkness. "I have Daddy's pistol in my jeans. If worse comes to worst, I can shoot up in the air and scare somebody."

"You've got a gun? You didn't tell me you were bringing a gun."

"I didn't want to make you nervous, darlin'."

I don't want to admit I was thinking the same thing. But it makes me a hell of a lot more nervous being out here knowing Ruby is planning on shooting up in the air when it might be too dark for her to tell where that is. I start getting a slight ache in the middle of my back where I imagine that bullet would end up.

The rain has been coming down long enough to keep our footsteps quiet through the brush. There are no lights on in the house as we duck between the split rails of the fence. You can tell there isn't much crime around here, because this isn't much of a fence. It's pretty enough, but if it can't keep us out, it's pointless.

I see the silhouettes of some outbuildings and the definite shape of a barn as we walk carefully across the wet field. There are large outcroppings of rocks that look like giants in the dark. It's hard to tell where the property ends and the sky begins. Going down the steep hill is kind of like falling into the sky.

There are no lights on in any of the buildings. The three of them are closed up tight. I signal to Ruby that we should check the building farthest to the left, but she pulls at my jacket and says, "That's the stable. I doubt if they put the shed in there."

Since I can't tell the difference between a stable and a chicken coop, I agree with her and we head toward the smallest building in the middle. The outline of the building on the far right is the standard barn shape. I guess we'll go there next if we don't find what we're looking for in the middle.

I use my hands to grope around and find a wood latch that opens easily. We slip inside. I'm grateful for the reprieve from the rain, which has gotten worse since we got out of the truck. I suppose it doesn't really make any difference now. There's a point of saturation that makes any more moisture redundant.

After Ruby closes the door behind us, we both turn on our flashlights. The building is set up with horse paraphernalia: saddles, brushes, bits, and even an old buggy. We both look carefully through the shadows along the walls but come up empty.

"If it's in here, I don't see it," Ruby says. "I guess we should try the barn next."

"If it's not in the barn, we may have to go into the stable," I tell her.

"I don't know if we should do that. Sometimes horses can get pretty loud if someone starts crawling through their stalls. It could wake someone up at the house."

"Okay. Let's get through the barn first and hope it's in there."

We sneak out of the small building and into the barn. The structure is huge, two floors with plenty of places to hide the wood and metal from a small shed. And that's if they kept the pieces from the shed together. I would've burned them.

"Glad! Come up here. I think I found it."

I hurry up the ladder and reach the light on the far end of the hayloft. Ruby holds up a piece of tin that I'd recognize anywhere as being part of that old shed. She pushes at the pile of lumber and metal with her foot. "What could be in this that makes any difference?" she asks. "The police went over it. What else can there be?"

"I'm not sure, but we better look at the whole thing. Frances risked a lot to bring it here. The fact that she hasn't destroyed it must mean something."

For twenty minutes, we look through every piece of wood, every scrap of metal. There's blood on some of it. I know it should be in police custody. They obviously didn't have a chance to take all of it with them.

It strikes me that we should call Frishburn and let him know we found the shed. He's going to know, without question, that his investigation has been compromised. That would be the safest—and probably the most productive—thing to do. It would also keep us from getting shot by the Masseys and possibly help find information that can be used to further the case. It's fine for us to play detective, but I really wouldn't have appreciated someone stepping on my case like this.

"I don't think there's anything here." Ruby sits down hard in the hay with an exasperated sigh. "I don't know why Frances wanted this old thing anyway."

I'm about to explain my idea about calling the police when a bright light shines in, blinding both of us. A loud click announces the presence of yet another gun, probably a shotgun, hopefully filled with salt. That way it won't kill us, just hurt like hell.

"What are you two doing out here?" Frances demands.

EIGHTEEN

Before I can think to stop her, Ruby steps forward with an attitude. "Did you think no one noticed that you took down the shed Ricky was killed in and sneaked it out here?"

Frances stares at her like she's crazy, but the shotgun stays steady, and it's aimed at Ruby's head. "You don't know what you're talking about. *And* you're trespassing. I could shoot you right now and no one would fault me. I knew you were trouble when you gave me back my license. I didn't get out in the front drive that day. You took that from my truck. You're a thief and a trespasser."

"Well, at least I'm not a murderer," Ruby returns. "You killed Ricky because you hated him after what happened to your baby."

Frances laughs. "I hated him a long time before that. But I didn't kill him."

Ruby laughs back at her. "If you didn't kill him, then why move the shed out here?"

"Because she was afraid *I* killed him." Paul Massey joins us as the rain outside becomes a thunderstorm, lightning illuminating the sky through the cracks in the old barn while thunder pounds the morning.

"Go back inside, Daddy," Frances says, not taking her eyes off me and Ruby. "I can handle this."

"You've already done too much," Massey says. "You could go to jail for moving that shed out here. I wouldn't want to live with that. You've been through enough."

"Never mind that, Daddy. We've both been through too much. I won't let them put you in jail."

Massey moves in front of his daughter, shielding us from her. "I didn't kill Ricky. There may have been a few times I wanted to, but I didn't kill him."

Frances starts crying. "I was there at the speedway. I was looking for you. They were delivering the new engine for Ricky's car. I saw John Staple there waiting for the crate to be opened. He was there and your alibi—that floozy from California—was there, but you and Ricky were off somewhere together. *She* told me that. What did you promise her if she'd lie for you?"

I look at Ruby, wondering if she's thinking what I'm thinking. Besides thinking that we should get the hell out of here while Massey and his daughter have a heart-to-heart chat, I'm thinking that the scene Frances is painting of the night Ricky was killed is different than we thought.

What was Jeanette doing out there? If she wasn't with Massey, why would she be there?

Massey counters his daughter's accusation. "I didn't promise her anything. That must've been when Derek told me he saw Bobby and Ricky playing poker in the old shed. All I did was tell Ricky to go to bed since he was driving the next day. I went back to the condo after that. Jeanette joined me a little while later."

Ruby barges in with the finesse of a monster truck. "So you and Jeanette probably have no alibi for when Ricky was actually killed?"

Both of the Masseys look at her in surprise. I guess they forgot about us for a few minutes. I wish it could've been a little longer, like until after we were back home. But no such luck.

"I'm not sure when Ricky was killed," Massey admits. "But Jeanette and I were together most of the night. We were at her RV until I got the call about the engine coming in. We walked down to the garage together, and then I went to find Ricky. We weren't apart more than an hour."

"Which was more than enough time to kill Ricky and make it look like Bobby did it." Ruby puts her hands on her ample hips and defies Massey to deny it.

"They know too much, Daddy." Frances holds the gun on us again. "Go back to the house. I'll make sure they don't tell anyone else."

"Don't be ridiculous, Frances. Put down that gun. If Ruby and Glad want to go to the police, let them. I didn't do anything wrong. I don't want you to get in any more trouble."

For a moment, I contemplate being a hero and snatching the gun away from Frances. That moment passes quickly as Massey starts pulling at the shotgun and Frances pulls back. The hero in me loses as I push Ruby down to the straw again, despite her angry look. There are more people shot accidentally in this kind of situation than intentionally in a cold-blooded shooting.

"No, Daddy," Frances sobs. "I won't lose you too."

"Maybe there's no reason to go any further with this." I walk toward them after giving Ruby a look that I hope she recognizes as *stay put*. I'm never sure about those looks, but I hope this time I get it right. "Something isn't adding up here. We want to get Bobby off the hook, but only by putting the right person behind bars. Massey, how well do you know Jeanette Almond?"

"Beyond the biblical sense?" he asks. "I've known her for years. Since before her husband, Phil, died. We only started seeing each other a few years ago, and then only at Lowe's. She's a good woman. A little flamboyant maybe, but she has a generous heart. You see the parties and such she puts on."

I'm not sure what it is I'm groping to put together here. If what Massey says is true, there was a short time between when he told Ricky to call it a night and when Ricky followed him out. Bobby came out right after him and went to Angel's.

Something made Ricky go back to the shed where he was murdered. Did he go back because he thought Bobby was still there? Did he see something, as Angel and Frishburn seem to think? If so, maybe Ricky went back to tell Bobby what he saw and the killer, realizing Ricky had seen something important, followed him back and killed him.

"What are you thinking, Glad?" Ruby glances at me, and then her eyes go back to the Masseys.

"I don't know yet. I'm still trying to piece this together."

"If it helps any, Frances and I are going to take this shed and give it to the police. I know we didn't have any part in killing Ricky. They can do whatever testing they want on it. They won't find anything from me or mine." Massey finally takes the gun from his daughter. "The two of you are free to go."

Frances sniffs. "Are you sure, Daddy?"

"Sure, baby girl. We made some mistakes, but we didn't kill that boy." He hugs her.

I can finally take a deep breath again. I think it's time for us to go. I help Ruby to her feet and brush some straw off of her backside. She takes a few steps, then turns back to the Masseys. "I'm sorry you've had such a hard time. I hope things get better for you."

"Nice words," I mutter, urging her out of the loft and down the ladder. "Now let's get the hell out of here."

We scramble out of the barn and climb up the hill the way we came. The thunderstorm has passed, and the rain has even stopped. The sky is getting light at the horizon. The smell of spring and earth surround us as we tromp across the sodden ground.

"Are you sure about this, Glad?" There's an edge of irritation to her voice.

"Pretty sure. We want to help Bobby, but we don't want the wrong person to take his place, do we? I don't think the Masseys are involved."

"Then who? We have a limited number of suspects."

"Staple had to be involved. You saw how he acted and what he did when he thought he might get caught."

"So the question you asked Massey about Jeanette was because of Frances saying Jeanette and Staple were out there together when the engine came in for Ricky's car."

"That's it." I open the doors as we reach the Ranger. "Staple was hiding something for someone else. I don't think he was involved beyond that."

"What about Spencer? Massey said he was out there ratting on Ricky."

"What was his motive?"

She shrugs. "What was Jeanette's motive?"

"I don't know yet. But Ricky was like nothing to Spencer. He was just a little fly who buzzed around on the same team. He had no reason to kill him."

"That you know of. The fact that he was there makes him a suspect to me."

"Maybe. Tell you what, when we get back to the RV, you can use the computer to look up all three of them—Staple, Spencer, and Jeanette. We'll see what you find out that could relate to Ricky's murder."

"But the Masseys are in the clear?"

"I think so. Let's see what you find out." I yawn. "In the morning."

I wade through a line of twenty people later that morning to get coffee and Krispy Kreme doughnuts for Ruby while she hunts down the bad guy on the computer. It may seem odd to some people that she's our technical whiz, but I would rather chew nails than spend time on the computer.

She gets on there and makes it look easy. So I take care of the incidentals while she takes care of business. Whatever she wants to eat, whatever music she wants to hear, I do that. I stop short of a pedicure. I'm sure she wouldn't want to see what her feet would look like when I got done, anyway.

When I get back with coffee and doughnuts, she's in the shower, singing as usual. It's often Dolly Parton, sometimes Loretta Lynn. This morning it's Faith Hill. I put the coffee and doughnuts on the kitchen table and wait outside the shower cubicle with a towel. I'd get in there with her if there was enough room. Once in a while between races we stay at a classy hotel that has room service and a Jacuzzi we can share. That's some sweet living.

The shower turns off, and Ruby emerges dripping wet and slightly pink from the hot water. I wrap the towel and my arms around her and kiss her. My mind wanders to other things we could be doing this morning instead of researching people on the computer.

She breaks my train of thought. "I think I may have found something. Come and look."

We walk by the bedroom and I gaze longingly at the bed. But Ruby's got her mind set to show me what she found. I follow her as she pads barefoot, leaving little wet footprints behind her. If I can keep from thinking about the fact that she's only wearing a green bath towel, I think I can manage.

"You may be right about Jeanette." She sits down at the laptop. "All this time we all thought she was rich. Her husband *was* rich, but when he died he left her a ton of bills and his company went bankrupt. She's doing all of this on her own. Where's she getting the money? Maybe Ricky saw the answer to that. Maybe she killed him because he knew what she was doing."

I scan the information on the screen and agree with her. "I think you might be right. This looks like it will be worth following up on."

She agrees. "Later. After coffee and doughnuts."

I kiss the back of her neck and slowly take off the green bath towel. "Much later."

After lunch, while everyone else in the world is getting ready for the Carquest Auto Parts 300 NASCAR Busch Series race that will start tonight, Ruby and I are looking at the computer. I suppose I only have myself to blame for distracting her. We could've been done and outside by now. But considering how great the distraction was, I don't really mind. We have plenty of time to go outside and see what's going on.

"You can see here that Jeanette's husband did have some money, but *she* definitely doesn't." Ruby shows me the online newspaper article from a few years ago. "She shouldn't have been able to buy that big custom RV or throw those parties for the entire infield."

"Maybe she has a big credit card."

"Maybe. But she doesn't work. Her husband died a pauper. His company was eaten up by his creditors. She lost her house and personal belongings. Who'd give her a credit card?"

"Do you have another theory?"

"Not really." She leans on one elbow in front of the laptop on the kitchen counter. "But she has to be getting money from somewhere."

"Maybe she has a rich uncle."

She glares at me. "Are you being serious? Isn't there some way to find out if she has any money?"

"If you were with the police, you could check her bank balance and trace back any large deposits. Even if you were a private detective, you might have the connections to do that. But sitting here in our RV, we're lucky we have Internet. I don't know anybody who could do this except Frishburn."

"Well, I guess that's that. I can't sit around here guessing how she gets her money. We'll have to find Frishburn and trade evidence."

I laugh, which is a mistake, of course. "Sorry. What evidence do we have to trade? We could tell him about the shed in the Masseys' barn, but they could tell him we broke in and put it there."

"What about what Angel said?"

"Frishburn said almost the same thing himself."

"You're not any help at all. What good is it to have an idea about Jeanette being responsible for Ricky's death if we can't prove it?"

I agree, but I don't know what to say about it. "Let's say that Jeanette killed Ricky for something illegal he saw her do. Whatever it is keeps her going. Let's say Staple got involved in it with her, but he wasn't willing to go the distance. He wasn't willing to kill for whatever it was."

"Okay." She starts clicking keys on the computer. "So maybe there was something in that crate that held Ricky's engine. What could it be?"

"Drugs?"

"Maybe. Although the crate doesn't seem big enough to hold the kind of score she'd need to live the lifestyle she's become accustomed to."

"I can't think of anything that small that could be that valuable."

"Where do the engines come from?" she asks, sitting back. "I mean, I know some of them come from around here. Where did Ricky's engine come from?"

"Wherever Team Massey gets their engines, I suppose."

Ruby types in "Massey Auto Sports," and their website comes up. "It should be here somewhere." As she searches through the site, pictures of Derek and Ricky come smiling out at us. "Bless his soul." She rubs a finger on Ricky's picture.

"There it is!" I can't believe I saw it first. "Click on that picture of the engine."

"You're right. Massey's engines come from Almond Engines and Transmission in Sonoma. What a coincidence!"

"Not that it really means anything." I hate to burst her bubble, but just because someone who *might* be in Jeanette's family owns a company that makes engines doesn't necessarily incriminate her.

"You mean the person who sent the crate that Ricky may have been killed for doesn't mean anything?" Ruby picks up the phone while she's talking. "Wait! Didn't Jeanette tell us her brother works on Massey's engines?"

"Yeah. Who are you calling?"

"I'm calling to find out if Jeanette is related to this boy, Brad, who's the general manager of Almond Engines." Someone answers the phone and she holds it out so I can hear too. "Hello? Is Jeanette there? I've been trying to get her on her cell phone."

"No, she's not here. I can let you speak to her brother, Mr. Brad Almond." The disembodied voice on the other end of the line gives Ruby her answer.

She thanks the woman and hangs up. "Now we're saying that Jeanette's brother owns the company that sent the crate to Massey with Ricky's engine—and maybe something else—in it. I think *that* might sound suspicious."

"Without having the crate, and with all the witnesses except Jeanette dead, I still don't see how we'll find out what was in it besides the engine."

"Let's see what we can find out about Almond Engines." Ruby is typing the name of the company into the computer.

A list of links to various sites involved with NASCAR comes back. Brad Almond has built race car engines for the last ten years for various teams. Nothing seems unusual or out of place.

"I don't see anything here that could give us a hint."

"Maybe you should try looking up Brad Almond without his company and see what comes up."

She tries Jeanette's brother's name, and a lot of the same sites come up again. "It looks like he likes to race cars too. But that's about it. Maybe he sends her money. Maybe Jeanette lives off what her brother makes."

"What's that?"

"Where?" She looks at where I'm pointing at the screen. "It looks like an old newspaper article. Let's pull it up."

The article is from Terre Haute, Indiana. It's dated January 12, 1986. It's about a man who was taken in for questioning by the Indiana State Police, who were looking for a missing shipment of uncut diamonds. The article said Almond was not charged.

"Oh my God!" Ruby almost bounces out of the chair. "There it is! He steals diamonds and sends them to her in the engine crates. She hangs out with the owners and mechanics and waits for the right moment. Maybe pays someone like Staple to look the other way. *That's* where she gets her money!"

"Hold on. We can't be sure it's the same man. Do you know how many Brad Almonds there probably are in this country?"

"Call the Indiana State Police. Ask them! You didn't mind telling the Arizona Highway Patrol about being an ex-cop, you can tell the Indiana State Police the same thing."

"That's *not* the same thing," I try to explain. "Getting out of a speeding ticket is one thing. Asking someone to look up information is another."

She hands me the cell phone. "Go ahead, Glad. They should know if it's the same boy. Then we'll know for sure."

I'm sure she's right, although I don't use the computer to look up the Indiana State Police. If anyone has that information, it's the police in Sonoma. Every time a problem child goes from one place to another, it's the resident police who end up with the information.

It takes a few minutes to talk my way around the sergeant who picks up the phone, but eventually I make my way up to a lieutenant who has a cousin who lives in Chicago. I make my request for information about Brad Almond and he laughs. "We've been watching him since he set up shop here twenty years ago. The state police in Indiana are still convinced he went into the engine business on money he got from those stolen diamonds. But they couldn't prove it and neither could we. We check in on him from time to time, but the guy is as clean as yesterday's laundry."

"Any recent diamond heists?"

"You know how that goes, Wycznewski," he responds. "There's always something going on. But Almond *seems* to keep his nose clean. At least we haven't caught him doing anything wrong. You know what I mean."

Which basically means the lieutenant thinks Almond is guilty of something but hasn't been able to prove it. I thank him and close the cell phone. "You may be right. It might be stolen diamonds that are keeping Jeanette ready to party with the infield."

"Whooee!" Ruby shouts and dances around the room. "We've got her!"

"Maybe. But we've got a few unanswered questions."

"We can give the whole mess over to Frishburn. Let him connect the dots."

"We can try that. But be ready for skepticism. Just because it makes sense to us doesn't mean it will make sense to him."

Someone pounds on the door, and I open it to see Andy and June Andersen's smiling faces on the other side.

"Are you two holed up in here?" June demands. "Jeanette is having a big pre-race barbecue. Everyone's invited. Come on out."

NINETEEN

THE GRANDSTANDS ARE STARTING to fill up with fans waiting for the 300 race. They look like tiny, colorful ants from down here. There is activity in pit road too as the drivers, mechanics, and crew chiefs get ready to show their stuff.

The pit crews in their matching jumpsuits are standing together, plotting their strategy on how they're going to get their drivers out of their pit stops in less time. A lengthy pit can mean the difference between who wins the race and who goes home second.

Everything is calculated as precisely as possible, down to how many laps each tire can go before it has to be changed. The cars may be very similar, but the variables include the driver, the pit crew, and the strategy. When all of those things are working at their peak, you have an unbeatable team.

In the meantime, before the cars actually take the field, I guess we'll go down to Jeanette's party and see what's going on. I don't expect to actually catch her doing anything illegal. She's been at this for a while, if our theory is correct, so I'm sure she's too clever to do anything out in the open.

But you never know. The smartest criminal still makes dumb mistakes. Maybe we'll get lucky. I'd like to wrap this up before the 600 race. I had a nightmare about chasing Ricky's faceless killer on the track, dodging the cars doing 190 miles per hour. That's not something I want to do while awake.

Ruby may be right. The best thing to do may be to hand over our investigation to Frishburn. But there are so many holes in it, North Carolina mud could slide right through. I wish we could close a few of them up before we pass it on. The next time I talk to Frishburn about this, I want it to end up with him smiling and shaking my hand.

I know. This can't be me thinking this. I didn't want to do this in the first place. But now that we might have an answer, I'd like to see it through. Of course, Ruby is ready to give it up just when I decide I'm ready to keep going. That's just the way it goes sometimes.

"So what do we do?" Ruby whispers as we get close enough to see Jeanette in her colorful dress.

"We eat some barbecue and drink some beer, I suppose. It's not like we're going to catch her handing the diamonds over to whoever her contact is. We'll have to take what we can get."

"We're doing this to have a good time before the race? There's nothing more to it?"

"That's about it. I think your theory is good. I think we should find Frishburn and tell him what we've figured out. He has the resources to check it all out."

Ruby nods and smiles at me. "That should take care of Bobby, right?"

"I hope so. Having a theory about something and proving it are two different things. The lieutenant in Sonoma thinks Brad Almond is smuggling diamonds too, but he can't prove it."

"So Bobby may not be in the clear?"

"I don't know. We'll have to wait and see."

"Welcome!" Jeanette flutters over to us like some big tropical bird. "Welcome to my party." She sees Ruby and looks a little doubtful, but the smile she gives me seems genuine. She looks away and goes to find someone else to welcome.

"I don't think she likes me," Ruby says. "She always acts funny around me."

"You did kind of threaten her," I remind her. "I'm sure she'll get over it."

"I don't know if I can stand here and eat barbecue knowing that she killed Ricky and that Bobby has had to suffer for it. I'm not good at that kind of thing."

Don't I know it! But I tell her she can do it, and we mix and mingle with the group. The barbecue is great and the beer is cold. The sounds and smells of cars getting ready for the track lend excitement to the gathering. There's no sign of rain, and the afternoon sky is clear and blue with high, puffy clouds. It's going to be a good race, even though Joe isn't racing in this one. After losing an engine, he'll wait for the big race tomorrow.

"Glad, Miss Ruby," Frishburn says, coming up behind us. "It's good to see you both."

"Just the man we were looking for." Ruby smiles at him. "Right, Glad?"

"Exactly." I shake his hand. "We have something to tell you."

"This wouldn't have anything to do with that old shed turning up back where it belongs, would it?"

"No, not exactly." The Masseys came through with their promise. "Is it standing or in pieces?"

"In pieces, but that's okay. At least it's back." He looks up at me, squinting into the sun that's dropping in the sky.

"Yeah, not exactly. We heard rumors, right, Ruby?"

"Right." She grins, looking totally guilty. "We heard about it. You know how the grapevine is."

"Okay. Fair enough. I just found it on my way over here, but if you heard about it sooner, I'm sure it means other people saw it and were talking about it. What do you want to tell me?"

"Not here." I glance around at the milling crowd of at least two hundred people. This isn't a good place to talk about diamonds. "Maybe it would be best after the race."

Frishburn nods and looks around us. "That's fine. I'm having the shed pieces picked up and hauled back to the police lab to check DNA and that kind of thing. I hope you've got a good theory, because I don't really expect them to find much on those pieces."

The party reaches a high point where it seems like there must be five hundred people or more. The barbecue and beer hold out as the grandstands continue to fill. The pace car starts going around the track, and the announcer starts welcoming people to the race.

A young man hesitantly gets on the microphone and asks his girlfriend, Carly, to marry him. She accepts, and they each get a ride around the track in the pace car. Thunderous applause accompanies their progress as an ambulance is called in to deliver a baby in the infield.

The crowd gets even more worked up when they announce that a baby is being born. Everything happens so quickly, and with so much going on, it's like a circus, or my first year as a rookie cop. Except without the bank robberies or carjackings.

"Welcome to the Carquest Auto Parts 300," the announcer says to a roar from the crowd. The cars begin to take the field behind the pace car. A couple of the big-name drivers are in this one. Junior is out there, and Jeremy Mayfield. David Stremme is out there with a pack of rookies I've never heard of. Greg Biffle and Kasey Kahne are in the front of the crowd.

It always starts out this way. The cars crowd around, trying to stay toward the front, two across, until the pace car leaves the field. Then they start jockeying for the lead. Sometimes whoever takes the lead here will hold on to it for the entire race. Sometimes not. It's a tricky mixture of knowing your car and knowing when to pit. The driver has to know what he can do and what the car can do.

Derek Spencer is in the lineup. He's the ninth car back. I can tell he's already looking for an opening to pass Kasey Kahne. Spencer isn't an aggressive driver like Kurt Busch, but he's good at pushing up in the field.

"Bobby should've been out there," Ruby mourns at my side. "He had his chance taken away from him by that hussy."

I squeeze her hand. "There will be other races if we can keep him out of prison. Bobby's a hard worker. He'll get there."

"Yeah." She smiles. "Even if he has to run over Spencer to do it."

The pace car leaves the field, and binoculars and video cameras go up from everywhere. It's a good crowd in the grandstand. It will be better tomorrow for the Coca-Cola 600. That's the granddaddy everyone is waiting for. Six hundred grueling miles during a night race when anything could happen. Everything else is leading up to that.

Joe's not driving, so I put on my headphones and listen to Jeremy Mayfield in the number 19 car as he communicates with his crew chief. I know Ruby is listening to Kasey Kahne. She likes him—not as much as Jimmie, but you have to pick someone else when your man isn't in the race.

Mayfield is in the lead, but Spencer is coming up right behind him. Mayfield tells his crew chief that his car is running good. I see Greg Biffle pushing Spencer, trying to pass at the same time that Mayfield's crew chief advises him of it. Junior looks like he's ready to make a move too, going on the inside of the track.

Spencer doesn't look too welcoming, and Biffle is looking for the right minute to buzz by him. He looks like a goldfish surrounded by sharks out there. Mayfield seems in charge. He's commanding the lead position without much opposition. The other three cars behind him are too busy with each other to work on him yet.

Suddenly Biffle makes his move. He tries to pass Spencer on the outside, but Spencer moves to block him. Junior sees him move from the inside track and takes advantage of the situation, taking the spot behind Mayfield. Spencer overcompensates on the steering and swings wide into the wall. His car spins around and Biffle taps him, sending him back into the wall again. Smoke pours out of Spencer's number 112 car, and the yellow caution flag comes down for the first time.

Ruby nudges me and points at the track to Kasey Kahne's car, which has sneaked up and taken third place away from Biffle. "The car is loose," she grumbles. "He can't handle it."

As I'm focused on the scene, something wet plops down right in the middle of my forehead. I glance up, praying it's not a bird, and realize that the beautiful blue sky has gone gray with some strong black clouds in it. The evening is coming on earlier than it should. Extra lights go on around the track.

"Rain," Ruby groans. "I can't believe it's raining."

"Maybe it will pass." But I already feel a spattering of drops.

Some of the thousands of people watching the race begin to duck for cover. Many more put on ponchos and bring out umbrellas. Tickets for the race are rain or shine. Unless officials call the race off or postpone it, they won't get their money back.

"It's getting worse!" Ruby shouts over the heavy thunder that follows several flashes of lightning.

"We better head for shelter." There's nothing else to do. You can fight mosquitoes, heat, cold, and not having any beer, but you can't fight a thunderstorm. Hopefully, the race will be postponed until after the storm passes. They might have to dry off the track.

We turn back toward Jeanette's RV to head for ours. It's really raining hard by now. I'm already soaked. Ruby is wearing my windbreaker. It looks better on her anyway. Andy and June were smarter and faster than us. There's no sign of them or the hundreds of partygoers who were just consuming beer and barbecue a little while ago.

I glance toward Jeanette's RV. I wouldn't have looked that way at all except for her bird-of-paradise outfit. Even in the rain, it stands out. She's there by the corner of her motor home, rain dripping down her face, plastering her clothes to her body, talking to some young guy.

Ruby is looking the same way. "I can't believe she's letting the rain ruin her hair and makeup like that. It probably took her hours to get that look."

I laugh, but I keep my eyes on Jeanette and her friend. I know it's too good to be true when she hands him a small package wrapped in newspaper and plastic.

"Is that what I think it is?" Ruby asks as quietly as she can in the middle of a thunderstorm.

"I don't know yet. Let's just hang out here for a few minutes like we think this rain is going to stop."

"We can't just stand here," Ruby objects. "We have to do something."

"Okay." I watch the obvious transaction going down at the corner of the RV. Jeanette glances around nervously and sees us. I know Ruby's right about doing something, but short of a jig, I don't know what to do.

Fortunately, Ruby is fast on her feet. She puts her arms around me and plants her wet mouth on mine. As diversions go, this is a good one. She's even positioned us so I can still see what's going on.

"Well?" she whispers a scant inch from my mouth. "What's happening?"

I can't help it. I look into her eyes. "You're a cold woman, Ruby Wycznewski. You shouldn't even be thinking about anything else while I'm kissing you."

"Well, I'm kissing you, and the only reason I'm doing it is so we can find out what she's doing. Don't go all testosteronic on me!"

I'm not even sure what that means. In fact, I'm pretty sure it's not even a word. I'd call her on it, but at that moment, the young man takes possession of the package from Jeanette and begins to walk calmly away from the RV.

"He's leaving," I hiss. "We have to follow him."

"We have to be careful. We don't want to tip off Jeanette before we get the diamonds."

I put my arm around Ruby's waist, and we both wave to Jeanette as we walk by like we have all the time in the world. The RV forest has swallowed up the man with the package.

Ruby and I separate and walk a little faster once we get out of Jeanette's line of sight. The rain has already turned the infield into a muddy mess. And lightning and all, some people are out mud wrestling, covered in North Carolina orange clay.

"I think he went to the right," Ruby insists. "I think we should go this way."

"I'm pretty sure he went left." I start tugging her with me that way.

"We're gonna lose him!"

"Not if we go this way."

"Okay. Fine." She sticks out her bottom lip, but I know she's going with me.

I start picking up the pace, running as fast as it's possible to run without joining the mud wrestling or sliding into the side of an RV. I'm sure I catch sight of his orange Jeff Gordon windbreaker as he rounds the last turn.

"I'm sure he's right there," I say to Ruby. "We're almost on him."

No response.

I glance back behind me. She's gone. She went right and I went left. She faked me out again. Only this time, she could be in danger. I know if she runs into this guy, she won't think twice about demanding the diamonds and trying to force him to stop.

"Damn!" I'm not sure at this point if I should follow her back to the right and hope to catch up or keep going this way and hope to get to him before she does.

"Is there a reason you're out in the rain, Wycznewski?" Frishburn's words are accompanied by an ominous crack of thunder that shakes the speedway.

There's no time to explain it all. "Ruby might be in danger. We saw a man take a package from Jeanette. We both followed in different directions."

"I can't believe you don't know better than to work with an amateur."

"Whatever. You run that way, I'll run this way."

Frishburn must be thinking some of what Ruby and I have been thinking, because he doesn't ask what kind of package we saw exchanged. Maybe we're on the right track. I just hope our paths converge before anything happens to Ruby.

I run down the left side of the RV forest without even a hint of caution. I'm sure I saw an orange blur this way that wasn't related to the color of the ground. I wish I had my Glock with me. I wish I had a good strong piece of wood. Anything I could hold in my hand and plan to use if I come around one of these corners and find that man hurting Ruby.

The rain continues, so hard it stings when it hits my face. My feet slip in the wet clay, rivers of orange water rushing across the infield where some scrub grass used to be. I keep running until my lungs feel like they're going to explode. Where is she? Has she found him yet?

I don't want to think about anything happening to Ruby. What was going through my head when I agreed to help look for Ricky's killer? If Ruby gets hurt, I'll never forgive myself. I knew what was involved and did it anyway. I shouldn't have let her talk me into it.

My cell phone rings on my side. I almost don't hear it in the storm, and when I finally do, I almost don't answer it. I pick it up and hold it to my ear.

"Where are you?" she demands in an irritated voice.

"Ruby!" I can barely say her name. My lungs feel like they're on fire, and I hardly have the breath to talk.

"Where are you? I told you that was the wrong way."

"What?" I wheeze into the phone.

"I'm next to the AOL trailer. Where are you?"

I look around me. "I'm next to the AOL trailer. Where the hell are you?"

"On the other side, I imagine. Would you mind coming around this way?"

I stay connected with her, holding the cell phone in my hand. Off to the right, I see Frishburn slide at least twenty feet through a pile of mud and land under someone's RV that says GRAPE EATER on the side. That had to hurt.

I come around the side of the AOL trailer and see Ruby sitting on top of the man who took the package from Jeanette. She's got his arm in an old wrestling hold that gets worse if he tries to get away. It looks like she's checking out her nails, although I can't swear to that because by now I'm angry.

"What are you doing?"

"Hey!" The man under her squirms and yelps as she tugs on his arm. "Get her off of me!"

"I went the right way." She shrugs. "So I caught the bad guy. I think I ruined my sandals though. And I broke a nail."

"Is anyone listening to me?" The man under her demands attention.

"Did it ever occur to you that I might be worried about you? You said you were going to follow me."

"I didn't say anything like that," she denies. "You were going the wrong way. Why would I follow you?"

"Teamwork, Ruby. It's all about teamwork. Every cop knows that."

She looks up at me with a splash of red mud on her face and smiles. "When you're a hairdresser, Glad, it's all about results. The team only works if you're the only hairdresser and the other team members are manicure and pedicure."

Frishburn limps over to us and gives me a painful stare. "We were supposed to be saving her, right?"

"Yeah." I close my cell phone and put it away before I grab the package wrapped in newspaper and plastic. "I don't know what you're thinking is in here."

"A girl's best friend, right?" Frishburn winks at Ruby. "I love that movie. Marilyn Monroe was one hot babe."

I take out my pocketknife and cut open the newspaper and plastic wrap. Frishburn, Ruby, and I peer into the package. A slanted ray of sunshine peeks down through the clouds, illuminating what we all know is wrapped inside.

"What is that?" Frishburn turns up his nose.

"Looks like liver mush to me," Ruby replies confidently. "Fried liver mush."

"What were you expecting?" the man under her asks. "Gold coins?"

TWENTY

"I AM SO SORRY," Ruby says, trying to get the mud off the man I help up. "None of this will stain. It will all wash right off."

I give him back his package of liver mush. It was an honest mistake. The question is, whose mistake? Is this the same man we saw take a package from Jeanette, or is this a different man? It was raining heavily, and one orange Jeff Gordon jacket looks pretty much like another. Did Jeanette give the man liver mush? Or is there another man with a package of diamonds?

"My arm is really sore, man." The victim moves his arm and hand, trying to make it feel better. He glares at Ruby. "You're like some kind of Amazon or something. What did you think I had?"

Ruby smiles at him and brushes off some mud that's hanging off his face. "Never mind. It wasn't anything. I'm really sorry."

Frishburn, covered from head to toe with mud as well, offers to arrest both of us. The man with the package decides his arm isn't hurt that badly. He glares at Ruby one more time, then takes off.

The speedway announcer tells the restless, wet crowd they will resume the race if they can get the track dried off. In the meantime, everyone is moving around, looking for food and hot coffee.

Frishburn laughs at me and Ruby. "You two really look like something else."

I don't want to say what *he* looks like. I would say out of the three of us, he's the worst for wear. But I'm not going to say that. Ruby and I could be in enough trouble already.

Frishburn continues on his righteous high. "I should take both of you in for obstruction and assault."

"Assault?" Ruby arches her eyebrows. "I didn't assault anyone. I was trying to catch a thief. Doing my duty as a good citizen of this country."

As they wrangle over it, I glance down at the wet ground. Something shiny catches my eye as a sunbeam dances across it. I reach down and touch it. "Damn! He got us!"

As I start running after liver-mush man, Ruby yelps, "What's wrong, Glad? Where are you going?"

"The diamonds are in the liver mush," I yell back at her. "Frishburn, close the speedway."

I can hear Frishburn yelling back at me about protocol and rules, but I know he'll find some way to get it done. If liver-mush man hasn't changed jackets, he should be easy to spot. Even in a sea of racing jackets, the orange stands out.

Of course, there's a tide of orange jackets milling around the infield. I can't stop every man who pulls for Gordon and see if he has a package of liver mush. I pause and look at the diamond in my hand. It's uncut. Probably stolen. I stuff it in the pocket of my jeans and keep going.

"Do you see him?" Ruby comes up behind me.

"Not yet. He might already be gone."

"Frishburn called security. No one is getting in or out of the infield. Maybe he's still here."

We both scan the crowd. Liver-mush man's face is fairly unremarkable. No scars. No piercings. No tattoos. Plain brown hair, brown eyes. Maybe five-ten or five-eleven, about 150 pounds.

Even as I'm thinking about his description, I see him. Incredibly, he's waiting in the line at the Bojangles. Unfortunately, he sees me too. I start moving toward him and he takes off through the crowd and across the safe-driving field. "Call Frishburn, Ruby. Tell him he's out this way."

"Wait for me, Glad!"

Liver-mush man and I are running, pounding hard across the flat, open area where they give driving lessons to teenagers when they aren't having a race. I remember this being another reason I gave up being a cop. I don't like chasing anyone, except maybe Ruby, and she's usually not trying this hard to get away. I don't like chasing people in cars, although I'd take that over chasing them on foot.

I'd yell out some cheesy cop line right now so liver-mush man would at least think I might shoot him. But he knows I'm not a cop, so that takes care of that idea. He's thin and fast, two things he's got over me. I won't go into the probably twenty-year difference between us.

The only thing I have going for me is a weight advantage, four years playing tackle on the Saint Stephen High School football team, and a willingness to hurt myself. I reach a point where I can throw myself bodily at him and do it.

"Get off me!" he yells. "I'm gonna press charges this time, you freak!"

"If there are no diamonds in that liver mush, you go right ahead." I automatically roll him on his chest, my knee in his back, and search on my belt for nonexistent handcuffs. For a minute there, I forget I'm not a cop anymore. I never want that to happen again.

"You got him!" Ruby runs up. "You looked so professional. I wish you still had one of your old uniforms."

I glance up at her, the suspect under control. "What for?"

She wiggles her eyebrows up and down and giggles. I'm not sure if I have an old uniform, but if I can find one, I'll be glad to put it on.

"Is this . . ." Frishburn comes up, breathing hard. "Is this him?"

"This is him." I toss Frishburn the package of liver mush. Then I hand him the single diamond that gave liver-mush man away.

Frishburn puts on a latex glove and runs his fingers through the liver mush. He brings out two or three small diamonds like the one I found. "We got him."

"What a waste of good liver mush," Ruby says, shaking her head. "I have to get Mama to make me some before we go. It's hard to get good fried liver mush anymore."

"Let me cuff him, Glad." Frishburn takes over. "Unless you'd like to do the honors for old time's sake?"

"No, that's okay." I move away from liver-mush man to let Frishburn do his thing.

"Unless he knows about more than these diamonds," Frishburn says, "this doesn't solve a thing for Ruby's brother."

"I know. But at least it's a start. Maybe one of them will confess." I don't really have any hope of that, but you never know.

"Yeah. Maybe." Frishburn puts the cuffs on liver-mush man as two squad cars pull up beside us. "I'll let you know how it goes. Thanks for your help."

Ruby and I watch them put liver-mush man into the back of one squad car as the speedway announcer tells the crowd that the 300 is ready to start up again. The crowd roars back its response with almost as much thunder as the race cars produce.

"What now?" Ruby asks me.

"We'll have to see what happens when Frishburn questions him. Until then, we might as well watch the rest of the race."

"What about Jeanette?"

"I'm sure he'll take her in for questioning too. We'll probably have to give some kind of statement about what we saw. But this doesn't clear Bobby of Ricky's murder. We have our theory about how it happened. Proving it is something different."

Ruby agrees, and we put our headphones on again to listen to the rest of the race. It's almost midnight before the race is over and Jeremy Mayfield spins doughnuts in the smooth green grass inside the track as he heads for victory lane. It's a good race despite the problems. I hope the 600 tomorrow runs smoother.

We head back to the RV, talking about stats and who pitted when they should have and who didn't. We're both still covered in mud, but so are most of the people around us. We walk past Jeanette's RV. There are no lights inside and no sign of her outside.

"You think Frishburn already took her in for questioning?" Ruby asks.

"I'm sure he didn't leave the infield without her."

"What are the chances she'll talk?"

I laugh at her cop-speak and put my arm around her. "I don't know. Sometimes people want to talk about it. She's been doing this for a while, if we're right. It may be Ricky is the first person she's ever killed. If so, a good interrogator can make her feel guilty enough to tell him what he needs to know. It's possible liver-mush man was involved in that too. If so, they could make a deal with him. We'll have to wait and see."

"There has to be *some* way to prove she did it." Ruby looks back at Jeanette's RV. "What about that black fuzzy stuff all over Ricky's jumpsuit? Maybe Jeanette has a sweater or something that it came off of."

"True. And if it did, the chances would be good forensics would find Ricky's blood on it from when she brushed up against him as she put him in the car."

"Exactly!"

"No way."

She looks at me. "What do you mean? The evidence that could save Bobby could be in that woman's closet. If the police don't have anything against her, they can't get a search warrant, right?"

"Let's not jump the gun. Frishburn is going to find some way to get in and search Jeanette's RV for diamonds if nothing else. We can put a little bug in his ear about looking for black fuzzy stuff. He can look for that too."

"It would be easier for us to do it right now." Ruby stops walking and stares at me with her boo-boo face.

"Oh no! That's not happening. I'll call the police and report us for breaking and entering before I do something like that again." She doesn't look convinced. "Besides, if we find the evidence, it won't be admissible in court. Then Frishburn would have to start all over again. Except that Jeanette could be long gone. We're not doing that, Ruby."

"Glad, I think we should do this. If Jeanette leaves before Frishburn gets a search warrant, the same thing will happen. We have to go in there now while they have her at the police station."

"I don't know how many ways I can say no. I think I can say it in three different languages. There's *nein. Nyet. Non*. No. We're not going into Jeanette's RV."

Ruby sighs and leans over to adjust her sandal. "Okay. Just let me fix my shoe."

I've been here before. Instead of falling for this, I lean down, pick her up, and put her across my shoulder. She squeals and slaps my back. "What are you doing? Put me down!"

"Did I ever tell you about my Uncle Lat? He was in the fire department back at the turn of the last century. They used to lift calves every day until they grew up to be cows so they could lift anyone in the fireman's cradle."

"Are you calling me a cow?" she demands, long legs flailing in the air.

"No. I'm saving you—*us*—from yourself. We can't break into Jeanette's RV. It could spoil everything. I know you don't understand—"

"Now you're talking down to me. When you put me down, I'm going to kick you so hard, you won't be able to sit down for a month of Sundays."

I recognize this threat from when we spent time with her grandmother. She used it every few minutes. I think she really meant it, if her boots were anything to go by. "You're mad now, sweetie, but you'll thank me later."

She doesn't say anything and stops flailing. I realize this is probably not a good thing, because it means she's thinking of all the terrible things she's going to do to me when I put her down. I open the door to our RV and set her inside on the floor.

She looks at me, anger darkening her eyes, and turns her head. "I'm going to take a shower. I plan to use all the hot water, so you should plan to sleep outside tonight."

"Ruby, this will all work out." I follow her toward the bathroom. She slams the door in my face. "Really. It would be a mistake to break into that RV. We could be accused of planting evidence if we find something. There could be a hundred complications."

I hear the shower start running and realize there's no point in saying anything else. For good measure, I lock the door to the RV. I can't sit down on anything with this mud all over me, so I put some newspaper on the floor and sit on it. It's been a long day and promises to be a longer night. And I don't mean that in a good way.

Ruby's smart and intuitive. She's right about that fuzzy black sweater, or whatever it is. It could tie Jeanette to the crime. No doubt people have seen her wearing it. There may even be pictures of her in it. Even if she washed it after she wore it, forensics could still pick up traces of blood on it.

But Frishburn has to be the one to take it out of the RV. There's no two ways about that. It won't take more than a phone call to point him in the right direction. It's important for him to know about it before he gets the search warrant. Just looking for diamonds won't cut it.

I'm still wearing these filthy clothes. I hate to change before I shower, but that looks like it could be a while. I could at least put on my robe. Then I could sit on the furniture. I strip off the muddy shirt and jeans, some of the dried clay flaking on the floor. Naked, I walk past the bathroom. The shower is still going strong. She wasn't kidding. There may not be any water at all when she gets done. I try to find my robe and realize it's hanging behind the door in the bathroom. I'll have to find some old shorts and a T-shirt until Ruby decides to come out.

It takes a few minutes to rummage around and find some old clothes. I put them on and walk past the bathroom again, wondering if she realizes how pruney she'll be when she comes out. That's about the only thing going my way tonight. It's cold comfort. And speaking of cold, there can't be any hot water left.

I knock on the door and it swings open. The shower is still running in the stall. But Ruby is gone.

It takes me a minute. I actually look behind the bathroom door, even though I know she can't fit back there with the toilet. I don't want to think about where she is. I know she couldn't be where I think she is. She has to be in the kitchen or the living room.

She's not, of course. She's trying to break into Jeanette's RV. "I should've married someone who listened to reason once in a while," I console myself as I put on my muddy tennis shoes. "I should've married someone too old to sneak out around me like this."

The infield campground is quiet for a change. Not that you can't hear the muted sounds of conversation and music around you, but nothing noisy. I slam the RV door closed just for the pleasure of it and storm toward Jeanette's RV.

With any luck, I'll have built up a really good anger that can make it through all that sweet talk and kissy-face stuff she uses to get around me. I'm really mad. I don't know if I've ever been this mad before. I'm so mad I could totally forget our anniversary this year.

Jeanette's RV is still dark. The door is closed but not locked. Maybe it wasn't locked before Ruby went in there. That way it wouldn't be quite as bad. At least Jeanette doesn't have an alarm. I can drag Ruby out without anyone knowing what happened.

I close the RV door quietly behind me. "Ruby! Where are you?"

There's no response, but I know she's in here somewhere. I walk quickly through the living room and bedroom until I hear a dull thud from a dark area to the right that I assume must be a closet.

Hoping I scare the crap out of her, I throw open the closet door, and there she is, holding up a pair of shoes. I'm so mad by this point that I'm speechless. I can only stare at her.

"Can you believe how tacky these shoes are? I wouldn't be caught dead wearing most of the stuff in here. Just because you have money is not a good excuse to dress badly."

"What are you doing? I can't believe you're in here after I gave you all those reasons not to do this. You shouldn't be here."

"All of those *were* good reasons." She tosses down the shoes she's holding. "But I have a better reason to be here. My brother is out on bail, Glad. This woman is not going to ruin his life. And look, I found the fuzzy black sweater. You know, she was just wearing this the day before yesterday. How brazen is that? Not only is there probably still blood on it somewhere, but she wore it while she killed Ricky. At least she could've thrown it away."

All I can do at this point is put my arms around her and kiss her. Like they say, bless her heart. I'm not sure what that's supposed to mean. But it seems applicable here.

The front door to the motor home opens and slams closed. The light in the front room turns on and shines into the bedroom.

"Quick! Into the closet!" I push both of us and the tacky shoes into the closet and close the doors.

"Brad, I'm telling you, I'm not waiting around to see what happens next." Jeanette's voice travels into the bedroom before I smell her perfume. "They questioned me about that stupid driver and the diamonds. I'm sorry the shipment was lost. But I'm not waiting around anymore. I'm leaving tonight."

Ruby and I are pressed together in the packed closet. I'm trying not to move or breathe. I know Ruby is doing the same.

"I'll come out there," Jeanette says, still talking on the phone. "They really don't have anything on me, or they wouldn't have let me go. They kept your pickup boy. He told them I gave him the diamonds, but they can't prove it."

The fuzzy black sweater, or something like it, is tickling my nose. I'm afraid to try to move it. A hanger or something might fall. Ruby is pressed against me like those old Colorform shapes used to stick to the background. I wish I had some clever idea of what to do right now. I hope the genius mastermind who got us into this has some way to get us out.

"No, they didn't even ask me about the driver. Don't yell at me, Brad! I did what needed to be done. You would've done the same thing if you were here. I'm packing up now and getting out. I'll call you when I'm on the road."

At this point, the best possible scenario would be Ruby and I sneaking to the door while Jeanette is driving and jumping out. We'll have to do it before she leaves the campground. Once she builds up speed, it could get ugly.

I can hear Jeanette throwing things around in the RV. She's running back and forth, getting ready to leave. Ruby was right. Frishburn didn't have enough to hold Jeanette. She's going to get away before they can search the RV.

"What should we do?" Ruby whispers when we hear Jeanette's footsteps at the front of the RV.

I tell her my plan of escape. "We'll have to do it as soon as possible. We can't wait too long."

"But she'll get away with killing Ricky. We heard her. She confessed."

"I'd like to tell you that matters. But right now, we have to think about getting out of here."

I know the sounds of getting an RV ready to travel. I know Ruby does too. We've done it a hundred times. Jeanette is close to climbing into her captain's chair and leaving the speedway. I'm thinking of how she'll get out of the infield. There's a better chance for us if we jump out on grass or at least dirt before she reaches the tunnel. Asphalt doesn't make for soft landings.

Someone bangs on the door as we hear the engine start. Jeanette rolls down the driver's-side window and demands to know what the person wants. I can't hear the reply, but the engine dies out and she walks toward the back of the RV again.

TWENTY-ONE

"Now what?" Ruby whispers.

Jeanette answers the door, and several other pairs of footsteps make the floor jiggle as at least two more people walk into the motor home. Once it's set up and stabilized, an RV is almost as solid as a house. But once you make it ready for the road again, it's a lot like stepping on a mattress. The floor moves and bounces when you walk on it.

I hear Jeanette talking to someone. They must be in the kitchen or living room. Hopefully, it's not someone looking for the messed-up diamond delivery. Someone somewhere can't be too happy about not getting that package. They're bound to complain to Jeanette or Brad. Since Jeanette is closer, my money is on her to take the complaints. I hope they don't get violent, at least not while we're here with her.

"What do you think she's doing?" Ruby wonders. "What's taking so long?"

"Someone may be searching the RV. It might be the owner of the diamonds."

"Great."

I can hear them coming closer, but I still can't understand what they're saying. It's definitely more than one voice. I hear Jeanette's voice, so I know she's not dead. That's a good thing.

I'm not sure what to do. We wouldn't make it to the door at this point. If they're searching the RV, they'll probably search the closet we're in. I'd like to have some kind of plan when that happens, but nothing comes to mind.

"When they open the closet door," Ruby says, "we'll rush out and hit them with shoes. There are plenty of them in here. Maybe that will surprise them enough that we can make a run for the door."

"Now there's a plan."

"Sorry. That's the best I can think of. I'm sorry I got us into this mess."

I kiss the top of her head. "That's okay. You were only trying to help Bobby. And I'd rather be in here with you than have you in here alone."

"Oh, Glad. I love you. I forgive you for that awful thing you did, picking me up like a sack of dog food. I hope we live long enough for you to make it up to me."

Even though I'm not sure diamond smugglers aren't about to shoot us, I have to smile. "I love you too, Ruby. And I hope we live long enough for you to make this up to me."

The voices come steadily closer. We're starting to be able to make out the words.

"There's nothing here," Jeanette says in a desperate, tear-filled voice. "You're wasting your time."

"It's ours to waste. Maybe you should just stay out of the way."

Ruby shivers. "That doesn't sound good. Feel around on the floor. I've got a few pairs of boots if you need one."

"You're talking to the wrong person." Jeanette has gone from desperation to pleading. "I have to leave. My brother is sick. Please let me go."

"Look," the same male voice responds. "Get back out of the way and let's get this over with. You're making it harder on yourself."

The footsteps and voices finally reach the bedroom. Someone switches on the bedroom light. At this point, the shoe idea isn't sounding so bad.

"This is crazy," Jeanette says. "Why would there be diamonds in my bedroom? That doesn't seem like a very smart place to hide them. People walk in and out of here all the time. It wouldn't be safe."

"People don't always do the logical thing, Ms. Almond," a familiar voice responds. "In fact, it's my experience that they do just the opposite."

Frishburn!

"What's in that closet?" the first male voice asks. It must be an officer helping him search the RV.

"My clothes," Jeanette replies. "I'm sure you won't find anything incriminating in there."

"Hah!" Ruby says loudly. "I think they will."

"Who's in there?" Jeanette demands. "Detective Frishburn, someone has obviously broken into my home and is hiding in my closet. I demand you arrest her."

"I'm afraid I probably know who it is." Frishburn throws open the closet door and shakes his head. "You two are giving me a permanent headache."

"Sorry about that," Ruby apologizes, holding the fuzzy black sweater as she climbs out of the closet. "But I think you'll find the fibers on this sweater will match the fuzzy black fibers that were on Ricky's jumpsuit after Jeanette killed him and put him in his race car."

I give her an A for dramatic effect. Her voice rings as true as Basil Rathbone in a Sherlock Holmes movie.

Jeanette is outraged. "You can't come in here and look for whatever you want! Unless I'm mistaken, the search warrant said *diamonds*. I don't see any diamonds on that sweater."

Frishburn considers the possibilities. "You're right, Ms. Almond. But I think we'll all sit down here for a few minutes while I call the DA's office to have another search warrant brought out here."

"That's an outrage! I won't stand for it. I want a lawyer." Jeanette glares at Ruby, then at me as I step out behind her.

"While you're at it," Ruby drawls, "you should get a search warrant for these shoes. It's a crime for anyone to own them."

"Welcome, everyone, to Lowe's Motor Speedway and the Coca-Cola 600 race!"

"So Jeanette was smuggling diamonds to buyers at races from her brother in California," Andy says, summing it up as we watch the pace car go around the track before the race.

"That's about it." I pick up my binoculars to check out how Joe is doing as the cars start out on the track. Junior is in the pole position, starting the field. Behind him are a bunch of competitive drivers ready to do anything to take his place. The lights of the speedway shine on the newly resurfaced track and the crowd of 160,000 fans that the announcer is kind enough to tell us about.

"She killed Ricky when he saw her get the diamonds out of his new engine," Ruby continues. "Staple was there. He knew what she did, but I guess she wasn't worried about him talking or she would've killed him too. He would've lost everything if he'd said anything. But then I guess he couldn't live with it."

Andy nods. "I heard they already arrested her brother, Brad. Too bad. He built good engines and she gave great parties. But I'm glad Bobby is clear, even if he won't get to race today. At least that cloud has been lifted."

"The only thing we aren't sure about," Ruby reminds me, "is who tried to run us down in the truck as we were leaving Speed Street."

I shrug and say, "It was obviously Jeanette. She was on to us."

"I don't think so, sweetie. I think it was Frances. She didn't own up to it, but she was ready to kill us in that barn."

As soon as I see that my man, Joe, looks like he's doing okay, I switch sights to Bobby, who is standing with his teammates at the side of pit road. He'll be in another race on another day, and, if he's hungry, he'll get some passing points and put on a show that will knock everyone's socks off. Rookies get noticed if they're willing to push it. Bobby still has that chance.

Ruby slips her arm around me as she puts on her headphones to hear Chad Knaus talk to Jimmie Johnson, who's coming up fast on Junior. She smiles at me. "I love you, Glad. But Jimmie is gonna kick Joe's butt today."

GLAD AND RUBY'S TRACK LOG

LOWE'S MOTOR SPEEDWAY
5555 Concord Parkway South
Concord, NC 28027
704-455-3200
www.lowesmotorspeedway.com

Every May and October, Lowe's Motor Speedway in Concord, North Carolina, a few miles north of Charlotte, is the place to be. With three NASCAR Nextel Cup Series events, two NASCAR Busch Series races, and the NASCAR Craftsman Truck Series, this track is exciting in spring and fall. The speedway is known for its night racing.

Many race fans consider the speedway to be the heart of NASCAR. Ninety percent of NASCAR teams are based within fifty miles of the facility. The addition of the NASCAR Hall of Fame in Charlotte is icing on the cake. Movies like *Days of Thunder*, *Speedway*, *Stroker Ace*, and *Talladega Nights* were filmed at the speedway.

Besides the 1.5-mile quad oval, the complex includes a 2.25-mile road course and a karting track in the infield. This was cleverly created by using a quarter-mile asphalt oval with part of the speedway's front stretch, pit road, and a one-fifth-mile oval located outside turn three of the speedway.

The speedway hosts other events on its tracks, including a weekly short-track series for Legends cars, Bandoleros, and Thunder Roadsters. The World Karting Association also holds regional, national, and international races there.

A clay oval dirt track was added across the street from the speedway. This facility can seat almost 15,000. It hosts the races for late models, modifieds, sprint cars, and monster trucks. Two of the largest car shows in the nation, the Food Lion Auto Fairs, are held at the track in April and September.

Lowe's Motor Speedway History

In 1959, Oakboro, North Carolina, native Bruton Smith and early stock-car-driving celebrity Curtis Turner came up with the idea of building a speedway in Concord. Together, the two men designed and built Charlotte Motor Speedway, which became known as Lowe's Motor Speedway in 1999 when Lowe's Home Improvement bought the right to name the speedway. The track became the first in the country with a corporate sponsor.

Smith was a car dealer and short-track stock-car-racing promoter at Concord Motor Speedway and Charlotte Fairgrounds. Turner, from Virginia, made his money in the lumber industry and became one of the first NASCAR drivers after the sanctioning body was created in 1949.

Their dream of a 1.5-mile superspeedway became reality on June 19, 1960, when the first World 600 race took place. Unfortunately, despite a strong beginning, the facility declared bankruptcy in 1961. Smith left the track—but not the dream—behind. In 1975, Smith became the majority stockholder in the speedway and resumed control of operations. He hired H. A. "Humpy" Wheeler as general manager, and the two began to design and rebuild the track as fans know it today.

Smith and Wheeler bought the $1.7 million, 1,200-fixture lighting system developed by Musco Lighting that uses mirrors to simulate daylight without light poles interfering in the watching of the race. The system was installed in 1992, making the speedway the first superspeedway to host night racing.

The speedway continues to grow. In May 2000, a 10,860-seat expansion of the Ford Grandstand on the front stretch was completed. The speedway's seating capacity is 167,000, with another 50,000 possible in the infield.

In 2005, a diamond grinding process used to smooth out bumps in the surface of the track caused tire problems during both NASCAR Nextel Cup events. There were a record twenty-two cautions at the Coca-Cola 600, making it the first Nextel Cup Series race to go more than five hours (excluding red flags) in twenty-five years. After that race, the speedway repaved with a new-generation asphalt.

Races

May

Quaker Steak & Lube 200 NASCAR Craftsman Truck Series
NASCAR Nextel All-Star Challenge
CTC Pole Night NASCAR Nextel Cup Qualifying
Carquest Auto Parts 300 NASCAR Busch Series
Coca-Cola 600 NASCAR Nextel Cup Series

October

Bojangles' Pole Night NASCAR Nextel Cup Qualifying
Dollar General 300 NASCAR Busch Series
Bank of America 500 NASCAR Nextel Cup

Other Activities

Note: During Race Week, the city of Concord can enlarge by more than 200,000 people, making it the third largest city in North Carolina at those times. Be sure to plan plenty of time for traffic and possible lines for any activity. Many of the activities listed here are free, but many require tickets or reservations. Call ahead or check websites before going.

THE RICHARD PETTY DRIVING EXPERIENCE

6022 Victory Lane
Concord, NC 28027
704-455-9443
www.1800bepetty.com

The Richard Petty Driving Experience provides ride-alongs following each NASCAR Nextel Cup race at Lowe's Motor Speedway. Each participant goes three laps in a NASCAR Nextel Cup–style stock car at the speeds championship drivers are used to. Even someone who has never been to a race can travel in a car at 160 miles per hour.

The cars are driven by professional instructors. Prices and times vary, so check ahead. Expect a waiting line, since this activity is very popular.

THE 5 OFF 5 ON PIT CREW FANTASY EXPERIENCE
156 Byers Creek Road
Mooresville, NC 28117
Main: 704-799-3869
Toll-Free: 866-563-3566
www.5off5on.com

The 5 Off 5 On Pit Crew Fantasy Experience lets you learn how a real pit crew works. A race car comes in to pit while you work with five other people, including coaches and real pit-crew staff. You'll suit up in a flame-retardant jumpsuit, gloves, and kneepads while you learn from the professionals. When it's over, you'll receive a certificate verifying your work. A must-do experience for any real NASCAR fan!

CONCORD MILLS
8111 Concord Mills Boulevard
Concord, NC 28027
704-979-3000
www.concordmills.com

Concord Mills is a 1.4-million-square-foot shopping mall located about a mile from Lowe's Motor Speedway. It is North Carolina's largest tourist attraction, drawing more than 15 million visitors a year. Large stores include Circuit City, Bass Pro Shops, and Books-A-Million. Factory outlet stores include Old Navy, Nike, and Nautica.

There is a large food court in the mall, as well as several sit-down restaurants. AMC Theaters has a twenty-four-screen facility in the mall, and there are plenty of other things to do too. There's a Jeepers for the kids, and NASCAR SpeedPark, a huge indoor-outdoor complex for kids and grown-ups alike. The SpeedPark has six go-karting tracks, a climbing wall, and a games facility. There is also an indoor NASCAR simulator called Silicon Speedway.

Museums

HENDRICK MOTORSPORTS MUSEUM
4400 Papa Joe Boulevard
Concord, NC 28262
Toll-Free: 877-467-4890
www.hendrickmotorsports.com

Rick Hendrick created Hendrick Motorsports in 1984 with an unsponsored car, five employees, and 5,000 square feet of working space. Twenty years later, Hendrick Motorsports has become one of NASCAR's top teams, with many championships and more than one hundred Nextel Cup victories. Jeff Gordon's Daytona 500 winner, Terry Labonte's Iron Man machine, the *Days of Thunder* Chevy Lumina, and other team cars are housed here. There are viewing areas for Hendrick Motorsports's race team shops, giving fans a behind-the-scenes perspective. The Hendrick Team Store offers collectibles from drivers Terry Labonte, Jeff Gordon, Jimmie Johnson, and Kyle Busch. Open weekdays, 9 a.m. to 5 p.m.

ROUSH RACING MUSEUM
4600 Roush Place
Concord, NC 28027
704-720-4600
www.roushracing.com

Ten minutes from Lowe's Motor Speedway is Roush Racing Museum and the team headquarters for Roush Racing. There is a self-guided tour of the museum, where you'll find team photos, trophies, race cars—some dating back to 1913—and other displays. Spend time watching Mark Martin, Greg Biffle, and Matt Kenseth get ready for weekend racing in the shops. Look through the store to find your favorite driver's Roush Racing apparel and other merchandise. Open weekdays, 10 a.m. to 5 p.m.

CURB MOTORSPORTS MUSEUM
218 Chestnut Avenue
Kannapolis, NC 28083
704-938-6121
www.mikecurb.com

Richard Petty won his last two races driving for Mike Curb and Curb Motorsports. The car Petty drove in his 199th winning race is on display, as is the car Dale Earnhardt drove in 1980 for his first Winston Cup Championship. Dale Jarrett's car from his first Busch win and Johnny Sauter's winning car from the September 2003 Richmond race are here as well. A total of twenty-one cars are on display in the museum. Open weekdays, 9 a.m. to 5 p.m.

Team Shops

DALE EARNHARDT INC.
1675 Coddle Creek Highway (State Highway 3)
Mooresville, NC 28115
Toll-Free: 877-DEI-ZONE
www.daleearnhardtinc.com

Dale Earnhardt Inc. is a massive complex that includes team shops for Martin Truex Jr., Dale Earnhardt Jr., and Paul Menard. A word of warning: there are no signs on the complex that tell what it is, so drive in the open gate at this address and you'll know you're here.

The showroom includes Dale Earnhardt exhibits and a gift shop. There is a large selection of other Earnhardt Inc. drivers' products, including caps, jackets, and T-shirts. Open weekdays, 9 a.m. to 5 p.m., and Saturday, 10 a.m. to 4 p.m.

CHIP GANASSI RACING WITH FELIX SABATES
8500 Westmoreland Drive
Concord, NC 28027
704-662-9642
www.chipganassiracing.com

Ganassi Racing is the home of drivers David Stremme, Reed Sorenson, and Casey Mears. There is a shop viewing area where the cars are put together for the weekend races. The gift shop includes items from Ganassi/Sabates Racing, as well as driver souvenirs. Open weekdays, 8:30 a.m. to 4:30 p.m. (Could be closed for lunch, so call ahead.)

EVERNHAM MOTORSPORTS
160 Munday Road
Statesville, NC 28677
704-924-9404
www.evernhammotorsports.com

The Evernham Motorsports Race Facility is a longer drive from the Lowe's Speedway area (about an hour), but it is a must-see for fans of Scott Riggs, Kasey Kahne, and Jeremy Mayfield. There is a showroom with collector's items. The race shop and viewing area are open to the public, so you can admire the spotless floors and hardworking mechanics while you're there. Open weekdays, 9 a.m. to 5 p.m. Closed 1 p.m. to 2 p.m. for lunch. Call ahead.

THE DALE TRAIL
Dale Earnhardt Tribute
Cannon Village
Kannapolis, NC 28081
704-938-3200
www.daletrail.com

North Carolina State Highway 3 was renamed in honor of Dale Earnhardt and has now become known as the Dale Trail. It stretches from Kannapolis, Earnhardt's hometown, to Mooresville at Earnhardt Inc. Marked by flags that proclaim it the Dale Trail, the road stretches through the heart of race country. Dale Earnhardt Plaza in Kannapolis holds a nine-foot, 900-pound bronze statue of Earnhardt. There is a granite monument contributed by Earnhardt fans from Vermont and New York as well. The Dale Earnhardt Tribute Center in Cannon Village contains artwork by motorsports artist Sam Bass. If you're an Earnhardt fan, you won't want to miss it.

NASCAR HALL OF FAME

The NASCAR Hall of Fame is the jewel in stock car racing's crown. When constructed, it will showcase the history of motorsports. A hard-fought battle between Atlanta, Charlotte, and several other cities ended in 2006 when it was announced that Charlotte would host the hall. The NASCAR Hall of Fame will be open by spring 2009, giving an area already rich in NASCAR heritage another reason to be proud of its roots.

Read on for an excerpt from the next
Stock Car Racing Mystery by Joyce & Jim Lavene

Hooked Up

COMING SOON FROM MIDNIGHT INK

ONE

"Who's that sleeping in my bed?"

"Shh! You'll wake him." Ruby drags me away from the bedroom door, *my* bedroom door, where some strange man is sleeping in our bed. I have just enough time to see that he's also wearing *my* pajamas.

"Wake him? I should get my gun out and shoot him! How did he get in there? And what's that big, black thing on the bed?"

Ruby keeps walking down the hall toward the kitchen of our 2000 Holiday Rambler Navigator. I follow her statuesque form, admiring the sway of her hips even as I work myself into a fine temper, as my Polish grandma used to call it. I mean, a man should have some inalienable rights. One of those should be *not* sharing his pajamas and his bed.

"He's a cat, Glad. His name is Malibu. Bill, his owner, was stranded out on the road. Mama and I picked them up. He was exhausted." Ruby pours a cup of coffee. "Bill needed a place to get himself together. He said he hadn't had a good night's sleep in days. What else could I do?"

Those big, blue eyes turn on me, so wide and innocent. But I'm not backing down. There are some things that should be private. "When did you pick him up? Your dad and I were right behind you the whole time. I didn't see anyone hitchhiking."

"He was at the last rest stop. You were too busy flirting with that woman in the '57 Chevy. Remember?" She smiles sweetly.

I vaguely remember the woman. The car was fantastic. It had everything. If I had time for something that sweet, it would be the car, not the woman. "I wasn't flirting with anyone. I can't even look at a car without you thinking I'm looking at another woman." I put my arms around her waist and pull her close. "I don't need another woman, sweetie. You're all I want and all I can handle."

She pouts and I kiss her sexy lower lip. Then I shake my head. "But you aren't getting out of this that easy. You can't pick up some bum from a rest stop and put him in our bed. And you gave him *my* pajamas. Don't you think that was taking kindness to an extreme?"

"Well, he couldn't wear *my* pajamas! If you could've seen him, you'd know why I did it."

"If I saw him, I might have given him a few bucks, but not the key to my RV."

"Glad, the good book says to give no matter what the person seems to be like. Remember the parable about the lepers?"

"Not right now. But I don't think it says anything about putting a stranger in your bed *after* you give him your husband's pajamas."

"Let me call Mama." Ruby edges away from me. "She'll back my story. She thought it was the right thing to do."

"While we're at it, let's call Oprah and see what she thinks." I can't believe she doesn't see any harm in what she's done.

"Fine." The word barely slips out of her pretty lips. "If that's the way you feel about it, I hope you're never alone, hurt, and exhausted and you have no one to turn to."

"I hope not too. But I'm not real worried about that right now. I'm going to get that guy out of my bed. Maybe you could find some disinfectant and someplace we can burn my pajamas."

"Oh, you're so dramatic! Everything will be fine after we wash the pajamas. You'll see."

"And while we're at Wal-Mart getting new pajamas, we can pick up a mattress cover to put on the bed." I start back toward the bedroom.

She stops me. "I'll go. I created the problem, and I'll take care of it. I don't want Bill to be upset when I tell him my big oaf of a husband has no Christian charity."

"Tell him whatever you want to. Just get him out of here." She's not going to make me feel guilty about this. No telling who this guy is or where he's been. I have to sleep in that bed tonight, if we eventually make it through this line of RVs waiting to get into Dover International Speedway.

Dover, the next race after Lowe's, isn't a bad drive from Charlotte, North Carolina, normally. Ruby and I make this circuit every year. I might have skipped the Monster Mile this year, since my driver, Joe Nemechek, isn't driving. I'm only a spectator, not a fan, when Front Row Joe isn't driving. When he's at a race, I'm out there with him. He may not win all the time, but he's one hell of a driver.

Now, Joe is a different story. I'd give *him* my pajamas, no problem.

Ruby's parents decided to join us on this trip. Her father, Zeke, hasn't been to a race since he was confined to a wheelchair a couple of years ago. Suddenly, he decides he wants to see his son race at Dover. He can't drive his RV anymore, and Ruby's mom has never driven it. That's how we decided to split up. If I'd known Ruby was going to take on passengers, I would've driven our RV and let her drive her parents' 1987 Coachman Shasta 280.

I don't have anything against Ruby's parents. I suppose they're like any other in-laws. Louise, Ruby's mom, has never called me by my name, and her father once chased me out of his yard with a shotgun. Seems he didn't care for the idea of his daughter marrying a Yankee.

There's a knock on the door and Louise steps inside. "There you are. I brought these by for Bill. Where's Ruby?"

"Asking Bill to leave." I reach for the plate of brownies in her hand. "I'll take those. Thanks."

She holds them back and glares at me. "I *said* they were for Bill. What do you mean Ruby's asking him to leave? Where will he go?"

"I don't care." I really can't believe Ruby and Louise are so touched by this man. What did he do that was so appealing? And thinking about the two women finding him so attractive makes me wonder what's going on back there in the bedroom with him and Ruby.

"All you people are the same." Louise says "you people," but she means Yankees. "This poor man needs our help. The good book says we have to give."

"Hold that thought." She's still got the brownies in her hand. They smell really good. Once we take care of Bill, maybe I can sweet-talk a few from her.

I'm normally not worried about Ruby with another man. She's loyal down to her Royal Carnation Pink toenails. It's the men I worry about. My Ruby is a very desirable woman.

In this case, though, I'm starting to worry that Bill hypnotized Louise and Ruby when he met them at the rest area. Nothing else makes sense. Okay, I don't believe it was *really* hypnosis, but I know there are drugs that can cause this kind of behavior.

Louise is glaring hard at my back as I walk to the bedroom, but I figure I can take her staring. It's when she follows me that I start getting nervous.

The bedroom door is closed. My heart starts beating fast. I trust Ruby. She's the best thing that ever happened to me. I know she wouldn't do anything to hurt me, at least not on purpose. But my last marriage ended when I found my first wife in our bed with her aerobics instructor, which pretty much signaled the end of our relationship. Standing here, wondering what I might find going on in my bed this time, is chipping a few years off what life I have left to live. I don't know if I can take finding Ruby in bed with Bill.

"Well? Why are you still standing there?" Louise demands from behind me. "Open the door."

She's right. I know she's right. But I can't bring myself to open the door. Every man has his limitations. This is mine.

I step to one side. "You open it."

Louise rolls her eyes and briskly steps forward. "You are one weird boy. What's wrong with you anyway?"

I take a deep breath and Louise opens the bedroom door. She peers inside and catches her breath. I'm too far on the right to see whatever she sees in the room. Short of pushing her out of the way, I'm stuck with her interpretation. "*What*? What's going on?"

"Oh, Ruby!" Louise shakes her head. "What are you doing?"

That's it. I slam the door open all the way with my forearm and step into the room. There are no lights on, and the blinds are drawn on the door and window. The shadows merge on the bed, becoming Ruby's form and the large, black cat I saw before.

"Isn't he adorable?" Ruby asks her mother. "He's so friendly too. Aren't you just so friendly?" She talks gibberish to the cat. "And you're so soft and fluffy."

I glance around the room, old senses taking control of my brain. I don't see Bill anywhere. I check the bathroom, but he's not there. I check the closet, but he's not there either. This is a nice RV, but you can only hide in so many places. "Where's Bill?"

"He was gone when I got back here," Ruby explains. "He probably heard you talking about him and left."

"I hope you're satisfied." Louise shakes her head and reaches down to pet the cat. "He's a beautiful animal. Didn't Bill leave a note or something about coming back for him?"

"I didn't see anything. All I could find were his ragged old clothes and Glad's pajamas that I gave him."

"Then what's he wearing?" I notice the bottom drawer of my dresser is open.

"Oh, he took those old jeans you should've given to Goodwill last year, and that old Talladega T-shirt. And those nasty moccasins you've been wearing since before I met you."

"In other words, your helpless stray stole my clothes. Did you check to see if he took anything else?" I take out my cell phone. "I'm calling the police."

"You put that thing away, Ruby's husband," Louise chimes in. "I'm sure you have plenty you can share with that poor man. You didn't see him. Someone had beaten him. He was lucky to escape with his life."

Ruby stares at me too, and I put the cell phone away. "I think both of you have lost your minds." I say this in the *kindest* way I can. "Let's at least put the cat outside."

Both women yell "No!" at the same time. Louise drops the brownies on the bed as she rushes to her daughter's side to protect the cat. Ruby clutches the animal to her ample bosom, a place usually reserved for me. "I'm sure Bill will be back for him," Ruby assures me as she and Louise laugh at the animal licking the brownies.

"I'm sure Bill has already forgotten his furry friend." I reach for the cat.

The animal looks up at me and hisses. Large, white fangs protrude from his pink mouth as half-inch-long claws show in his front paw, which he uses to scratch my hand.

"No wonder he left it here." I pull my mutilated hand back and look at the damage. "That cat better have a rabies shot. Good thing I had that tetanus booster last year."

"Calm down, Glad." Ruby gets off the bed and hands me a tissue. "He's wearing a collar with his name and his shot record on it."

"I hope it has an address on it too, because it can't live here."

Before I can acknowledge that my ultimatum will be largely ignored, RV horns start blowing. It means traffic is finally moving. I have to get back to the Furrs' RV. For good measure, I add, "I'd like that thing to be gone when I get back."

Ruby and Louise glare at me, and the cat snarls. Not a great beginning for race weekend.

I slam the door on my way out and stalk up to the Furrs' RV. Zeke is waiting for me at the door. "Where the hell have you been,

Glad? I thought I was going to have to get out and push this thing. What's going on that couldn't wait?"

I don't know where to start, but it all tumbles out as I pull the RV forward. I'm actually close enough to see our parking spaces, and I pull the Coachman into one of them. It will be another hour before it's all set up, but that's another story.

Zeke agrees with me. "A man shouldn't have to share his bed with a stranger," he says. "Unless she's a pretty little honey."

I appreciate Zeke's support. At least someone besides me isn't crazy. I don't want to think about Zeke being in bed with Louise, much less a pretty little honey.

By this time, Ruby has pulled our RV into the space beside us. I decide to work at getting back on her good side before I set up anything. Ruby is one of those people with a long memory. I could find myself sleeping in one of the Furrs' captain's chairs tonight if I'm not careful.

Outside is chaos. Everyone is moving at the same time. Late-arriving drivers are getting their cars in place for practice runs, and fans are getting RVs set up while they yell at friends across the parking lot. A hundred different vendors are setting up their striped tents.

Ruby steps out of the Navigator with Louise right behind her. Louise gives me an evil look and then goes inside her RV.

I ignore her and go over to Ruby. "Let's not stay angry over this." I come up from behind and put my arms around her. "I love you. I know you did what you thought was right."

"Even if it wasn't?"

At last she's beginning to see the light. I guess the evil spell, or drugs—whatever it was that Bill and his cat did to her—is over.

"That's right. We all do wrong things for good reasons. I don't hold it against you, sweetie."

"Thank you, honey. You're such a wonderful husband. So kind and forgiving." She smiles at me, and I fall for it.

"That's okay. As long as we're on the right track."

"We're on the right track." She moves away from me. "Unfortunately, we're at different tracks. *Your* truck is sleeping in the truck tonight while Malibu and I share our filthy, disgusting bed that probably saved a man's life."

"Ruby . . ."

"Excuse me." She brushes by me. "I'm going to level the RV."

"Fine. I'll unhitch the truck and get your parents' RV set up."

She's mad, and there's nothing I can do about it right now. I'm not sleeping in the truck, but it won't be a good night anyway.

"Hey! My two biggest fans!" Ruby's brother, Bobby, speeds up in his 1966 Mustang with his friend John Paxton, another rookie driver. "You made it. Where's Mama and Daddy? I hope you had a good trip."

"Hi, Glad! Hi, Ruby!" John shakes my hand as Ruby squeals and runs over to hug him. She adopted him after meeting him at Lowe's. He's another one of her sob stories. Something about dead parents and barely being able to keep his race car going. He doesn't have a big team like Roush sponsoring him, and that can be a problem.

I admire Bobby's ride for a minute (who wouldn't?). Then I retreat to unhitch the truck. Let Ruby explain what happened. I've got my money on Bobby backing me and Zeke. He wouldn't want Bill in his pajamas either.

At that moment, we hear the first scream. Information runs like dust off a track through the spectator crowd. There is no grapevine here. It's more like instant messaging.

"Someone's dead on the track!" a man in a golf cart yells as he drives by.

"Someone fell off the DuPont Bridge," a woman shouts from a cab of a Chevy Silverado.

I look back at Ruby, and she's already in the car with Bobby and John. I run and jump in the back seat next to her. The tires squeal as Bobby pulls in front of oncoming traffic to head up to the track.

Bobby pulls the Mustang right up to the gate, and we jump out. People are filling the grandstands, rushing out to the fence that borders the track. The DuPont Bridge that crosses one side of the track is empty, waiting for the movers and shakers with invitations who will fill it during the race.

Underneath it is a body. From the angle of the legs and arms, I can tell he's in bad shape. His face is up, open eyes staring at the blue sky beyond the bridge. I estimate the fall at about thirty feet. The chances are that the crowd is right and the man is dead.

Ruby and Bobby stare at the scene until Ruby gets a strange look on her face. She steps away from her brother and puts her hand on mine. "Glad, do you recognize that shirt?"

ABOUT THE AUTHORS

NASCAR fans Joyce and Jim Lavene are a husband-and-wife writing team who co-author several mystery series, including the Sharyn Howard Mysteries and Peggy Lee Garden Mysteries. They live outside of Charlotte, North Carolina, just twenty miles away from Lowe's Motor Speedway. Find out more at www.nascarmysteries.com.